STRUCTURAL
DAMAGE

Copyright © 2023 by Sloan Spencer

All rights reserved.

No part of this publication may be reproduced, distributed, or transmitted in any form or by any means, including photocopying, recording, or other electronic or mechanical methods, without the prior written permission of the publisher, except as permitted by U.S. copyright law. For permission requests, contact sloan.spencer.author@gmail.com

The story, all names, characters, and incidents portrayed in this production are fictitious. No identification with actual persons (living or deceased), places, buildings, and products is intended or should be inferred.

Book Cover & Illustrations by Vera Osipchik

First Edition 2023

Contents

Dedication	V
Author's Note	VI
Epigraph	VII
1. Carefree	1
2. You're Kidding Me	21
3. The First Week	32
4. A Reluctant Massage	43
5. Too Deep	57
6. Princess Play	61
7. Digging My Own Grave	73
8. The Holiday Party	80
9. The Holiday Party	85
10. Erotic Audio	91

11.	Parental Support	98
12.	Workout	108
13.	Indecent Proposal	119
14.	Brunch	144
15.	The Nightmare	150
16.	Piping Hot Tea	155
17.	Let's Get Wet	161
18.	Smile for the Camera	182
19.	Wise Advice	195
20.	Inspection	203
21.	Oh, She's Rich	224
22.	The Cottage	235
23.	Bare	242
24.	Opening Up	250
25.	The Date	255
26.	Christmas Morning	271
27.	New Year's Eve	277
28.	Recoil	286
Acknowledgements		294
Trigger Warnings		296
About the Author		297

For Rachel—Thank you for recklessly hyping me up and convincing me I could write my own romance novel.

Author's Note

I understand the importance of trigger warnings, but in my opinion, reading them will spoil this story. If you know there are certain themes that are uncomfortable for you, then please read them in the back after the acknowledgements section. But rest assured, there is no trauma around body image, nor body-shaming.

"If you want to reach a state of bliss... make a decision to relinquish the need to control, and the need to be approved, the need to judge."
—Deepak Chopra

Chapter 1

Carefree

Cora

Well, tonight was already shaping up to be very different from my usual Friday. That was the plan, after all. My best friend Angie, in all her infinite wisdom and charm, had convinced me to go out with her to rekindle our glory days. It wasn't that we were pretending to be twenty-one again; it was that we were pretending to have little responsibility, a carefree attitude, and just be the silly girls who wanted a buzz and some fun.

On a normal Friday night, I'd be working in the office until 6:30 pm, visiting my mother, then grabbing takeout on my way home and curling up with Netflix and my gray, polydactyl, storm cloud of a cat, George. At least, that was my new normal since my separation and now official divorce.

And that's what has brought us here tonight, in a tight little bar in downtown Manayunk, a cute hipster neighborhood in Philadelphia. We are celebrating my divorce, even though part of me is still broken and will probably never heal. But, like I said, Angie can be very convincing.

As I finish my first drink, a strong cucumber and herb vodka soda, I can recognize that she was correct. I needed to get out and forget about Theo. Forget about the man who totally blindsided me, cut me open, and rubbed salt so deep in my heart that I would never be the same.

"My darling, can we have another round and cash out?" Angie calls to the pixie of a bartender behind the counter.

"We're cashing out already? Wasn't this your idea to go out and get weird?" I ask her with a confused look and gesture around the room.

"Girl, we are staying out until we see the sun, calm down. But we're not staying in one bar all night." Angie smooths out her fitted skirt and shimmies. "I didn't dress up like this not to show it off. So, let's finish this next drink and head to the next bar, then the next one, and maybe get some nachos on the way."

"Maybe?" I say incredulously.

Angie giggles, "Okay, okay, definitely, one hundred percent chance we are getting those corn 'chos that we love."

"Now *that's* a plan I can get behind." Accepting my second drink from the bartender, I clink Angie's glass.

We down our refreshments after only a few minutes, excited to start our journey to the next bar. As I standup from the faux-leather bar stool, my bare legs essentially ripping themselves off, I wince and turn my torso around to inspect the back of them. "Are they red?" I ask her. "I probably shouldn't have worn this dress. It's too short and flouncy. I'm going to end up flashing my panties to someone."

The summer dress is pale blue which I think compliments my long wild brunette curls. It has thin spaghetti straps and is tight enough around the chest that I didn't have to wear a bra with it—also known as a dream dress for us card-carrying Big Titty Committee members.

"With any luck," she smirks.

As we head for the exit of the bar, shaking my head, I grouse, "You're incorrigible. But that's not the plan tonight. It's you and me and—*oh my god, a puppy!*" I shriek so loud, I'm sure if we weren't already leaving, we'd be asked to. I zero my line of sight on the tiny bulldog puppy and immediately go in to cup its face and nuzzle my nose to its fuzzy body.

Yup, I'm definitely buzzed because I know better than to pet a random dog without permission.

With my tiny creature/mother hen voice, I gently whisper, "Oh my goodness, you sweet baby puppy, I could just eat you up!" And I continue to make kissy sounds.

"Wow, what would I have to do to get a reception like that?" a low voice says from very close to me. Strangely close.

I slowly look up and realize I'm standing mere inches away from a tall, golden-skinned man with dark hair that falls forward over his brow. He's wearing an olive T-shirt that fits damn well over his chest and arms. A man who is holding a bulldog puppy in his hands against said chest... right in front of my face. My eyes go wide, and I take a big step back, covering my mouth with my hands, embarrassed that I basically assaulted this man's personal space. I didn't even see him because I was so focused on this tiny angel in his arms.

"I am so sorry. I don't know what I was thinking. That was so rude of me to pet your dog without permission and—"

He grins at me with a beautiful smile and chuckles. "It's okay, believe me. I'm supposed to be helping my friend socialize his new puppy anyway." He tips his head, gesturing over to another man with a mess of dark blonde shoulder-length hair, a crisp white short-sleeve button-down that hugs his arms, and what can only be described as 'sexy glasses.' He's sitting at the bar's outdoor seating with–

"ANOTHER BULLDOG?" Angie squeals and leaps for it, lying down at its owner's feet. This one is full-grown and clearly tired. She stops short and looks at the other man as if realizing she needs to not make the same mistake I just did. "May I pet your dog?"

The man smiles and nods his head, "Sure. Her name is Fiona. My name is Noah," he says and points back to the puppy in tall-dark-and-golden's arms. "His name is Duke."

Angie proceeds to lie on the ground next to Fiona as if laying on a dirty concrete sidewalk is no different than a sofa.

"To be clear, this little guy is Duke," the man in front of me says, as he bounces the pup in his arms. "I'm Jay. And if you tell me your name, I'll let you hold him."

"I–" I start.

But the other man, Noah, sitting next to Fiona and Angie, pipes up, "He's talking about himself, not the dog."

Jay and I both chuckle, "I'm Cora, and this is the best deal ever." I step closer to Jay and take Duke from his hands. Jay looks to be Asian, but I can't place it. It's probably for the best that I don't ask right now; not the ideal time to play '*Guess the Ethnicity*' while drunk.

He smiles brightly. "To be clear, I'm totally fine with you holding me, too. Everyone likes to be the little spoon."

I smile and give him an arched eyebrow while I hold Duke close to my face, and he chomps his tiny mouth over my nose. I could die happy right here. What's better than puppy breath and snuggles? I squeal more as the puppy bites and licks my nose. I look over at Angie rubbing Fiona's belly and panting with her tongue out, mimicking the dog.

"Ugh, girl, do we have to keep bar hopping?" I groan. "I'd

gladly give up cocktails and 'chos for puppies."

Angie laughs and agrees. "I know, right?"

"What are *'chos?*" Jay asks.

"Nachos," I answer, looking up at him while shamelessly smelling the tiny cherub in my hands. "There's a place down the road that has amazing nachos, and they put corn in the homemade cheese sauce. Corn! It's what dreams are made of."

"Oh, I know the place you're talking about," Noah chimes. "I live nearby."

Jay laughs at me, turns to his friend, and says, "Well, what do you think, Noah? Should we join these ladies for some drinks and 'chos?"

"Quite presumptuous, aren't you?" Angie asks.

"We'll buy?" Jay asks Angie and turns to me. "It's the least you could let us do after assaulting our dogs," he smirks.

"*My* dogs," Noah adds.

"Whatever. When beautiful women want to talk to you, you keep that shit going as long as you can, man."

Angie and I look at each other. She smiles, and I remember why we're here in the first place: to be carefree and have fun. Old Cora wouldn't have thought twice about meeting strangers and striking up a party. I smile back at her and look at Jay. Fuck, he's pretty. Strong eyebrows, deep dark eyes, full lips, and a jawline that would make a Calvin Klein model jealous.

"Alright, fine," I roll my eyes dramatically with a grin. "We will let you guys pay for our drinks and 'chos."

We spend the next couple of hours meandering through downtown, going from bar to bar. Noah took the dogs to his apartment and met back up with us in time to finally indulge in our mess of corn cheese nachos. Eating could not have come at a better moment because I need to sober up a bit. I am having too much fun. At some point, Jay put his arm around my shoulder as we walked, and I wrapped mine around his waist. He smells like sweet and spicy citrus in a way that envelops my senses in a warm hug. It feels so natural, and I realize I miss this kind of easy. Laughing with each other, flirting, teasing. It's exciting and comforting.

Noah and Angie seem to be in a similar state. She and I keep smiling at each other as if to say *how is this happening to us?*

As the four of us are sitting together, digging into the food, I ask, "So, how do you boys know each other?"

Noah gives Jay a devious look. "We used to date. Didn't work out, but we're good friends now."

I'm pretty sure my mouth is on the floor. Wow, I misread this whole situation. No wonder I was having such an easy time with him. He's non-threatening, flippantly flirtatious, and so freaking hot. God, I'm blind.

Jay chuckles and leans down to me in the booth seat next to him and whispers with a smirk, "Don't look so shocked, Cora. You still have a chance with me tonight." Then he places his hand on my knee and slowly drags it up my bare thigh. "I can play for any team."

I immediately turn red and grab his hand to stop him from going any farther. *Jesus*, the confidence of this man! I mean, I'm into this, but I do not want to play a game of chicken in this very public restaurant.

Angie clears her throat and—not very casually—asks Noah, "And, ahem, uhh, what about you? Do you have a, um, a team?"

Smooth, Ang.

Noah leans over to cup her face, and grins, "I'm sorry babe, I'm as gay as they make 'em."

"Damn. I knew you were too good to be true," she mutters, shifting her gaze.

"Aww, come on, you're not gonna dump us now, are you?"

Noah feigns with a sarcastic pout. "Let me make it up to you by taking you dancing at the club down the street. My treat."

"Oh, hell yeah!" Angie and I say in unison, like the cultured and sophisticated women we are.

Both men laugh with us while Jay slides his hand around my lower back, gently grabbing my hip, and whispers in my ear, "Mmm, this I'm really going to enjoy." Chills run down my body, and butterflies erupt in my belly at the low timbre of his voice. I'm pretty sure I just did an involuntary Keagle.

As we leave the restaurant, Noah carries Angie on his back, her skirt just long enough to cover her ass. I walk with Jay, arm in arm behind them, to make sure her skirt stays down.

"So, what do you do for a living, Cora?" Jay asks. "Tell me everything about you."

So far, I've been pretty forthcoming about myself, but I don't want to give Jay the wrong impression. I'm out here for one night. I'm not looking for a relationship. I have too much going on in my life as it is. Between my mother and career, I'm hyper focused on succeeding at both. Not to mention the mental mess I would bring to a relationship now. Knowing just by giving him my first name, plus architect, plus Philadelphia, and entering that into a search bar, he could easily find me. Good thing my social media accounts are private already.

I lie to him and blurt, "I'm a dental hygienist." Grateful for the cleaning I had done yesterday, so that job was at the tip of my tongue.

"That must be why you have a radiant smile."

Blushing, I look away and then back up at him, asking, "And what about you? What do you do?"

"I'm in Human Resources."

"Do you enjoy it?"

"God, yes. I find it fascinating. There is nothing I love more than getting that piping hot tea directly from the source, you know? I know it's petty, but I love gossip, and I always want to get to the bottom of it. What better way than to make it your job to know people's business?" He chuckles to himself, "I swear I don't go spreading their dirty laundry around. I keep it locked up from other employees. But man, do I have juicy stories."

"Can you tell me any?"

"Well, there was this one time I had just started with this company and didn't know everyone that well yet. I walked into this meeting that I was briefly prepped for, about a newly married husband and wife, who both work for the company, asking about what they need to do to be on each other's insurance and all that benefits merging stuff, you know? So they walk in, and all three of us stand shocked to see one another. Turns out, I had made out with both of them before they were ever together."

"Shut up!" I exclaim, stopping in my tracks and turning to look at him head-on. "No way."

"Can't make that shit up."

"Oh my god. That *is* juicy," I beam as we arrive at the nightclub line.

He steps a little closer so we're chest to chest, and he smooths his hands down my back and squeezes my ass, "That's the way I like it, Cora."

Holy shit—that innuendo is not lost on me.

"Come on, guys, we're heading in!" Noah yells back to us, yanking me out of my sexy real-life daydream. Jay takes my hand, lacing our fingers, and pulls me into the dark club. Apparently, Noah knows the bouncer, so we were able to cut in front of the small line.

Once we're in, Jay asks, "Can I get you a drink?"

"Honestly, I think I need to stop with alcohol. The 'chos helped with soaking up the booze, and I'm feeling really good.

I want to ride this out now. Maybe water would be a good choice." Jay leads me to the bar. Pressing my front against the rail, he leans his tall frame against me with his hands on my hips. He grabs the bartender's attention and orders two waters; all the while, he's stroking my hips and thighs. He leaves a tip, and we chug our waters, leaving the cups and heading to the dance floor.

Noah and Angie are already dancing to the music. It's some dance remix to ABBA's *Gimme! Gimme! Gimme!* And they are really getting after it, grinding on each other and laughing.

Before we reach the dance floor, I lean close to Jay and exclaim over the club sounds, "I adore ABBA!"

He leans back with a big smile and yells, "Who doesn't?" And then he lifts me up in a hug, twirling me around.

I giggle and scream, "Liars, that's who!"

God, I want to kiss him right now. I was never one to make the first move but fuck it. Carefree Cora is here and having the best night ever. And Jay has been more than obvious with his attention and touches and flirtations tonight.

I'm going for it.

As he sets me down, my arms quickly grab the back of his neck to keep him from standing back up straight, and I look into his eyes with what feels like a permanent smile from this evening. "Kiss me, Jay."

His eyes light up, and he immediately closes the gap and firmly presses his lips to mine. We both inhale, and I'm pretty sure time has stopped. The world has stopped. Nothing else exists at this moment except our mouths crashing into each other.

I feel him requesting more access, so I open my mouth as he gently slides his tongue against mine, tasting me. He moves one hand to my lower back, and the other goes to the back of my neck, pulling me against his body and deepening the kiss. I can feel his erection against my stomach, taunting me and driving me wild.

Ugh, this kiss! It feels like fireworks are going off in my body. "Cora," Jay groans. "You taste like heaven."

As the beat continues to thump in my chest, we kiss for what feels like hours. God, he tastes so good. His lips are so full, and desire is coursing through my veins with every lick and nibble. I'm consumed by this man.

When we come to, the song has changed to something sexy and slow. "Come on, dance with me, Jay."

We start to move our bodies against each other to the beat of the music. I move my hands over his shoulders, and he drags his eyes over my face and chest, slowly moving his hand from my neck, over my shoulder, and lays it flat on my breast while the other hand grabs my ass cheek. What we're doing right now is positively indecent, but the club is crowded, and no one seems to mind.

Jay whispers in my ear, "You may taste like heaven, but you dance like sin."

Jesus, I think my panties have dissolved, and I've been set on fire.

Who am I right now? I'm certainly not the workaholic control freak who never makes time for herself. I'm not the stressed-out woman who's been dealing with divorce lawyers and wallowing in any spare moment I have.

No, tonight I am free and unencumbered. Jay makes me feel like I'm floating in a pool of desire and ecstasy.

As much as I never want this feeling to end, I know it's only for tonight. And if that's the case, then I'm going to make the most of it. I'm going to let him worship my body tonight and fuck his brains out.

After a few more songs, I turn to look at Angie, and she gives me the wink and head nod combo, secretly telling me to *go ahead, get it*. I turn my head back to Jay and smile sweetly at him, slowing my gyrating down. I reach my hand in between us and palm his erection. His jaw drops, and his pupils seem to explode.

In my most sultry and seductive voice, I ask him, "And what are we going to do about this?"

He crashes his mouth against mine, moaning into my mouth. Breathlessly he asks, "Dirty club bathroom or my car? It's parked at Noah's apartment close by."

"Car. Definitely. I need you."

He grabs my hand and begins dragging me through the crowd of people and outside. At this point, we are full-on running and giggling the whole way. Jay's erection is prominent in his jeans, but he doesn't seem to care that anyone we pass by can see. My tits are bouncing like crazy, and I wrap my free hand against them, wishing I had a sports bra on at this moment.

We round the corner of a building, and he leads me to his SUV, which is tucked between two other cars and a brick wall in front. He leans me against the door and presses the full weight of his hard body against mine, grinding his cock against my center. The friction is absolutely maddening. He grabs my waist and dips his mouth to my neck, licking and nibbling at my pulse.

"Open the damn door, Jay," I pant into his ear.

"Yes, ma'am," he says, fumbling for his key fob in his pocket. I notice all the windows are tinted dark, thank god.

Once the locks beep, he whips open the rear passenger seat door and hops in first, sitting on a soft leather bench seat. He reaches a hand out for me to grab, and I hoist myself in and immediately straddle his lap.

Thank fuck it's clean in here. There is no greater turn-off

than a messy car.

Jay makes quick work of pulling down the zipper in the back of my dress and then pushing the straps over my shoulders and tugging the bodice down, freeing my breasts.

Groaning, he grabs them both, cupping and massaging them. He leans in and nuzzles his face right in my cleavage. He inhales a deep guttural breath as my back arches, allowing him better access. "Fucking hell, Cora, these tits are perfect. If you wanted to smother me with them, I'd thank you."

I giggle, but it quickly turns into a moan as he tweaks my nipples in his fingers.

"Oh my... is someone aroused?" Jay asks with hooded eyes and a positively sinful look on his face. "Does nipple play get you going, Cora?"

Panting, I whisper, "I didn't know it did until right now."

Jay smiles and leans in to gently lick one of my nipples, running his flat tongue over my areola, too. He continues this and starts to add sucking pressure, all while gently tugging and caressing my other breast.

I wasn't lying before. I really didn't think I was one of those women who got turned on by nipple stimulation. I have no idea what's going on with me tonight. It's like everything he does, everything he says has a direct connection to my pussy, making it throb with need.

I can't stand it any longer. I need to relieve this ache. I need to feel his hot flesh against my inner walls, filling me.

"Please tell me you have protection, Jay."

"Yes, of course. Sit up, turn around, and grab one from the center console."

I do as he says, and he takes the opportunity to pull his zipper down and shimmy his jeans and briefs down to his ankles. I hand him the condom that I've already ripped open, and he quickly takes it and sheaths his—*whoa*—very large cock.

"Holy shit, Jay... how... I... whoa." I can't even string together a coherent sentence. I've never been with a man this big before.

"I know, baby. It's okay. I'll warm you up, don't worry." I straddle him again and nod. "Can I touch you and make you feel better? Make you ready?" His voice is so gravelly and confident. I can't help but give him what he's asking for.

"Yes, please," I whisper to him.

He gently reaches under the skirt of my dress and cups his hand against my sex, stroking his fingers against the seam over my panties.

"You're so wet, baby. Oh my god, is this all for me? How bad do you need me?"

"Fuck, Jay. Really bad. Please make me feel good." I can't think straight anymore. Whatever he wants, whatever he says, I'll agree if it means he can make me come.

Jay then moves my skimpy panties to the side and runs the pad of his finger straight to my clit, gently circling and pushing on it. He works my body for a while, and I can feel my climax building. He adds his thumb and starts to pull on the sensitive peak, causing me to hunch forward with my forehead pressed to his.

"Yes, Jay! Yes, yes, yes. Don't stop. *Oh fuck*. Fuck, I'm coming!"

Then without notice, he uses his other hand and thrusts his fingers inside of me, and begins stroking my G-spot while still rubbing my clit. I wasn't even done with that orgasm before he brought another one rolling out like a tidal wave.

Jay brings his lips to mine as I moan and whimper into his mouth and contract around his fingers. "That's a good girl. Fuck, you're so beautiful."

I giggle into his face and let out a deep sigh as my orgasm fades away. "Welp, I got what I needed. See ya."

"What?" Jay exclaims with a smile as I pretend to lift myself off him. He quickly pulls me back down and tickles my sides.

Squirming uncontrollably, I laugh deeply and muster out, "I was kidding! I was kidding!"

When he stops torturing me, he brings both of his hands to my face and pulls me in for a drugging kiss, both of us relaxing into each other. He pulls back and softly says, "I didn't mean it like that; I'm sorry. If you want to stop, we can."

"No. I don't want to stop, Jay. I want to make you feel good, too."

"Only if you're sure..." he trails off, and I quickly nod my assurance. He blinks, and his hesitancy turns back into lust at my consent. "Then put your hand on my cock and guide it to that dripping wet pussy. Let me fill you up."

I reach down between us and wrap my hand around his rock-hard erection, still sheathed in the condom from earlier. Bringing it to my center, I run the tip along the seam and then rock slowly, coating his length in my wetness.

Jay's eyes are locked on mine, our breathing in sync, mouths parted as I slowly lower myself on him. Already feeling full, I stop my movements and bring both hands around his neck, closing my eyes and leaning against his forehead.

"Oh my god. That's so much, Jay. Please, just... just give me a moment."

I feel the breath from a silent chuckle on my face. "That's only half of it, sweetheart."

"Holy shit."

"It's okay. We're going to go slow until you feel ready. Rock your hips against me, and sink down at your own pace," Jay coaches while stroking my back and smoothing his hands over my hips and thighs. "That's it, Cora. Good girl. You're doing so well," he purrs in my ear.

His praise sends a truckload of dopamine to my brain as I finally get fully seated on his dick.

"Yeeeeees, baby," Jay groans and throws his head back, squeezing my hips. "Now come on, rock on me. Make yourself feel good. Use me."

As I do, I feel better and better, grinding my clit against his taut pelvis, but it's not enough. Whimpering, I ask, "Can you help? I need more."

"You need me to take control, Cora?" he asks through gritted teeth, his voice rumbling through me.

"Please. I'm begging you."

He starts with a few shallow thrusts, hands on my waist, pulling me down when he needs to. "Is that okay, baby? Can you take more?"

"Yes, Jay. Please. More." I pant, still holding his neck for balance.

"Okay, sweetheart, hold on tight." Without any more hesitation, Jay slams into me from below. Thrusting and slapping against me, causing my tits to bounce in his face. I can feel my orgasm building already, but I want more. I move a hand to my clit and start playing with it, and Jay grits out, "Oh yes, beautiful. Play with yourself. That's it. *Fuck*, that's hot. Do you like to be spanked, baby?"

I have never been spanked in the throes of it before, but my deep seeded desires have decided to manifest themselves right here, right now, and before I can think about any kind of judgment, I moan, "Yes. Please spank me."

Jay quickly flips my skirt up and bunches it with one hand while the other—*Crack! Crack! Crack!*—rapidly smacks my ass, making me clench so hard around his punishing cock.

Goddammit, that feels amazing.

"Holy shit, Cora, I'm not gonna make it much longer. You're squeezing me so tight, baby."

"Come for me, Jay. I'm almost there. Keep spanking me." *Crack! Crack! Crack!* "That's it! Oh fuck, I'm... I'm..." I then quickly change from rubbing my clit to using my fingernails to pinch my labia so hard that I think I might be drawing blood. "Fuck, yes. I'm coming!" I scream.

Jay's thrusts become erratic and without rhythm as he wraps his arms under my shoulders and pulls me tight to him, sealing our mouths together in a clash of teeth and grunts. "That's my good... fucking... girl..."

Jay finally slows and steadies himself and me. Panting heavily, the windows are fogged up, and the air is thick with arousal. I don't know where my mind is, but it's gone. My body is limp and sweaty against his.

Holy. Shit.

"Cora. Baby, are you okay? Tell me how you're feeling."

Still lying against him, my head in the crook of his neck, I let out an exasperated gasp and giggle. "I am spent. Happy. Relieved."

"Good. That was incredible." He sighs and reaches to put a hand on my head and wrap his arm around me, holding me tight. So comforting I could cry.

"Come on, pretty lady, let's get cleaned up and go get some Late Night Cookies down the road. They're open until 1:00 am, so we can probably catch them before they close."

I was supposed to get out of this one-night stand with a clean break, but I'm sorry, warm cookies are now on the table? Hell yeah.

I laugh and extract myself from Jay, moving my panties back in place and him removing the condom, tying it up, and wrapping it in a napkin to toss later. We hop out of the car, the summer night air a cool shock to the sex sauna we made. Grabbing my tiny purse from the back seat, I take my phone out and see a string of texts from Angie.

> Angie: Are you safe? Text me your location, slut.

> Angie: Bitch, I gave you permission to ditch me for dick, so you better reply.

> Cora: Lol yes, I'm safe. We just had wild sex in his car <fire emoji> <eggplant emoji> Walking to Late Night Cookies right now.

> Angie: Get it, girl! I'm actually in line there right now! I'll buy some cookies for you guys.

> Cora: Awesome. Hey, when we get there, can you make an excuse for us to leave right away? I'm not sure how to end this...

> Angie: Lol what are best friends for? <wink emoji>

"Angie is already there and will meet us," I tell Jay as we start walking.

"Wait, wait, wait," Jay urges, stopping me in my quest for warm, gooey treats. He wraps his arms around me and presses my head against his shoulder. "Let me hold you for just a moment longer. I–I'm sorry," he chuckles. "I can get a little needy and affectionate right after sex."

Wow, this is unexpected. I've never done random hookups, but wasn't the guy always supposed to be trying to get out of the situation as fast as possible? I guess that could be said for women, too. Hell, if it weren't for the cookies waiting for me, I'd be doing that.

Jay is giving tender boyfriend vibes right now, and if I wanted a relationship, I would revel in this kind of intimacy. But that can't happen. There is absolutely no room in my life for a relationship despite this sweet and sexy man holding me tight and breathing deeply into my hair.

"God, what is this shampoo, Cora? Fuck, it smells good."

I sigh and pull away slightly. "I think it's tea tree oil and rosemary." Wanting to end this too comforting embrace, I smile and pat him on the chest. "Come on, you owe me cookies after that romp."

With a deep laugh, he turns and puts his arm over my shoulder, just as he did earlier in the night, and we start walking. "A romp? Who says that?"

"Um, women who don't have romps very often?" I reply with total humiliating honesty.

"Could have fooled me," he smirks. "And I mean this is the most respectful way possible—that was professional level, hun." Gasping, I pinch his side, and he squirms away, chuckling in that low voice.

We make it another block or two to the shop and see Angie waiting for us outside with a box of warm cookies and bottles of milk. She gives us a knowing look and leads us to a bench close by.

"Where's Noah?" Jay asks Angie. We open the warm box and the aroma of butter, sugar, and cocoa wafts to our noses.

"I don't really know. We were at the club, and I lost him."

"Damn it. He's probably hooking up with that piece of shit bouncer friend of his. God, he treats Noah like trash." He takes a bite of a peanut butter cup cookie and groans the same way I heard him do not fifteen minutes ago. I shiver, remembering the beautiful man falling apart at my touch.

"Oh, Cora, our Uber will be here in two minutes," Angie says, looking at her phone, pulling me out of my sexy dream state.

Jay jerks his head in my direction with a concerned look, furrowing his full eyebrows. "I—damn. I've had the best night. Can I get your number, Cora?"

I hesitate, panic rolling through me. I need a clean break, but I'm also not one to disappoint people. How do people do this regularly?

If I give him a fake number, he'll probably text me immediately and notice it doesn't come through. Then the idea hits me: I can give him my real number but block him tomorrow. Yup, that's the plan.

"Sure, give me your phone." He smiles so big and bright it makes me feel guilty. I'm going to hurt him, and that hurts me. "Just send a text to your number with your name and your favorite emoji," he says. I can hear Angie quietly snort next to me as if to say *you are so fucked, girl*.

I enter it and send it with a chocolate chip cookie emoji, handing him the phone back with a smile.

"Uber's here!" Angie chimes and stands up, folding the box and taking it with her as she heads toward the Toyota Camry in front of us.

Jay grabs my hand and brings it to his lips, kissing it and staring directly into my eyes. "I'll call you. I had an amazing night, Cora. Please don't disappear on me."

With my gut dropping from guilt and butterflies coursing

through my body, I smile and whisper, "Okay. I had a great night, too."

He leans in and kisses me one last time. A gentle, tender kiss that breaks me.

Sighing, he stands up, pulls me with him, and walks me to the car. I slide in next to Angie and gulp, "Goodnight, Jay."

With positively puppy dog-like eyes, he smiles. "Goodnight, Cora. Talk soon." And he gently shuts the door.

Not a minute later, I get a text from a new number.

> Unknown number: Like I'll be able to sleep tonight after meeting the most delicious woman ever. Text me when u get home so I know ur safe?

With a heavy heart, I go into the info section of the contact and hover my thumb over the *Block Caller* prompt. I sigh, close my eyes, and press it.

CHAPTER 2

You're Kidding Me

CORA

Two And A Half Years Later

The meeting reminder trills and pops up on my desktop screen, indicating my Monday morning weekly check-in starts now. *Shit.* I hate being late. It's so unprofessional. It's the last thing I want to appear as, especially in front of Jonathan. But since I had to get into the office at 6:30 this morning so I could get a head start on the new auditorium renovation proposal, I've been sucked in and lost track of time.

I hurriedly undock my laptop and grab my notebook and sketchbook, tucking them under my arm and rushing to the conference room. I look around the office as I quickly make my way, my dark green palazzo pants billowing in my wake. I see almost everyone is at their desks and small breakout stations with coffees. Some people are looking over large rolls of prints, and another small group has a zoomed-in image of a foundation cutout, pointing to it and marking it with edits directly on the interactive smart screen.

I know exactly what they're discussing from this far away, and I sigh with dread.

Approaching the frosted glass conference room door, I push it open, and everyone quiets down, looking up at me. Jonathan, our CFO—and pain in my ass—mutters under his breath, but just loud enough for everyone to hear, "About time." His salt and pepper hair is cut short, the same way it's been since I met him fifteen years ago.

I make my way to the head of the large conference room table, setting my stuff down and collecting myself, "Sorry I'm late. Let's begin. First thing's first," I sit down in my chair and look up to our Legal Counsel, Horatio, "where are we with the lawsuit?"

Then my eyes suddenly catch on the new person sitting next to him.

What the hell? Why is Jay here?

His eyes are huge, and his look of shock is certainly mirroring mine.

"Our legal team is preparing..." Horatio starts with a confident tone, but my mind is reeling, and his words disappear in the fog of my confusion. I open my notebook and start to take notes because I cannot look in that direction right now. I pretend to jot down what is being said, but I just keep writing *WTF WTF WTF.*

You know, most people would probably forget about their one-night stands from over two years ago, but not me, as hard as I've tried. I've kept myself insanely busy whether I like it or not. Between my mother going into assisted living for Alzheimer's over a year ago and my father unexpectedly passing away shortly after, leaving me in charge of this architecture firm he had spent his whole life building, I've been going nonstop. So here I am, trying to prove my abilities as CEO and senior architect. At thirty-one years old, I can't believe this is the hand I've been dealt sometimes.

But as busy as I've stayed, I never forgot about that night. His lips. His hands. His warm citrus smell.

"Cora? Do you have any questions?" Horatio asks me as I lift my head up and pretend I was listening. I'm sure Sue will send the meeting notes later, and I'll read them to catch up with what Legal just said.

Okay, act like you were paying attention, Cora.

"Not at this time, Mr. Alvarez. Of course, please let me know if you need anything from us. We're here to help you as much as you're helping us."

I see Jay lean over to listen to something Katie, our heavily pregnant Office Manager, is whispering to him.

Needing to put myself out of this curious misery, I speak up, "Katie, can you please introduce us?"

Katie looks at me and pulls away from whispering. "Of course." She gestures to Jay and announces, "This is Jay Bishop. He's our new Human Resources Director."

Fucking hell.

I now vaguely remember seeing a resume come across my desk about a new HR Director applicant named Jay Bishop. As much as I have thought about him at night, alone in my bed, I did not compute that *this* Jay was one and the same. I think I mostly looked at his experience and approved the hire.

Katie looks at him and asks, "Would you like to say anything?"

Jay's wearing a fitted dark blue suit and a white dress shirt with tiny light pink polka dots, almost imperceptible in size.

He waves his hand in greeting and announces to the room, "Good morning, everyone. From what Legal has told me just now, it looks like I'm going to have my hands full."

An image of Jay squeezing my ass and cupping my breasts plays in my head. Oh god, this is doubly not appropriate to be fantasizing about my new employee and HR Director.

"Anyway, I hope to get to know you all, and thanks for bringing me onto the team." Jay looks at me with a sheepish smile and sits back in his chair.

"Cora, are you still good with giving Jay a tour today?" Katie asks.

Goddammit.

I forgot about that tradition. My father always took the new hires on a tour of the office and got lunch with them one-on-one. Everyone from new executives to interns. He always said it was a great way to show that you value each person as more than an employee. To let them know they shouldn't be intimidated to talk to you.

As much as I never thought I'd be in a situation like this, I want to uphold that sentiment and make my father proud.

"Of course. Jay, I'll come by your office at 11:30 for the tour. Will that work for you?"

"Yes, ma'am," he says, jotting a note down.

Oh, no, he did not just say that. Once again, taking me back to our wild night in his car.

Schooling my features, I reply, "I'll see you then."

The rest of the meeting passes as usual; discussing our Requests For Proposals and Requests For Quotes, where we are with current projects, and the upcoming holiday party.

When the meeting ends, I quickly grab my things and book it out of there before anyone can stop me. I'm going to hole myself up in my office and scream into my couch cushions until, hopefully, I spontaneously combust.

As I walk toward Jay's new office, I stop in the bathroom to look at myself. My long sleeve white blouse is tucked into my dramatic high-waisted evergreen pants. I untuck it, stare at myself, and tuck it back in. I long ago decided to accentuate my ample curves after falling in love with women in Renaissance paintings. Granted, I'm larger, but I'm just as soft and beautifully plump as them. So instead of trying to hide or shrink myself, I tastefully show it off. I have spent too much time worrying about my body in my younger days. Freeing myself from that mental prison was one of the best things I've ever done.

My long chestnut hair is pulled back in a high pony, holding back my mass of curls, and my makeup is simple with a striking black eyeliner wing.

Jeez, why am I fussing over my appearance? It's not like I'm trying to impress him. If anything, I should be making myself unappealing.

Shaking my head and looking the exact same as I did a couple of minutes ago, I storm out of the bathroom and take a deep breath.

You can do this, Cora. You're a professional. You're in control.

I repeat this mantra until I approach Jay's office, where the door is propped open. The glass wall and door of his office are completely frosted. Being in HR, we made sure each person in that department had complete privacy.

"Knock, knock," I say by way of greeting, meeting his dark eyes as they turn from his computer to me.

Leaning back in his chair with his strong arms crossed, he tilts his head to the side, narrows his gaze. "Well, well, well. Isn't this something out of a comedy?"

"Okay, yes. I'll just get this over with now." I sigh deeply and spew the apology I know he deserves. "What I did was shitty, and you didn't deserve that. I didn't know how to be upfront with you about that—" I turn back to look for anyone coming down the hall and step into his office further. "—about that night being a one-time thing. I wasn't in a position to have a relationship of any kind. I'm really sorry, Jay."

Something resembling sorrow crosses his face. "Not even a friendship? I thought we had a really fun night. If you would have said that before, I still would have liked to hang out regardless... as friends."

I don't know what to say. That wasn't the response I was anticipating. We're basically stuck with each other now, so I might as well mend the bridge.

I pull my phone from my pocket and tap the screen several times. I'm sure he probably thinks I'm being rude as hell, but he won't in a second.

I find what I'm looking for and show him my phone screen. "Is this your number?" I ask, pointing to what I assume is his, showing him the Blocked Callers list.

"Yeah, that's it," he mumbles.

I bring the phone back into my view and tap *Unblock*. I give him a smile, "There. Unblocked." Then I quickly send him a text.

> Cora: This is your boss.

Jay reaches for his phone on his desk, looks at it, and chuckles. "Thanks, boss."

The corners of my lips curl up. "Let's work on a professional relationship first before we dive into a friendship, okay?"

"Alright," he agrees and nods his head. "So, are you going to give me this tour or what?"

Smiling, I gesture for the door. "Of course. Follow me."

I led us around the entire facility, showing him the trendy office area filled with architects, interior designers, civil engineers, soil engineers, accounting, and everyone else in between. I explain how we schedule conference rooms and breakout spaces. I take him through the whole office space, break room, supply closet, server room, and modest gym with adjoining locker rooms.

When he sees the gym, he beams. "Nice! This is definitely a perk. I don't always get time to go to my normal gym across the city."

"Yeah, you'd be surprised how many people don't use this," I say. "You might be the only one if you come here."

An image of Jay pops into my traitorous brain of him in low-hung shorts and no shirt, glistening with sweat, doing bicep curls.

Get your head in the game, girl!
You're a professional.
You're in control.

I repeat that mantra until we get to our final destination in the printing room. It's a large space with plotters, 3D printers, and traditional printers. There are closets tucked into the walls housing all kinds of paper and printing materials.

"Wow. You'd think in our digital age you'd utilize less printing," he says as we slowly make our way through the room.

I smile and agree. "Architects still heavily rely on it. We take our printing pretty seri—*Ouch!*" I wince as I bang my hip into a protruding side table attached to one of the plotters.

"Are you okay?" Jay comes to my side and reaches his hands out for me, pulling me away from the table corner and steadying me. But before he lets go of me, my body warms from his simple touch. He's simply gripping behind my elbows with our forearms touching. There's nothing inherently sensual about it, but I can't help the horny little vixen in my brain from squealing.

I shake him off and step away on solid footing. Not looking him in the eyes, I shrug. "Yeah, I'm okay. Thanks." Smoothing out my pants and righting myself, I finally look at him and ask, "Should we grab our coats and head to lunch then? Katie told you about that, right?"

He nods. "Yeah, sounds good. Let's go."

As we sit across from each other at the bougie quick-service salad restaurant down the street, we open the tan biodegradable containers and start to dig in.

"You know, I'm all for recycling and composting," Jay contemplates, "but there's something so right about eating a salad from a giant clear plastic bowl. I blame the Kardashians."

I giggle at that. The image of a stoic Kourtney eating from a salad bowl three times the size of her head playing in my mind.

Smiling, I reply, "I think there are a number of societal problems that might stem from the Kardashians."

He lets out a small huff, "Maybe."

Moving the conversation back to a professional topic, I ask him, "So, why did you apply for this job? Give me the honest answer, not the contrived one that strokes executives' egos."

"Fair enough." He stabs around his salad and grins. "At my last job, I was an HR Representative. I actually have a degree in Mechanical Engineering and one in Business Administration. I worked as an ME for a year before I realized I was bored out of my mind. I found pleasure in talking with people, learning about them, and yes," he rolls his eyes and continues, "collecting gossip."

I smirk, remembering him telling me about the tea. "Anyway, I made the transition to Human Resources. When I switched companies to the one I was at for the last five years, I already had a few years of experience as an HR Rep." Jay sighs. "I watched my last HR Manager get replaced four times while I was there. They kept bringing in these morons, and they never stuck. Meanwhile, there I was, picking up the slack of every lost manager and doing their work. I eagerly volunteered to take the job every chance I could, but the powers-that-be wanted to keep me right where I was.

"So, here I am, taking the job that I know I can do with a company that actually believes in me."

Jay arches his eyebrows quickly and looks down at his salad, taking a bite.

Well, damn.

When I meet his gaze, I offer him something I once heard my dad say, "I think everyone needs to take responsibility for their own career trajectory. Sure, sometimes opportunities fall right into our laps, and privilege can have a lot to do with that, but it's up to each person to make the most of it and steer themselves to success the best way they can. Sometimes that's leaning on a network of people, and sometimes that's forging your own path."

When he smiles back at me, I add, "I'm happy you're forging your own path."

"Thank you, Cora. That actually means a lot to me."

With a curious thought popping into my head, I follow up with another question. "So, you didn't know I was the CEO and senior architect of this firm? I'm on our website."

He grins and folds over, covering his eyes with his palms and leaning on the table. Groaning, he mutters, "Okay, you caught me. I didn't research the firm that thoroughly."

I laugh and put him at ease. "It's okay. A tempting job opportunity was dangling in your face, and you had tunnel vision."

He was a tempting opportunity that I had tunnel vision for... Fuck, Cora. Control yourself.

He chuckles, "I suppose you're right. My boyfriend kept hyping me up, and I guess I spent too much time already envisioning myself as the Director here."

What did he say? I think my brain is buffering.

Boyfriend?

I shouldn't be shocked. This should be a good thing. One more very important barrier to add to the list of reasons I can't have a relationship with this man. This beautiful, smoking hot, sweet man...

Pull it together, boss lady.

No, no, no. This *is* a good thing. He's taken. I'm not looking for a relationship, and I'm certainly not a homewrecker. He wants to be friends. This all equals a healthy start to a friendship.

Yup. That's where I'm driving this train of thought. This can work.

Circling back to the conversation *outside* my brain, I smile, probably too big, and tell him, "I'm glad to hear you have such a great support system. That's so important to have."

Nice recovery.

We then finish our salads, and he asks, "Shall we head back? I think my team has a kind of meet and greet set up for me to get to know them."

"Of course!" I cheer, then tone it down and casually add, "I have a mountain of work and legal stuff to get through anyway."

We toss our containers, bundle up and exit the building into the blustery winter day. The cold air is like a shock to my system, reminding me to keep it profesh.

Chapter 3

The First Week

Jay

By the end of my first week at Define Architectural Group, the initial shock of seeing Cora again still hasn't totally worn off. I am still trying to come to terms with the fact that she is not only in my life on a full-time basis now, but also *my boss*.

And damn, she looks every bit as beautiful as the night I met her.

Even though she hurt me, I've thought about that night often since it happened. I even told my boyfriend about it back when we were just friends, swapping stories about people we've slept with. That's always been a topic both of us still feel comfortable talking about, even now that we're together. We're monogamous, but we can still point out people we find attractive and reminisce about flings without jealousy and without fear of the other leaving.

However, I haven't brought up that Cora is my new boss

with him yet. A part of me is afraid this might be the very thing that could tip those perfectly balanced scales in favor of concern. Several times I've gone into detail about my incredible night and feelings for Cora with him. I told him how hurt I was when I discovered she blocked my number. To be honest, I didn't realize how salty I still felt about it until I saw her. The bitterness resurfaced once again.

But being here, around her, it's making me feel warm towards her—of course, in a platonic way. I'm not and never have been a cheater, but I can appreciate her beauty in the meantime, right?

What I have noticed this week, though, is that she is not the same vivacious and bright woman she was when I met her. She holds this air of sadness around her. She's obviously stressed, too. Between fielding constant questions, approving designs, working with Legal on the lawsuit, and taking backhanded remarks from Jonathan, I'm sure she needs a reprieve. I hope she has some kind of outlet for that.

As my stomach rumbles, pulling me out of my Cora-infused thoughts, I glance at the time. Almost 1:00 pm. I should definitely eat before my next meeting.

I walk to the break room, where I see a couple of people chatting and eating their lunches. The person in the suit has an evaluative look of concern on their face from what the guy next to them is whispering. I smile at them both and walk up to their table, extending my hand to the guy.

"Hi, I'm Jay, the new HR Director. Sorry to interrupt, but I'm trying to get to know everyone."

Standing up and extending his hand, the guy jerks his chin, "I'm Chris. Soil Engineer. Nice to meet you." He's got that short king vibe. Light brown pompadour hair and a square jaw. He's wearing jeans, nice tan leather hiking boots, a forest green casual knit sweater, and a thin L.L. Bean puffer vest.

I then turn to the person he's having lunch with and shake their hand, too. "I'm Dayo, they/them. Director of Interior Design. Welcome to the team." They have dark skin with short tight curls cropped close to their head. Thick green statement glasses take up the majority of their face. They have on a gray suit with large pleated pants and a matching double-breasted blazer with gold buttons.

Damn, Dayo has the androgynous look down to an art form.

Stepping away, I gesture for them to continue eating, "Well, I won't keep you. Let me know if there is anything I can do for you or if you just want to talk. Enjoy your lunch."

As I turn towards the refrigerators to grab mine, I see Cora pouring coffee into her mug and reaching for the tiny flavored creamers. She's wearing tight dark wash jeans, a burgundy oversized silk button-down shirt that she has tucked into the front of her waistband, and her sleeves rolled up. Her hair is pulled up in a massive curly bun.

God help me; I want to touch her. I want to run my hands all over that silk.

"Hi. I hope you're drinking that coffee as a digestif from lunch and not as a replacement meal."

Really, Jay? Are you really asking about her bowel movements? The fuck is wrong with me?

"Oh. Hi." She lets out a small huff and bites her lower lip. "Um, kind of, yeah. I was just going to grab a protein bar from the vending machine and head back to my office."

Closing the refrigerator door, I peek in my lunch bag. "Come on, Cora. That's not a proper meal. My boyfriend made me too much food anyway. I'll share it with you."

When she hesitates, I think I might have to add something to this to make it more professionally palatable to her. "We can eat in your office, and I can recap my first week with you."

I can see that idea rolling around in her mind as she nods, "Yeah, let's do that. You can tell me your first impressions. That's a great idea."

"Lead the way," I gesture, following her.

Don't look at her ass.
Don't look at her ass.
Don't look at her ass.

Her office is like a fishbowl, much like the rest of the offices here, with clear window walls and a city view of Philadelphia. Everything in here is incredibly tidy and well organized, save for the old-school drafting table against the wall with old drawings fixed to it and a lamp attached to the top. It looks well used.

"This is a fun couch," I assess, running my hands against the mauve fabric as she sits in one of the matching armchairs across from me.

"It's called the Cube Sofa from Herman Miller, and it makes me happy," she says with an affectionate smile. "Architecture is still very much a man's world, so I like to disrupt that nonsense however I can. Not that color should denote someone's sex or gender. I just won't apologize for liking what I like."

"I gotcha," I say as I unpack my lunch on the sleek coffee table in front of us. A huge Caesar salad wrap with chickpeas already sliced down the middle, cut strawberries in a glass container, slices of raw bell peppers, and hummus. *Ooh!* And a Reese's Peanut Butter Cup Christmas tree?

Damn, babe. Someone wants to get some tonight.

I start to separate the wrap and put it on the napkin from my bag, sliding it over to her. "No, really, Jay. I don't need to eat your food. I'm fine. Although this is quite the spread. Does your boyfriend always do this?"

"Make too much food and pack my lunch?" I note with an arched eyebrow and a grin. "Yeah, pretty much."

I grab the Reese's and lift it up to her line of sight, waving it around a little. "Would you like the Reese's Christmas tree?" I croon with a devilish smirk.

"Oh my god, I'm not even going to act shy about this. Of course, I want the tree." She beams as she reaches for it, and I pull it back.

"I'll give it to you, but you have to eat half of my wrap," I tease.

"Oh, you don't play fair."

"So, what'll it be?" I ask.

"Fine," she drawls with an eye roll.

I pass the Caesar wrap and peanut butter tree to her with a smirk.

After taking my first bite, I nod over to the drafting table behind her. "That looks pretty old. Do you still use one? I thought architects mostly use computers these days."

She swallows and wipes at the corner of her mouth before nodding, "You're right. Most architects don't use drafting tables anymore. But it was my father's since he was in college, and it has sentimental value to me. His name was Paul." She furrows her brow and looks at me. "He passed away about a year ago from esophageal cancer and put me in charge as CEO. I'm not sure if anyone told you about that yet?"

My face drops. I feel totally caught off guard. "No. I'm so sorry. I didn't know that. Cora, that's awful."

"Thanks. And yeah... it is awful. He started this company when he got out of college with another architect he studied under, and they built it into what it is today. It went from just the two of them to over two hundred employees, plus a dozen or so partnering companies that rely on our business for their own." She smiles to herself and adds, "He was such an inspiration to me growing up. I didn't even mind that he pushed me into this career because I absolutely love it." Her smile fades, and she adds, "I just didn't think I'd be in charge so young, or honestly at all. He was only fifty-nine."

"You didn't think you'd succeed him as CEO?" I ask, pushing the strawberries toward her.

"The plan had always been for Jonathan to take over as CEO when my father retired. But once he was diagnosed with late-stage esophageal cancer, he decided he wanted me to take over. Despite my attempts at discouraging that move, he made me realize I do have what it takes.

"Now, Jonathan, on the other hand, is still pissed about the whole thing and makes that very clear around me. Not sure if you picked up on that."

"Yeah, I did notice that... but wasn't sure why until now. If he's so salty about it, why doesn't he just find another job? Or, I don't know, get over it?"

"Great question. He does good work, but I can't exactly fire him for snide comments. That seems a little petty," Cora says, reaching for a strawberry and popping it into her mouth.

I arch an eyebrow. "I mean, if he has a bad attitude that affects his own or other people's work, then yeah, it's possible. It can also be classified as disrespect."

She takes another bite of the wrap and contemplates what I said. "That's something to think about, I guess. It's nothing I can't handle at this point."

"Okay. But please let me know if it becomes too much. I'm not afraid of stepping up and telling *you* when I think his behavior has crossed a line, either."

She smiles at that. "I think we made the right choice hiring you. The last director, Erin, was kind of a pushover. She just did what she was asked and no more."

"Good, I'm glad I'm here, too." And I mean it more than she

probably realizes. I shouldn't admit that to myself, if I'm being honest.

"So, I've heard tidbits here and there about the lawsuit, but I've mostly been meeting people and going through new hire training. Can you tell me about it?"

Cora lets out a long sigh. "Right after my dad was diagnosed, he was heading this new condominium project that he already had drawings for. They were set in a beautiful location atop a bluff just outside the city." She looks down and shakes her head as if racking her brain and continues, "All the soil reports came back in support of what he had planned."

Looking back up at me, she continues, "So, construction began, and we were on track. Then my dad got so sick and had to take a leave of absence. Most of his work was already completed, so the smaller stuff that had to be done was split amongst the rest of the architecture staff.

"I took a lot of time off to be with him and my mother—gosh, that's a whole other story—and after he died, I took over as CEO. Then, as if my emotional load wasn't enough to begin with, right before the final inspections, the entire building shifted and fell down the hillside."

My eyes go wide at her and a flood of questions fly through my head.

"Oh my god, Cora!"

"I know. It was all over the news."

How did I miss that?

"Was anyone hurt?" I ask, still my eyes glued to her.

"Yeah. There were some workers inside doing finishing touches like painting and trim work, installing railings, that type of stuff. They felt the building shift, and a few crew members fell off scaffolding resulting in some injuries, but everyone got out of the building quickly. However, the building careened into a road at the base of the hill. A few cars were hit, but the drivers survived, and the road was blocked for over a week while crews cleared it.

"If this would have happened just a month or more afterward, the occupants could have died, not to mention anyone in its wake."

I'm stunned. Speechless. I feel awful for her. This is a monumental disaster she's carrying the weight of without the support of her father anymore.

"It's so bad, Jay. Every morning since this happened, I wake up worried and all day rack my brain for anything that could explain what happened. I've seen my father's drawings and notes, and *I* would have approved that design myself. The soil reports showed approval, and we were given the green light to build."

She leans back in her chair and looks up at the ceiling. "Best case scenario," she huffs, "we're found not guilty of gross negligence and a litany of other things, but we still have to deal with our reputation."

She moves her stare from the ceiling back to me, "How does anyone trust us after this? Even *if* this was a freak accident, no one is going to hire the firm that had a building slide down a bluff."

She lets out an exasperated huff. "So, that's where we are."

If I could take her in my arms right now and hold her, I would. Does she have anyone that can comfort her? Wait, what did she say about her mother?

"Do you have anyone to talk to about this? I mean that in a personal sense. Maybe your mom? This sounds like a pretty heavy burden you're shouldering."

She takes the last bite of her wrap and swallows. "If I'm going to talk about my mom, I'm going to need that Reese's Christmas tree for support." With a sorrowful grin, I hand her the treat, and she unwraps it and takes a bite. "Mmm. Yup, that is definitely temporarily solving my problems."

We smile at each other, and hers fades.

"My mom, Connie, is in an assisted living facility with Alzheimer's disease. My father decided to move her in when she became a danger to have at home. I remember him being so distraught over it, but she was going to hurt someone or herself. She left the gas stove on several times. Their dog ran away because she left the front door open. She's wandered out of the house many times, getting lost and scaring us. She's at the point now that, most days, she doesn't remember me or her sister, Shelly. We're all she has at this point. I go visit her on the weekends and for about thirty minutes after work each day, just before visiting hours are over.

"I haven't really seen any friends since she went into the home and my father died. But I still talk with Angie over the phone when I remember. It's just hard for me to make time to actually see her."

"Oh, yeah. I remember her. She was so much fun. I'm glad she's still in your life. It sounds like you have a lot going on, Cora. When was the last time you took some time for yourself?"

"Um..." She stops and thinks for about a minute. "Last week, I went to Sephora and bought some moisturizer and mascara?"

I bend forward, putting my elbows on my knees and clasping my hands together. I give her a serious look. "I don't want this to come off as judgmental, but you bought a couple of staple beauty items, and you're calling that self-care?"

"I don't have the time. Too many people depend on me. There's too much work to be done. I need to save this firm—"

"You need to save yourself, Cora," I say gently with sympathetic eyes. "You need to take some time and recharge. You're going to burn out if you haven't already."

She sighs deeply. "You're probably right, Jay. Honestly, if I wasn't in the thick of it, I'd tell someone else in my shoes this very thing."

An idea pops into my head.

"You know, I was reading through the employee benefits this week and saw that everyone is offered one free massage a month as part of the medical benefits package. Have you ever utilized that?"

"Honestly, no, I haven't."

With a smirk, I pull out my phone and dial a number I have programmed into my phone. The line trills, and Cora is looking at me with a confused expression.

"Do you have plans tonight after visiting your mom?" I ask her while holding the phone to my ear.

Cora shakes her head.

The line picks up, and I hear, "Thank you for calling Revive Wellness Spa. This is Cheryl; how can I help you?"

"Hi Cheryl, it's Jay."

"Jay!" She cheers, "Oh my gosh, I haven't seen you in a while; how are you?"

"I'm great. Hey, I'm wondering if you happen to have any openings this evening, by chance? This would be for a friend of mine, Cora Dalton." I wink at her, and she begins to protest.

I can hear Cheryl humming, and I know she's looking at the schedule on the computer in front of her.

"Yes, Marco actually had his last appointment cancel on him for 7:30 tonight. Want me to book her?"

I raise my eyebrows and smile at Cora, "Can you do 7:30 tonight?"

She chews her lip.

"Hold on one second, Cheryl," I blurt into the phone and mute it.

"Cora, as your Human Resources Director, I am urging you to take time for yourself. You're no help to others if you're stressed." I pause and ask, "When are visiting hours over?"

"Seven," she mutters, and I can sense her giving in.

"Come on. Take it. Take this time for yourself."

She curls the corners of her lips and rolls her eyes. "Okay... you win."

"Yes!" I exclaim in a hushed tone and pump my fist. Tapping the mute button once again, I say, "Sorry, Cheryl, I'm back. Yes, please book Ms. Dalton."

She needs this.

This is a good thing.

I think.

Chapter 4

A Reluctant Massage

Cora

What did I just agree to? I instantly regretted accepting Jay's offer, and guilt washed over me at the thought of taking time for myself. I mean, I had to get home and feed George. Granted, she has an automatic feeder and water fountain at her disposal, but she likes when I talk to her while she eats.

Okay, that's a lie. George is a moody puss who throws shade at any inconvenience she comes across. Honestly, I'm sure if I were to arrive later than normal, she wouldn't even notice. Sometimes she gives me an attitude for arriving home early, as if *I* had the nerve to disrupt her schedule.

Okay, so George wasn't the real issue here.

It was late in the work day, and I was nervous about this massage. What Jay asked really struck a chord with me. *When was the last time I took real time for myself?* It certainly wasn't a vacation in the last year and a half or so. All my paid time off had accumulated and zeroed out at the end of the year because I never felt like it was worth taking time off for. Being the CEO of a company that you're not wholly prepared for is daunting and I've been trying my best to show I'm worthy.

Fuckin' Jonathan.

It kind of reminds me of whenever a president takes time to go golfing, and half the country is up in arms because they're taking some downtime from—*hello*—the most stressful job ever. I really couldn't remember the last time I took time for myself.

You've had a lot going on, girl.

Like gross and vicarious negligence.

Then I think of Angie, and the night we met Jay and Noah. That could have easily been the last time I felt free, wild, and out of control in the best way possible. That night had started as a bittersweet beginning after my divorce. But meeting Jay and having him quite literally sweep me off my feet felt magical. It felt impossibly good to let go of my anger, sadness, and responsibilities and give in to his warmth and charm.

Fuck, his charm... the man was smooth and charismatic, and he knew it. An absolutely lethal combination.

I pull away from staring at the latest design concept for the auditorium we are pitching to the arts center and tap my phone to call Angie. Just thinking about her makes me miss her. It has probably been about a month since we last spoke, but we're always able to pick up right where we left off.

She picks up on the second ring in a gasp. "Girl! Did I ever tell you about that guy I went out with, Lance, who lived on a boat? This was from, like, a couple years ago?"

I chuckle at the entire lack of phone etiquette. "Yeah, I remember. He made you pay after asking *you* out on a date and said he was saving money for his year-long trip to Peru. Didn't he ask you to go with him after the dinner?"

"Oh my god, he did," she groans. "I'm pretty sure he was just trying to woo me so I'd sleep with him that night on his boat. Thank you for reminding me."

I laugh and ask, "Why are you asking if I remember him?"

"He reached back out to me and asked if I was available to *catch up* this weekend. And I was contemplating it, but after talking to you, you've made me remember it all so clearly. He was such a tool."

See, picking up like no time had passed at all.

These were the friendships I loved the most.

"But hey, you called me Cora, babe. What's up?"

I hesitate but remind myself I need a sounding board. One I can trust. One that knew my life then and now. "Speaking of men we used to know..." I lead. "Do you remember Jay from that night we went out dancing in Manayunk?"

"Gasp! Yes, of course. Also known as the best dick you ever had, sure. Go on."

"I never said that," I counter.

"You said, and I quote, 'It's never gonna be better than that, Ang.'"

I grimace, but I know she's right. "Well, uh... he sort of works for me now... as my Director of Human Resources."

"I'm sorry, what?" she bellows in that too-shocked-to-comprehend baritone she pulls out for occasions such as this.

I go on to tell her about the whole debacle of his accidental hiring and our meeting again. I tell her he has a boyfriend, and he's actually a good hire, but it's definitely weird seeing him again.

"Anyway, I told him about my parents, the lawsuit, and

he can already see right through me. He was like, 'You're so stressed. Take time for yourself. Let me schedule you a massage for today.' Uhh! Can you believe that?"

"First of all, spot-on impression, girl," she quips. "Second, he has a point."

"Not you, too," I groan and spin in my chair, head bent back.

"You work yourself to the bone five days a week. Then when you're done, you go visit your mom. And on the weekends, you either take work to the assisted living home so you can do both all day long, or you work in the office half the day and still visit Connie afterward."

Where is she going with this? Because to me, that makes me look like a devoted daughter who takes her work seriously, too.

"Let me ask you this: if your dad was still alive and healthy, and he was working like you are, spread out as thin as possible, dealing with a lawsuit and still visiting your mom every spare second, wouldn't you tell him to take a damn break once in a while?"

Sigh.

"And let me remind you, your Aunt Shelly visits her like four times a week, too. She's retired and has the time. Plus, you have thousands of cousins that show up all week long, right?" Angie points out, alluding to the eight children Aunt Shelly and Uncle Martin have, plus their spouses, who all live within an hour's drive of the city.

Sigh again.

Angie knows too much.

She continues, "Paul would want you to stop taking yourself so seriously, honey. He was so generous and kind. He cared about the people in his life and their wellbeing. Is your *being* well?"

And that's it, the kill shot. This lady is so smart and insightful that it astounds me sometimes.

I relent, not wanting her to dig any deeper into my past and bring up triggering subjects. "Fine. I'll go."

"Yes! God, I should really go into sales."

I laugh. "You could, but I think you're right where you need to be as a youth counselor. You clearly know how to counsel me."

"Bah, it's only because I was the oldest of five siblings with no mother figure and had to fill in as the voice of reason and emotional support," she spews out quickly with sarcasm like it's the millionth time she's said it.

She's definitely done a lot of work on herself in the twelve years I've known her, and I know she's comfortable with accepting her past and setting boundaries with her siblings these days.

I'm amazed by her and her family. They've been through so much together, and even though she has set hard boundaries with them, they're still all present in each other's lives.

I've always been envious of that kind of large family. I never liked being an only child, but I did always have my cousins close by. I loved going over to their house in all its glorious chaos. I knew even as a child that I wanted to have exactly that someday. I would have a loving husband and lots of children to overflow our home with. I wanted abundant art and giggling and love from a family.

Wanted. Past tense.

I very nearly had that.

"So, is he still as sexy as when you met him?" Angie asks suggestively, pulling me out of my spiral.

"Like I said, he has a boyfriend," I reply with a flat tone.

"That's not what I asked," she persists and it's like I can hear her smirk.

"He's my employee."

"Bitch, answer my question," Angie blurts, cutting to the chase.

Just then, Jay walks past my office and stops in front of the door, tapping his watch with exaggeration and his brows rising high. Giving me a *you better get out of here soon* look and smiles as he walks away, waving his hand goodbye. *What a goof.*

I wait another few seconds before I whisper to Angie, "He's just as fine as the night we met. Maybe more so."

I hear my friend giggle like a gossiping schoolgirl on the other line, but cut her off, "None of that now. There will be no heinous homewrecker thoughts on my end *or yours*! Shut it down."

"Okay, okay," Angie concedes. "I hope you have a good massage later. You absolutely deserve this, and I won't hear otherwise. Please enjoy yourself and relax."

I smile and accept her orders. "I will. Thanks, babe. I love you."

"I love you, too."

As I walk into Revive Wellness Spa, the reception area is clean and tranquil. The walls are tan with a scattering of green plant decals and macramé planters hanging throughout. There's soft, soothing music playing low throughout the space, and warm light is cast from sconces.

After the hard visit I had with my mom tonight, this is certainly welcome. I mean, I know she doesn't remember me, but tonight was especially difficult. She got angry at me, accusing me of sleeping with her husband as I sat there playing gin rummy with her. A game where I have to explain the rules every single time the cards are dealt.

It was a lot to deal with.

"Welcome to Revive. I'm Cheryl. You must be Cora?" the bright blonde receptionist greets. She has round cheeks and a sweet smile.

"Yes, I am. Hi."

"Wonderful. This is your first time with us, right? I'll have you take this tablet and fill out the new patient paperwork. This will go over any areas of focus you'd like, areas to avoid, pressure preference, insurance information, and a brief medical history." I take the tablet from her, and she chimes, "If you'd like to follow me into our serenity room, you can have a seat and fill this all out."

She leads me into a small seating area with low light and a deep tan color on the walls. More macrame planters hang in the corners, and an electric fireplace is situated in the center of the lounge seating.

Okay, this is nice and cozy. I'm already relaxing.

"Please feel free to make yourself a cup of tea or cucumber water right over there," and she gestures to the little counter station with a beautiful assortment of herbal teas in a wooden box and clean mugs stacked next to them. Cucumber water is in a beautiful spouted carafe on a tall, elegant stand next to a hot water dispenser.

Don't mind if I do...

Cheryl continues with her welcome spiel. "Marco will be with you shortly and will take you back to the room. If you have any questions, please let me or him know."

I fill a glass of cucumber water and look back at her. "Will do. Thank you."

Cheryl steps back towards the door to the reception area and grins, "Alright, have a wonderful massage, Cora. I'll see you when you check out."

Sipping my infused water, I sit down with the tablet and fill out all my information. This isn't my first massage ever, but it is the first one in several years.

Deep pressure? *Yes, please.*

Don't touch my stomach or face... No allergies...

When I finish, I set my tablet down and sit back. Taking a deep breath, I close my eyes, listening to the tranquil music.

Okay, yes, I'm glad I'm here. Angie is right; if my dad saw me now, he'd be worried about how thin I've spread myself.

"Cora?" a deep gruff voice croons.

I open my eyes to see a large muscular man smiling at me. He has dark brown hair that curls into a pile on the top of his head, spilling a little over his forehead, and the rest is cut into a fade. His eyes are bright blue, and his face, with its high cheekbones and very short beard, is both rugged and beautiful. And even though it's December, his skin is still slightly tan, almost an olive skin tone. He's wearing what I assume is a uniform of a black polo and matching slacks with a belt. His waist is trim, and his shoulders are broad. He has stunning tattoos that pour down both arms like a geometric waterfall, ending at his wrist.

I clear my throat with a small huff and stammer, "Y-yes. You're Marco?"

He nods with that beaming smile which seems like such a juxtaposition to his gruff look. "I am. Would you like to follow me back to the room?"

Okay, yeah, no big deal: just the hottest massage therapist that's ever lived right in front of me, and we're going to be alone in a room together for an hour.

Cool. Cool. Cool.

Why couldn't I have a woman named Helga from Latvia with the muscle strength and appeal of a buffalo? At least *then*, I could turn off my brain and actually relax. Now I'm going to be thinking about Marco and his gorgeous, powerful body this whole time.

I stand up and walk behind him, trying my best not to look at his mountain of a back and the way his pants hug his tight ass.

Trying is the operative word. *Failing* is the accurate one.

When he turns and stops at one of the open doors, he gestures with his arm for me to enter. As I walk past him, he smells like sandalwood and... lavender? Why does that work so well? I guess he does work in a spa. He probably always smells good.

The room is the same deep tan with low lighting as the rest of the spa. The massage table is in the center of the space, with a soft navy blue blanket and white sheets peeking out. There's a small counter with a cabinet in one of the corners with a sink, oils, and a mini fridge that probably has hot towels in it.

Marco moves in and shuts the door gently. I move to stand by the chair in the other corner and look at him.

Jeez, he's so tall. He's at least a whole head taller than me.

"So, what brings you in today, Cora?" He asks in that deep voice that has my senses quivering. He gestures to the tablet tucked under my arm, and I hand it to him.

I sigh and answer, "Stress relief." Then muttering under my breath, I add, "Apparently, it's obvious to some people."

Looking over my information on the screen, he nods. "Okay. And I see here you like deep pressure, which I can definitely do for you, just let me know if it's ever too much or not enough."

He keeps scrolling through my details, humming his acknowledgment. "Okay, Cora, this all looks good to me. Do you have any questions before I step out and let you change?"

Yeah, could you find Helga?

"No, I don't think so," I say instead.

"Alright then. I'll step out for a few minutes to let you

change. Please undress to your comfort level and then lay on your stomach on the table with your face in the hole here." He taps the headrest at the top of the table. "I'll knock on the door before entering at your discretion." He smiles and opens the door to step out, and again, gently latches the door closed.

Exhaling my relief that he's gone, I shrug off my coat, shoes, and clothes except my panties and slip under the sheet and blanket. *Ooh, there's a heating pad*. Nice touch. My breasts press flat against the table under my weight, spilling out to my collarbone and armpits.

Dainty little thing, aren't I? I laugh to myself.

When I hear a double knock on the door, I lift my head and call out, "Come in."

The door cracks slightly, and I hear Marco announce softly, "All set, Cora?"

"I am," I call, and I lay my face back into the cradle.

I can see the carpeted floor, and the lights dim even further. Spa music still plays in the background.

"So, Cora, you're here for stress relief—" *fuck me*, could his voice be any deeper? He continues, "—so that will be my entire purpose with you here today. I'm going to grab your ankle in a second and gently squeeze my hands up your body through the blanket before I bring it down to your waist and begin on your neck and shoulders. Is that okay?"

"Y-yes."

"Okay." Then he takes both hands—whoa, *big hands*—and firmly squeezes my ankles, heels, calves, thighs, and hips before setting his hands on my lower back, quickly smoothing them up to my shoulders and down my arms.

He hasn't even touched my skin yet, but I'm already in heaven.

He begins to slowly roll the blanket and top sheet down to

my waist.

"Let me know if the table is too warm or not warm enough. I can adjust it," he says as he begins to pump oil into his hands and presses into my trapezius muscles.

Trying to stifle a moan, I tell him with a small giggle, "It's winter and I'm a woman; of course, I want it warmer."

He gives me a small chuckle. "You got it. It's set at medium heat, so I'll turn it all the way up." Without stopping his hands from their delicious pressure, he clicks a floor pedal that must turn up the heat.

Standing at my head, pulling the muscle at the crook of my neck and shoulder with his thumb and forefinger, Marco drawls, "So, it's up to you, but if you'd like to talk the whole time, or not, I can make that happen."

I think in most relaxing circumstances such as this, I would not want to talk. However, I fear that if we don't, my mind will wander to dirty things, and we simply don't need that here and now. I don't need to be accidentally moaning.

I also think if I have him talking, I'll eventually discover something weird or off about him that will snap me out of this sexy image I have conjured. No one can be that hot, gentle, and cool to talk to. Something's gotta give. Maybe he's a total dumb-dumb or he has a passion for doll collecting.

I giggle at my own thoughts.

"I'd like to talk if that's okay with you," I tremble, mouth still pointed to the floor as he rubs his knuckles down each shoulder in a slow, borderline tortuous manner.

Yeeeees. The harder, the better, Marco. Mama likes.

"Okay," he says. "How's the pressure so far? You said you wanted deep, but if it's not enough, I still have more in me if you need."

"Give me everything you have, Marco. I have a pretty high

pain tolerance."

"Uhh, well," he stutters. "The-the goal of a stress relief massage shouldn't be pressure to the point of almost pain."

"Says you."

He huffs a small laugh. "Yeah, says me, the professionally trained massage therapist."

"Trust me, I can handle it, and I'm asking for it. Let me see what you got."

"Alright, Cora. But please tell me if it's too much. I can also read your body language, and if you're squirming, I'm going to back off. I don't want other muscles tensing while others are being worked. Ready?"

"Yes."

"Okay, here we go." He digs in deep, just below my neck, and—*holy fucking shit. Yes. This.* It's definitely painful but in the most pleasurable way. "Speak to me, Cora. How is it?"

Words are hard to form at the moment, but if I don't try, I know he's going to back off, and I do *not* want that.

"Perfect," I muster out. "Just... like that." Wanting him to keep talking so I don't have to, I ask, "So... how'd you... get into this line of work?"

"Well," he sighs, "I was in the Army for a while, and it was pretty hard on me mentally. As it is with literally everyone, whether they think so or not. And when I got out, I wanted nothing to do with that part of me anymore. I wanted the opposite. I wanted peace and calm. I wanted to make people feel good and safe. Relaxed.

"So, when I got back, I enrolled in a massage therapy training program and got licensed. I've been happy with my decision since then. I get to work in a quiet, peaceful environment and I get to help people unwind and reset. I couldn't have made a better career choice for myself."

Well, dang. That's really nice. And it totally explains the dichotomy between his rough intimidating presence mixed with a peaceful, beautiful one.

Enough of that. I need to find out what's wrong with this man. "That's admirable," I admit as he starts to dig his thumbs on either side of my spine and slowly drags them down and back up. *Jesus*. The blood flow in my body feels like it's taken on a whole new life. His large hands are warm, and the skin-on-skin contact is intoxicating.

Before he can ask me what I do, because I don't want to try and form coherent sentences while he tenderizes my body, I ask, "So, the Army... you must have moved around a lot. Are you from here originally?"

I can't detect the awful but amusing Philly accent with him, but that's not to say he's not from here, too.

"Kinda. I grew up in Norristown. Didn't exactly come from the best neighborhood, ya know? The Army was kind of my way out, or so I thought when I enlisted after high school." There's a long pause, and then he asks, "Cora, are you alright? Are you too warm? You're sweating."

Oops. Yeah, I totally am.

I'm sweating from the pain, not the tantalizing heat radiating from the table. It's like when I go get my coochie waxed on occasion, I always end up sweating through my clothes and thin paper sheet from the pain. I definitely don't keep going there to maintain my pussy for anyone to see. It's just a sick little pain rush I love. You can't have thick hair like mine without some deep follicles *everywhere*.

"No, no, I'm not too warm. I'm fine. I'm great. Keep going. Tell me more about... yourself. What are... your hobbies? Your interests?" God, anything to get him to stop asking me questions.

Marco goes on to tell me about how he loves to cook, his big Italian family, and then I kind of black out after a while. I don't realize he stopped talking until he covers up my back with the blanket again and begins to roll it up around my leg, exposing it from foot to hip. He starts massaging my leg as deeply as he was everywhere else. Now that we're not talking, my mind is running wild with thoughts of him rubbing my ass and digging those strong fingers everywhere... inside me. Pinching me.

My mind has its own agenda, and I can't remember why I thought distracting myself from this naughty fantasy was a good idea before. *This* is so much more fun. This is—

"Ahh!" I hiss as he pulls his hands away from my hip. The same hip I bruised earlier this week when I was giving Jay a tour of the printing room. That sharp hit of pain mixed with my internal sexcapade was the most action I've seen since... well, a long time.

"I'm so sorry! Are you okay?" he asks, his voice laced with worry.

"Totally. It's fine. It felt good. Please, keep going."

"Oh. Did you know you have a large bruise here?" he asks, lightly skimming my skin.

"I got it a few days ago. Bumped into a table. I bruise like a peach, but it's okay; you can still massage it. Still felt good," I admit, desperately needing him to dig back in.

Please keep massaging it for the love of Christ.

CHAPTER 5

Too Deep

MARCO

That's it. I'm going fucking insane here.

"Um, no, I really can't. I could make the bruise worse, especially with this kind of pressure, and break even more blood vessels."

I went from a half-chub to a full-chub just now.

Thank god she's still lying face down and can't see my dick tenting my pants.

"Do you have any more bruises I should be aware of?" I ask her, already mentally chastising myself if I think about pushing on them any more than I already am. The professional in me knows I can't do that. But the sadist in me... fuck him for being so turned on at the thought of this.

"No, no other bruises," she says softly and a little out of breath—and I know *exactly* why she's out of breath.

"Okay, good."

This woman has been torturing me since I first saw her. First of all, those curves? Her pale skin against all that dark curly hair? I wanna wrap my hands in it and pull.

Second, the very obvious pleasure she's getting out of this brutal massage... *fuck,* it's hot. I rarely use this kind of pressure on anyone. This is sick, but I can't tell her that. I don't want to make her feel bad for liking it.

But the sweating? The wanting me to continue pressing the sensitive bruise because it *felt good?* She's a damn masochist, and I hate that I can recognize that in this gorgeous woman.

This *client, asshole.* Remember, she's your *client.*

I'm always a professional. This has never happened to me before, I swear. Sure, I find women attractive, but that's about the extent of it. Very surface level. But this one... *Jesus Christ, save me.*

Think about something else, I tell myself.

Think about Nonna naked.

Ugh. Nasty.

"So, what are your plans this weekend?" she asks.

Yes, talk about your niece's birthday party, you sick freak. That should return the blood to my brain.

"I'm going over to my sister's house for my niece Viera's fourth birthday party. She's requested a Winnie-the-Pooh themed party this year and is forcing me to wear a Tigger costume because, as she puts it, *Uncle Marco can jump the highest.*" I chuckle at the thought. Whatever Viera wants, that girl gets from me.

"What about you, Cora? Have any plans for this weekend?"

When she doesn't answer right away, I wait a bit longer. It's not always easy to read someone when you can't see their face.

"Cora?"

Did she fall asleep? Wouldn't be the first time that's happened with a client.

Then I feel her shaking. I take my hands away, and I hear a little sob coming from her. "Is everything okay? Did I hurt you?"

"I'm so sorry; this is so embarrassing." Her quiet sob has now turned into a full cry.

Oh god, what have I done?

"Cora, please answer me. Did I hurt you? Are you uncomfortable?"

"No, nothing like that," her voice breaks.

I go to the head of the table and squat down so my head is closer to hers, bringing a tissue with me that I swiped from the counter. I push the loose strands of hair falling around the cradle cushion behind her ear and offer, "Cora, I'm right here. What is it? Talk to me so I can help."

She lifts her head from the cradle, and I extend the tissue to her. She takes it quickly and covers her eyes with the whole thing, her brows pinched tight.

"Fuck. This is... I'm so... It's nothing you did, Marco."

That can't be right. She was perfectly fine before, albeit visibly aroused, but fine.

"It's just me," she continues, still crying. "I just remembered something, and it got the best of me." She takes several forced deep breaths to calm her sobs. "I'd rather not talk about it if it's all the same."

"Okay. May I bring you a cup of tea or a glass of water? I can give you some space to collect your thoughts... or cry it out if you want. This time is yours. Whatever you need."

In reality, I want to hold this perfect stranger. I want to pick her up and sit her on my lap as I stroke my hand through her hair. I've always been a nurturer by default, and that's exactly what I want to do now—but as professionally as possible.

With her eyes still buried in her tissue, she relents. "Um,

yeah, water would be nice. Just give me a few minutes to collect myself, please?"

"Of course. I'll go get that and be back in five."

I stand up and exit the room, closing the door behind me. I tuck my stupid boner into my waistband as I take a couple steps across the hall and lean my forehead against it. What did I just do? I've never had a client cry in front of me before. This whole situation is disconcerting.

Pushing off the wall, I walk back to the serenity room and fill a glass of cucumber water for Cora. No one is in there, so I take a seat and wait.

I don't know how to fix this. I guess I'll just go back in there and try to resume my work? Making her feel good is why I'm here, after all. That's what I need to do.

After a few minutes more, I get up and walk back to the room with her water. I'm about to knock on the door when it opens, revealing a clothed Cora, no longer sobbing, but her eyes are definitely red and watery.

"I'm sorry to cut this short, but I have to go. I'm... I have to go. Thank you, Marco. I, uh, I left a tip on the counter there." She moves past me quickly and heads towards the reception desk. "Thank you. Again, I'm so sorry."

I stand there stunned, holding her water and utterly confused.

Chapter 6

Princess Play

Jay

I come home from work Friday, knowing I need to tell him about Cora. I just need to figure out how to approach this and make sure we stay on solid ground. I could be overthinking it. Maybe everything will be fine, and this won't be any different than when we talk about other people we find attractive.

I can only hope.

I busy myself in the kitchen, putting away the dishes and thinking of ways to start the conversation.

Hey, babe, remember that hottie I had car sex with a couple years ago, she ghosted me immediately, and I never really got over it? Well, she's my new boss.

Nope. Not like that.

So funny story, my new boss is that sex goddess...

Definitely not.

Just then, I hear the backdoor open, and I see him walk in. He doesn't look like himself. He's usually so calm when he comes home, but he looks worried like his mind is racing.

I close the dishwasher and walk up to him as he's shucking his coat off and boots.

"Baby, what's wrong?" I ask, taking his coat from him and hanging it on the hook. I wrap my arms around his torso, and he does the same to me. He closes his eyes and presses his forehead against mine.

This is weird. Something is wrong. Something is eating at him.

This is not my sweet boyfriend.

This is not the Marco Borrelli I know and love.

I pull him in and kiss his full lips, trying to reassure him that whatever is going on, I'll be here for him.

"Come and sit down, baby." I release him from the embrace but grab his hand and lead him to the living room. "Tell me what's going on."

I sit him down on our deep light gray sectional and situate myself on his lap so I'm straddling him. His hands instinctively go to my hips and rest there as his head hangs down.

God, whatever this is, I need to make it better.

Reaching my hands behind his neck, I smooth over his olive skin and plead softly, "Baby, please tell me what's going on. I'm here for you."

"Okay," he relents, lifting his eyes to mine and exhaling. "I had a very bizarre session today, and I'm pretty rattled about it. It was my last client for the night, and... she was *so* beautiful, Jay. You would have thought so, too."

Oh no. He's talking about Cora.

"Okay, so what happened?" I ask nervously, but I'm trying my best to appear calm and supportive.

"She wanted deep pressure, but like... *really* deep. Painfully so. She kept sweating but told me it was a relaxing pressure, and she liked it. Then I accidentally massaged a bruise she had on her hip..." he shakes his head and flings it back over the couch. "She gasped in pain and told me... *fuck*, she told me it *felt good*, and she wanted me to keep going."

Oh, I see where this is going.

I knew from the night I shared with Cora that she was a little kinky, but obviously, I didn't get the chance to find out just how much. And a man like Marco has very specific tastes in the bedroom. Tastes that, based on the very little information he's told me, might line up with his, too.

"I definitely crossed a line, and I feel like shit about it." He groans and brings his head back up to look at me but closes his eyes and admits, "I had an erection basically the whole time. God, I hope she didn't notice. But then..." he pauses. His eyes pop open, and his mouth drops. "Oh no... I didn't even think about that at the time..."

"What?" I ask.

"I'm not really sure what happened, but all of a sudden, she started bawling. I obviously stopped and asked what was wrong, if I hurt her, ya know? But she said no. I squatted down by her head to soothe her and gave her a tissue. *Fuck*, she might have seen my erection! I left the room to get her some water, and when I returned, she was dressed and left in a rush. *Ugh*, I'm gonna get fired, *fuck!*" he groans.

Holy shit. Cora basically opened up Marco's vault of kinks and didn't even know it. Well, she might have if she actually saw his dick.

"Whoa, relax. Maybe she didn't see it. You have black pants on, and those rooms have such low lighting. There's a very real chance she didn't see it."

"Baby, I am so sorry about this. This not only crossed a huge professional line, but it crossed a personal one as well. I know we've always been able to talk about this stuff, but it's always been just that, talk." Then he grabs my face with both hands and bores his bright blue eyes into mine. "Please believe me when I say I would never have gone further. You're my everything."

The look in his eyes tells me he means every single word.

"I know, baby. It's okay." I lay over him and hug him, breathing in that sandalwood and lavender smell I adore.

He wraps his big arms around me and murmurs in my neck, "Are you sure?"

"I'm positive."

Then the most delicious idea comes to me, and I unwrap from his neck and start sliding my hands over his thick pectorals. I pull my head away to look at him. I kiss him and linger there, waiting for his sigh of relief that comes after a few seconds.

With a smirk, I suggest, "Why don't we go take a shower, and you can relieve some of this pent-up energy on me?"

When I can feel him smiling against my mouth, I know I've got him.

"I'm the luckiest man," he whispers and squeezes my ass. "What did I do to deserve you?"

"It's the big Daddy energy, honestly," I quip, and I know what's coming next.

He slaps my ass once and growls in my mouth, "You better run and get in that shower before me, you fucking tease."

With fire igniting in my lower belly, I know better than to keep him waiting, so I scramble off him and head for the stairs, taking them three at a time.

When I get to the bathroom, I start the shower right away and start to peel off my clothes, and toss them in the hamper. Marco is a stickler for cleanliness and organization and I remember the first time we had a scene, he beat my ass raw for throwing my clothes on the ground and not folding them. So they're either folded neatly or in the hamper they go.

I can hear his steps getting closer, so I hop in the shower even though the water isn't warm yet, and I get on my knees with my hands folded behind me in the box position. When he walks into the bathroom, he peeks through the shower door at me shivering, and asks with a smirk, "Are you warming it up for me?"

With my head bowed, I stammer, "Y-y-yes, Sir."

He reaches in, lowers his head, pulls my chin to his face, and whispers against my lips, "Good boy." Then he backs away and begins undressing slowly.

The water is finally warm when he steps in. Dark hair dusts the tops of his bare feet, which are almost touching my knees.

"You're so perfect like this, my prince," he croons down to me.

He's not going to think so in a second when I disrupt his plans with a suggestion.

"Permission to speak, Sir?"

"You may," he allows.

"I know you had a tough day, Sir, so I was thinking maybe you'd like to pretend I was Co—" I cut myself off before saying her name. He didn't reveal that to me downstairs. "—your client from tonight."

Without even seeing the rest of his body, I can feel him tense, and he steps back a little.

"Excuse me?" he asks with a gruff accusatory tone.

"Sir, I only mean for this to be fun. I just thought maybe you'd like to enact the desires you had for this client with me. Use me like you wanted to use her. Help me like you wanted to help her."

This is definitely out of our wheelhouse a bit. Of course, we've role played in the past, but never about someone we both know. Well, at least one that he thinks only he knows.

He crouches down and runs his hand through my wet hair, and asks, "Are you sure you're comfortable with that, prince?"

Okay with this? Hell yeah. The thought of Cora and Marco together... my dick twitches in enthusiastic agreement with that. I can see his massive throbbing erection in front of me, so clearly, he's into this, too.

"Yes, Sir. Please."

With a fierce grip, he grabs my jaw and tilts my head to his, and growls, "Don't think that since you asked so nicely that you're going to get out of this without a punishment for changing my plans."

"Never, Sir. Please, let me do this for you," I beg.

He stands, dragging me with him, and pushes my back against the tile wall. "Well then, let's start by finding those marks I left earlier, shall we? Put your hands flat against the wall at your hips," he demands, trailing his big hands down my chest and circling my nipples with his fingertips. There are several red marks peppered around them from previous bites. He wastes no time and starts to pinch them as I wince and drop open my mouth, shuttering at the pain.

"Oh, is that too much, or are you a *good girl*?" he asks with a sadistic smile.

"No, Sir. No, please keep going," I whimper.

Still pinching me, he says through gritted teeth, "You're so fucking twisted, you know that? You wanna feel pain because it makes you feel good?"

"Mhmm," I murmur.

Marco then moves his hands to the outsides of my pecs and pushes them together as much as he can, and begins to bite over the marks, sending a jolt of pleasure and pain straight to my groin. "You like it when I bite your titties, you little slut?"

He laps his tongue over the now redder marks and kisses them fervently.

While still biting my chest, he runs his hands down to my thighs, where he begins pushing on the many finger-sized bruises that are almost always there. My legs want to give out at this point, but then he stands to his full height, just an inch taller than me, and pushes his body against mine. He hikes my leg up around him, and our dicks are straining against one another.

Nipping at my jaw and still squeezing my thigh, digging into the bruises—*the bruises he left*—he growls, "I love to hear you whimper, but I want to see you cry. Get on your knees."

I immediately drop down, excitement thrumming through my whole body.

"Put your hands on my hips, princess."

I do so, but I don't dare make another move without his explicit direction.

With hooded eyes, his voice drops impossibly lower. "Open your mouth and stick out that pretty tongue. You're gonna take this cock, and you're going to be thankful."

I nod eagerly, but before I can say anything, he's shoving all nine inches deep into my throat, gagging me at the invasion.

Marco thrusts into me as he holds my head, tears already forming in my eyes as I stare at him. He's fucking my mouth without mercy, but I know he trusts me to safe out if needed. But seeing him like this, his raw need on full display, his fantasy playing out, I'd do anything to keep this up for him.

Before him, I had never been with someone who had a crying kink. It doesn't matter if we're in a scene or if I'm actually sad, that man gets a woody regardless.

"That's a good girl. You're so pretty when you cry," he grunts, fire burning in his eyes. "Hold out your hand."

He grabs the bottle of lube we keep in the shower and pumps

it onto my fingers. "Get yourself ready for me."

I bring my hand around to my ass and begin to rub the lube around the small hole. He slows his thrusts down to allow me the time to enter myself with one finger at first. I give several exploratory pushes with my fingertip and then slowly enter myself to the bottom knuckle.

"Mmm, you're so fucking needy, aren't you? You wanna take my big cock in that little pussy?" he muses, and *fuck me*, if being called a good little girl and referencing my imaginary pussy doesn't turn me on.

Then I have the thought of Cora in my place, sucking off Marco and crying for him. Her long curly hair fisted in his hands. Her round ass on full display.

Goddammit, that's hot.

I get lost in the thought of her and moan around Marco's thick length, closing my eyes and adding a second finger, scissoring them to make room for him.

"Are those fingers enough for you, princess? Or do you need your sir to take care of you?" he asks, pulling his hard, saliva-coated dick out of my mouth.

"It's not enough, Sir," I pant and start to frantically kiss along his shaft and balls. "Please, please make me feel good. I need you."

"Up," he commands. "Chest and hands against the wall."

I get up, arching my back and sticking my ass out for him. I hear him apply lube to his hand and lather it on himself and me. He presses his chest to my back, his erection nuzzling into my ass, and he whispers in my left ear, "Don't think I forgot about your punishment, prince." And then he bites my earlobe and pulls at it, sending a zap of lightning down my wet, trembling body.

He switches to the right ear and purrs, "Are you ready for me, princess?" He notches the crown of his dick into my waiting hole and holds steady. "Are you gonna let Daddy in?"

"Yes, Sir. Please, use me," I beg. "Use my... my pussy."

He growls in my ear and begins his shallow thrusts. "That's a gooooood girl," he croons gently. His other hand slides over my ass and hip like I'm a fucking horse he's trying to soothe. His cock rocks in and out, creating a tight pressure that I'm trying to adjust to. Slowly the tightness begins to fade, and it's replaced with blooming pleasure.

Even with the water pouring on us, I can feel the sweat start to form when he's fully seated in me. I know he sees it, too, because as he starts to move in earnest, his hands on my hips, he starts to lick the sweat from my neck and shoulder.

Her neck and shoulder.

I can't help but moan and cry for him as he now pounds into me.

"That's it, princess. *Goddammit*, you're so tight. Let me make you feel good. Let me take care of you."

Then he moves his mouth back to my left ear and whispers, "Count to ten for me, prince."

Oh, shit.

Crack! He slaps my ass hard.

"One!" I cry out. Fuck, that first one is always a surprise.

Crack! Again, in the same spot.

"Two." I can feel myself clenching around his cock at every spank.

Crack!

"Three," I whisper.

His free hand grabs the front of my neck, and he holds me close. "I can't hear you, prince," he growls in my ear. "Do we need to start over?"

"No, Sir," I shout. "Please, I'll be good. Please. Please."

Crack! Crack! Crack!

"Four! Five! Six!" Actual tears are coming down my face now. Pain coursing through my body and setting it on fire. But never does he stop thrusting into me, never relenting.

He switches to my right and nuzzles and licks *her* ear, still holding my neck. "How do you feel, princess?"

"I—I need more, Sir."

"You need more?" he growls. "You need me to play with that little clit of yours? I bet it's throbbing by now." He reaches around and grabs the tip of my cock head in his hand. Massaging it and rubbing his thumb and forefinger around the slit. That, mixed with his thunderous fucking and the pain, start to create my orgasm at the base of my spine. My balls are so fucking tight right now. Just a few more thrusts and—

Crack! Crack!

"Seven!" I sob. "Eight! Sir, I'm going to come. Please, can I come for you?"

"Yes, princess. Come for me."

Crack!

"Nine!" That's it. I can't stop it, my orgasm washes over me as I weep and shoot ropes of cum on the shower wall. "Thank you, Sir. Oh my god... *fuck*."

Crack!

"Ten! Yes... yes..." I can't stop crying. I'm overwhelmed in the best sense. My ass feels like a million little needles are stinging it, and my body shakes from pleasure.

He whispers in my right ear, "Take it, you little pain slut." His pumping is getting erratic, and I know he's almost there. I'm just gonna hammer this last nail in the coffin...

"Please fill me up, Sir. Please fill my pussy."

He groans and gives a few more deep, powerful jabs, his hands digging into my hips, pulling me into him each time as he finishes inside me.

"Good girl." He kisses the base of my neck on my spine and hums his appreciation against my skin, and adds, "Good boy."

After a few more moments pass with us catching our breath, he pulls out and turns me around to face him. With a sated smile we both wear, I rest my head on his shoulder, and he wraps his arms around me.

"How are you feeling, prince? That was new for us."

With my arms dangling down, he holds on to me tightly, and I feel like a blanket he's clinging to. "I feel incredible. That was intense but fun," I answer honestly. "What about you?"

"That was certainly surprising for me, but, yeah, it was fun." He sighs again, his breathing slowly returning to normal. He grabs the shampoo while I lay against him and lathers it into my hair. "How are you feeling emotionally?"

I know what he means. He wants to know if I regret this scenario. If I regret setting a scene with Cora, his client, as the focal point. "I feel good about it. No regrets. You?"

Closing my eyes as he leans me towards the spray and rinses my hair. "No, my love. Thank you. This was very special."

Marco tenderly washes my body and conditions my hair as well as his own. He turns the water off and steps out of the shower, grabbing two towels. He wraps one around me after drying my head and then wraps his low on his waist before taking my hand to lead me out.

He steers me to the bed and takes my towel off. "Lay down, please," he says softly and leans over to the nightstand to grab the healing balm. "I'm sorry if I was too rough, baby." He begins to gently rub it into my skin. I'm sure there were unhealed marks on my ass before he spanked me tonight, so it has to be a red and swollen mess down there. "But you look so beautiful like this."

That makes me smile. "You know I'll tell you if it's too much.

And you know I love it."

"I love you," he says, leaning down to kiss me.

"I love you, too."

"Let me go get you some water and aspirin. Stay right here." When he returns, the balm has soaked in enough that I can feel it tingling. He sits me up and hands me the pills and water to drink. When I finish, he takes the glass and sets it down on the nightstand coaster. He peels the comforter back and tucks us in bed, wrapping his body against mine like a koala.

"I don't deserve you, Jay," he murmurs into my hair. "But I am thankful for you."

"Hush," I playfully chastise. I lean back so I can see his face when I ask, "Was that a cheesy spinach quiche I saw in the fridge earlier?" He smiles and nods. "I'm the one who doesn't deserve you."

Chapter 7

Digging My Own Grave

Jay

When I arrive at work on Monday, I feel like I have a double dirty secret. Not only have I not told Marco about working for Cora, but she certainly doesn't know how we fucked with her as the focal point.

I know I should have told him about her this weekend. But the more I put it off, the harder it was to bring it up after our shower together. The next day we went to Marco's sister's house for Viera's fourth birthday party, and showing up in costume as Tigger and Christopher Robin was a pretty good distraction, but by the time Sunday rolled around, I was downright too scared to bring it up.

After I set my things down in my office and get ready for the day, I head to the large conference room for the bi-weekly check-in meeting with all the department heads. I take a seat and unbutton my navy blue suit jacket. When Jonathan comes in and takes Cora's usual spot at the head of the table, I furrow my brow in confusion. I know I haven't been here long, but that seems like a purposeful power move.

At exactly 9:00 am on the dot, Jonathan, wearing a dark gray suit and a scowl, announces, "Cora won't be joining us today, so I'll be leading the meeting. Sue, make sure the notes reflect that."

"Where is she?" I ask since he doesn't seem to want to divulge that information.

Dayo speaks up. "She had an early meeting with the auditorium project team on site," they reply simply. "She's getting more measurements and asking more questions so that our quote to them is accurate."

Jonathan huffs. "She could have scheduled it at a better time."

"They're our potential client, and they requested the meeting," Dayo retorts pointedly but professionally.

He looks down at his notebook and opens it, flipping to a blank page, and then clicks his pen. "It's neither here nor there, and we've wasted all this time talking about something that's not important. Let's get started. Legal, where are we?"

Horatio goes into the status of the lawsuit and who he needs to talk to this week. I talk about how the benefits open enrollment period has come to a close. All the departments take their turn, and we end with Katie reminding us that the holiday party is this Saturday and that we all need to make sure our respective departments show up and have a great time.

After the meeting, I get to my office and sit down at my desk.

"Hey, Jay," Dayo announces, standing in the doorway. "Do you have a minute to talk?" They're wearing a large geometric black and white print sweater with a matching loose skirt going to their calves. Paired with shiny blue Doc Martens boots and matching glasses with blunt small square frames.

"Yeah, of course." I nod and gesture to the door. "Close it if you think it's necessary, and have a seat."

They shut the door and turn back to sit at one of the chairs in front of my desk. They sit back and put their arms up on the armrests. "I wanted to talk about Jonathan and what you heard in the meeting today."

"About Cora not being here for the meeting?"

Dayo sighs, "Yeah. I don't know if anyone has told you about him, but he was supposed to take over as CEO when Paul left, er... died." They lean their head over to their hand and rub their temple. "May he rest in peace."

With a serious look, they continue, "Anyway, ever since Cora took over, Jonathan has been like this. Passive aggressive. Blaming her for anything he can. Making her look bad by twisting the situation. I'm not the only one that's noticed, but I am concerned he's trying to get people on his side with this slander. I'm not sure if he has an agenda or not. I just don't like seeing a capable and professional person being messed with like this."

It's my job to listen and provide reassurance in situations like this. While I can't confirm or deny any similar statements to them, I can say, "I see. I'm going to take note of this and see if anything else pops up about this. Do you think you could do me a favor and send me any instances of this happening in the past and future? An email will suffice, but send it to me directly."

"You got it," Dayo replies and stands up to leave. "Thank you for listening, Jay. I'm just trying to look out for her."

"Of course," I say with a smile, and they open the door and walk out, waving.

An hour or so later, I see Cora walk past my open door, presumably headed towards her office. I want to go talk with her, but I wait a bit and give her time to get settled in.

When I walk to her office, she's engrossed in her computer, dragging her mouse and clicking the keyboard with her other hand. She must be drafting. She's wearing a brown tweed blazer and a sky-blue blouse with a V cut. Her hair is down, and long strands of bouncy curls overflow her shoulders. She could look up and easily see me standing here, but she bites her lip and furrows her brow. She's so cute when she's concentrating.

I clear my throat, and she shakes out of her work and looks up. "Oh, hey. Sorry if you've been standing there long. I got carried away making these changes to the auditorium mock-up. What's up?"

"Nothing pressing. Just wanted to know how your weekend was." Perversely, I want her to tell me about the massage. I know she won't tell me the kind of intimate details Marco did, but I want to hear something.

"I spent Saturday and Sunday visiting my mom mostly. Saw my aunt when I was there. The two of them beat me in cards like it was their job." She smiles. "How was your weekend?"

Still standing in her doorway, I smile and nod. "That sounds nice. I went to a birthday party with my boyfriend. But I'm more interested in knowing if you actually went to your appointment Friday night or not."

I know I'm goading her. But then I immediately remember she left that appointment in tears. Shit. What if I trigger something in her? She probably doesn't want to talk about this. But then again, maybe she'll give me some information about Marco, and I can see where her head is at.

Did she see his erection?

Did he do something she didn't like?

Maybe it's all a misunderstanding, and I can put his mind at ease. After all, I *will* be telling him about Cora. I have to.

She smirks and parts her lips before whispering, "Close the door and have a seat."

Yes ma'am. Give me the tea.

I shut the door and sit in front of her desk with my elbows on my knees. "What happened?" I solicit.

She turns in her chair to face me completely and leans on her desk. "So, you've been to that spa before?"

I mean, she saw me dial their number from my contacts list, so she must have deduced this. "Yes," I answer, trying not to give away too much information.

"Have you ever had a massage therapist named Marco? He's like, really big and muscular and has tattoos down his arms?" Her body kind of shimmies when she says it, and she licks the inside of her lower lip.

Oh my god, I am in gossip heaven right now.

"Um, yeah, I've had him before." *Really had him, girl.*

Her eyebrows arch up, and her eyes go big. She bites her lower lip and shakes her head. "Holy shit, he's so hot, Jay. I tried to keep it together, but it was hard to concentrate."

My mind is like a hurricane right now. Adrenaline, anxiety, and pleasure are all ripping through my body at her words.

She thinks my boyfriend is hot.

I should feel anger. I should feel possessive. I should feel territorial. But I don't.

Cora keeps going, thankfully unaware of the turmoil in my head. "But it was the best massage I've ever had. I really want to thank you for setting it up for me."

"Oh, sure. No problem. Do you think you'll go back?"

"I'd love to, but I think I made a fool out of myself, so I might have to find a new place or a new massage therapist."

"What happened? Was it something Marco did?"

"Oh, no. It was just me. I can't really get into that, but he was great. And even though I was kind of... in a mood, he did his best to calm me down. He's very easy to talk to. But I definitely embarrassed myself, and he probably doesn't want to see me again," she huffs with a little self-deprecating laugh.

"I'm sure he doesn't think that," I offer because I know that for a fact.

"Well, regardless, I am glad I went. Thank you for forcing me," she says with a smile that doesn't quite reach her eyes.

"You're welcome, Cora." I'm so glad she didn't get upset at something he thinks *he* did. That's a relief.

She sits back in her chair and sighs with a smile. "So, what did I miss in the morning meeting? I see Sue sent notes, but I haven't read through them yet."

I briefly fill her in about everything, but at the end I bring up Jonathan and tell her what he said. She shakes her head in annoyance. My conversation with Dayo fresh in my mind, I ask, "Do you think he's trying to cause trouble on purpose? Maybe he could be trying to recruit people to his side of things, so to say."

"I don't know what his motive is or if he even has one."

"Someone talked to me about this very thing. This person is concerned Jonathan is trying to purposefully make you look bad and get others on his side. I've asked this person to send me any more instances of this happening if they hear or see it."

"Thanks for looking out for me. For the company. I appreciate it, Jay."

"It's not just my job; I really do care about what happens," I affirm.

Cora's computer trills. "Oh, I have a meeting in five minutes. But hey, before you go, you're planning on going to the holiday party this Saturday, right?"

"Yeah, I'll be there," I say with a quirk of my lips as I stand up.

"Good. Make sure you bring your boyfriend, too. I'd like to meet him," she suggests casually as she scoots her chair back into place in front of her multiple computer displays.

"Uhh... yeah. Yeah, I will. Have a good day, boss." I walk out of her office and head toward mine. The thought of them seeing each other at the party both worries and thrills me. Maybe I should just see how that plays out instead of telling either of them.

Chapter 8

The Holiday Party

Cora

The company holiday party has always been one of my favorite things. I've been coming to this event since I was eighteen, along with my mother, as my father would charm his way through the crowds of employees and their dates.

The event had been held at various locations throughout the decades, but this year, it's at a swanky historic hotel. You can't have a big event like this at a run-of-the-mill event space. I can't have dozens of creatives who specialize in architecture and interior design at a boring venue. They wouldn't be able to relax and have fun. They'd spend the whole time pointing out flaws and critiquing the architecture of the building, or lack thereof.

Every year, we invite several of our smaller partnering companies to join us. It's not like a bribery thing; it's just expanding the party. Taking smaller companies that might have small holiday parties and combining them so everyone can be a part of a bigger, grander event. Each company pays its portion, of course.

THE HOLIDAY PARTY

This year Valley Forge Construction, LLC and Green-Growth Urban Planning joined us again for the third year in a row. With all of us and our dates, we have about six hundred people attending.

While people mingle and sip their cocktails, I'm standing in the women's bathroom reading my note cards for tonight's speech. I don't mind talking in front of a large crowd, especially one that has been supporting me and the company's goals. I truly want to thank them for everything they did this year.

But as I stand here, staring at my cards, I can't register the words. All I can think about is seeing Jay and meeting his boyfriend. Things are going to go one of two ways: either I meet his boyfriend and see them together, and this stupid little crush fizzles out, or I'll be blindly jealous. I'm not going to deny the fact that I'm attracted to Jay. I'm just trying to control it the best way I can, and it's working. The crush *will* fizzle out.

I step out of the stall and look at myself in the huge, gilded mirror. I'm wearing a classic black velvet gown that hugs my curves all the way down to my thighs, where it flares out slightly and hangs to the floor. It's strapless, and the bodice has a slight sweetheart neckline. I've paired it with black patent leather pointed-toe heels and gold earrings. My hair is up in a beautiful romantic twist that starts at my ears and forms a low bun.

I want to look confident and commanding because, Lord knows, I'm *not* on the inside. I'm a nervous wreck with the anticipation of seeing Jay.

I take a deep breath, stuffing my notes into my tiny black studded clutch and swing open the door. I walk by several employees and wave at them as I make my way to the stage.

I'm in the hallway outside of the ballroom, and I know the doors that I stand in front of will open, and I'll walk out on the stage and begin my speech once Katie gives me the signal.

I wait there in the alcove of the hallway, and David, the CEO of the construction company, comes up to stand with me. He's my height, and he's wearing a nice black suit with a crisp white shirt and a ridiculous novelty Christmas tie with Rudolph front and center.

I can tell he saw me eyeing the tie, and he says, "I know. My six-year-old son said I had to wear it or else Santa wouldn't know we were true believers."

We both smile at that as I lean in to whisper, "Well, then I retract my thought. You went from ridiculous to adorable in three seconds."

"Have you seen Sierra?" he asks, referring to the CEO of GreenGrowth. "I think we're due on stage in a minute or two."

As if summoned by his words, Sierra comes running over with a glass of champagne in her hand. She has light brown skin and gorgeous natural hair that has been twisted in a crown around her head. She's slender and just as bubbly as her drink she's almost spilling. She's wearing a silver gown that's modest in front, covering everything from her neck to her toes, but the back is completely open from her shoulders to her lower back. She looks incredible. I've always been envious of women who can wear open backs. Me? I always have to wear a bra or make sure the dress is structured in a way that holds my jubblies up.

"Sorry I'm late," Sierra sings as she comes to a stop in front of us. "I had to make sure the DJ had Mariah Carey on the playlist."

"Good call," David says, surprising both me and Sierra. "What? Everyone loves Mariah Carey," he states matter-of-factly.

Just then the door opens and Katie steps forward. "Alright, it's your time to shine." The three of us follow Katie to the stage and she stops at the stairs and gestures for us to walk up and take our places.

The music lowers, and everyone in the room claps for our arrival. I take the microphone from one of the stage attendants and try to look out at the crowd, but the lights are so bright it's hard to see. I have my speech more or less memorized, so I leave my notes in my clutch.

"Good evening, everyone! Thank you so much for being here tonight to celebrate not only this joyous holiday season but also our successes. We would not be here if it weren't for you, our dedicated—"

I cut myself off as my eyes start to adjust fully to the lights, and I can see the room of people. There are large round tables everywhere, and the one closest to the stage, directly in front of me, sits Jay in a dark blue velvet suit jacket, black slacks, white dress shirt, and finished with a black bow tie and pocket square. He looks so chic and handsome. His chair is turned around, so he sits facing me.

Then I notice the man sitting right next to him, his arm around Jay's shoulder.

Marco?

What the fuck is my massage therapist doing here with Jay?

Marco is wearing a beautiful burgundy three-piece suit and a shocked look on his face, his mouth agape and eyes unblinking. I look over at Jay, and he gives me a positively lewd smile, then places his hand on Marco's thick thigh and rubs his fingers over his leg.

I think my brain has short-circuited.

Am I still talking? I can't hear anything except my own thoughts.

David nudges me, and I look at him. I have no idea what my face looks like right now, but he takes the microphone from my hand and takes over. "I think what Cora was trying to say is we wouldn't be here without you, our dedicated employees. We're so thankful for your hard work..." David keeps talking and going into his portion of the speech, but I stop listening.

Marco is sitting with Jay.

Jay has his hand on Marco's thigh. They're... together?

The memory of me telling Jay about my hottie massage therapist comes to mind, and I inwardly berate myself.

Great. Now Jay probably hates me for ogling his boyfriend and *telling him about it.*

Fuck, this is what I get for letting go just a little bit.

Before I realize it, the crowd is clapping, and Sierra hands the mic to the stagehand and tucks her elbow into mine, hauling me off stage. She brings me to the corner of the room where David stands and asks, "Is everything okay? You look like you saw a ghost."

I stammer, "I-I'm fine. I just remembered something, and my mind went blank. Thank you for covering for me. I don't really know what happened."

David puts his hand on my shoulder and gives me a little squeeze. "It's okay, Cora. Would you like a drink to calm your nerves?"

I nod. "Yeah. But it's okay, I'll get it. I have to make my rounds anyway. Thanks again, you guys. Enjoy the party."

The two of them disperse as I make my way to the closest bar and order a glass of champagne and down it.

It's going to be a long night of avoiding them.

Chapter 9

The Holiday Party

Marco

"Jay, holy fuck, that was my client from the other night!" I whisper shout at him as I push him into an empty event room down the hall. "She definitely saw me. I think that's why she lost her words. Wait, is she your boss?" I ask, panic pouring out of me like a burst dam.

Jay closes both doors to the room and turns around to face me with a grimace. "Yeah, she is. And um... to make matters more complicated," he sighs, taking a long pause. "Do you remember that woman I had a one-night stand with a couple years back? The one I met that night I was with Noah, and we went dancing and had sex in my car?"

My eyes narrow in speculation before I nod. "Yeah... you were heartbroken she blocked your number."

Jay arches his eyebrows and bites his bottom lip. "She's the same person. That's Cora. That's my boss. That was your client."

My mind is buffering at this information. There's a lot of dots to connect and I'm not sure I'm connecting all of them. "Wait a minute. Did you know she was my client before tonight?"

"Yeah. I kind of set up the appointment for her." He winces and then rushes to add, "But I swear I didn't know she would be any different than a normal client for you. It just so happened that you were the only one available that evening because you had a client cancel."

My mouth is agape, and I don't think I've blinked since I saw Cora on stage. "Why didn't you tell me she was your boss? How did this even happen?"

"Well, I was hired by different people, and I didn't exactly do extensive research to learn about the CEO. So, when I arrived on my first day, I met her and... well, it was awkward as hell to be honest." He gives me a sad smile and reaches for my lapels, smoothing them down. "I'm sorry I didn't tell you earlier. It's just... I didn't know how to bring it up after you came home that night after meeting her. Then the more time passed, the harder it was. I figured tonight we could rip the Band Aid off, you know?"

I sigh and grab his waist and bring it to mine. "Let me just think about this for a minute." Jay gives me the time as he wraps his arms under my shoulders and palms my back.

I can't believe this is happening. I can't believe Jay would hide something like this from me. I know this woman was a lot more to him than a one-night stand. The operative word being *was*. I know what we have is unbreakable, and we've always been upfront and honest with each other. He must have really been in a strange mental state if he held out telling me for this long.

Once I've calmed down enough, I ask, "How do you feel about seeing her again? Working for her?"

Jay lays his head on my shoulder and speaks softly, "It was

awkward at first, sure. But I've been trying to be a friend to her. She's so stressed and I just want to help."

"And?" I ask, knowing there has to be more.

He huffs out a little laugh. "And it's been really hard seeing her again. She's fucking hot, *you've seen her*. And as much as I am trying to tamp down my memories of her, they still boil up to the surface." He sighs and continues, "That night in the shower was as much for you as it was for me."

Jay pulls back and looks at me in the eyes and quickly adds, "But I swear, baby, I would never act on those thoughts. You're my world and I wouldn't risk what we have for her or anyone."

"I know, prince," I sigh as I comb my fingers through his hair. "But damn, she's gorgeous. I don't know how you get work done with her around."

Jay chuckles, "I lock myself in my office a lot."

With a smirk, I grab the back of his neck and bring his lips to mine. "And do what? Do you stroke yourself thinking about her? Thinking about you and her? Me and her? Oooh, the *three* of us?"

He smiles against the kiss and murmurs, "I'm not that unprofessional to masturbate at work." He kisses me back, opening my mouth and tasting me. Rolling his tongue against mine. I bite his full bottom lip and let go as he drawls, "But I'd be lying if I said I haven't thought about the three of us. *God, could you even imagine?*"

I kiss along his jaw and whisper, "Her soft curves..."

Jay hums his agreement, closing his eyes and giving me more access. "Her tits," he muses.

I kiss down his neck and murmur, "Her plump ass..."

"Her long hair..."

"Her sad eyes..."

"Her tight pussy..."

Then the full idea forms in my brain and I hesitate to ask, "Do you think she'd go for something like this?" I stop my kissing and hold his face, staring at him.

"Like, be a unicorn?" Jay asks with a worried look on his face.

"Yeah, unless you don't want to. We've never entertained something like this. Plus, she's your boss, so that adds a whole extra level—"

He cuts me off. "Oh, no I love this idea. And afterward, you and I can talk about it and see how we're feeling. You know, make sure we still feel safe and prioritized. That seems like the healthy thing to do."

I nod. "Absolutely. I think this could be fun. Plus, didn't you say she's stressed? If she's the CEO she probably needs something in her life to not be the boss of." I smirk and waggle my eyebrows. "This might be good for her."

"You know," Jay drawls, "I asked her on Monday how her massage was, and she said her massage therapist was really hot and she couldn't concentrate. Oh, also, you're totally in the clear about her possibly seeing your boner. She didn't say anything about that."

"Thank fuck," I groan. "But she thinks I'm hot? She told you that?" Damn, I sound like a teenager right now.

"Oh yeah." He laughs and then tries to mimic her voice, "You know that big muscular tattooed massage therapist? Oh my god, he's soooo dreamy."

I'm sure I'm blushing as I grin from ear to ear. "She did not say that."

"More or less."

Bringing the conversation back to our little proposition, I ask, "You really think she might go for something like this?"

Jay puts his hands on my chest and gives me a look. "Alright, let's hold our horses. We'll need to present this to her in a very strategic manner—and *not* tonight. She obviously freaked out on stage when she saw us."

"You're right. And as much as I want to take you right here and now," I say as I grab his ass and squeeze. "Let's get out of here and meet your coworkers. Show me off like your prize pony."

"More like a prize stallion," Jay replies, waggling his eyebrows.

I swat his ass and he leaps towards the double doors to open one. When he does, he stops with the door only cracked. "What's wrong?" I ask, stepping over to him and brushing my chest to his back.

He puts his finger up and whispers, "Shh!"

From outside the doors, we can hear what sounds like a couple men talking.

"The lawsuit is heating up, man. This is a lot more than everyone anticipated," one voice states.

"Relax. That bitch is going down. I've been..." the other voice trails off as I assume the two men are walking away.

"Holy shit," Jay exhales. "I think that was about Cora."

"What lawsuit?" I ask.

Jay pushes open the door and we step out, no one in sight. "I'll tell you about it when we get home."

"Did you recognize those voices?"

"Not really. It could have been people I work with but maybe I haven't been there long enough because I can't quite place them."

"Did I hear them call her a *bitch?*"

"It must have been her. There's no other woman dealing with the lawsuit like she is. She has the most to lose." He pulls out his phone and opens the notes app and begins to type. "I'm going to record this for future reference. It might be useful later."

When he's done, he pockets his phone and sighs, "Okay, let's go mingle, stallion."

We start to walk back to our ballroom, and I roll my eyes. "This is not a new nickname, is it?"

"Oh, I quite like it. It's staying," he proclaims, wrapping his arm around my waist as we stride into the room.

I lean over and whisper in his ear, "You'll pay for it later, prince."

"Thank god you're a man of your word."

Chapter 10

Erotic Audio

Cora

Even though it's the weekend, and the holiday party was just yesterday, I am in the office bright and early. It's Sunday and no one is here, but that only means I can get some real work done.

I have to prepare my deposition, even though the trial is weeks away, and finalize my quote for the auditorium remodel which is due this week. Technically, we have junior architects do work like this and I can give final approval, but I am hyper-focused on every quote coming from us these days. With the lawsuit underway, a tarnished reputation is already sprouting. I can feel it. I need to make sure everything we quote is flawless. Sure, changes will be needed as we go, if we are awarded the project, but I don't want anything getting in our way. We have to prove we are trustworthy and top-tier.

Gross and vicarious negligence.

I've worked with this client before on a couple smaller projects on their fine arts campus, but nothing as big as this. The client, Maureen Hansel and her board of trustees, loved what we did for them previously. Certainly, I knew that was not enough to be selected again, so I absolutely couldn't rely on that to win us this bid. This RFQ had to be on point.

As I'm estimating costs for the renovation, my phone buzzes on my desk and I see a picture of Angie pop up on the screen. It's a ridiculous photo of us dressed as Wayne and Garth from *Wayne's World* on Halloween from years ago and it's been her contact photo ever since. I smile at the memory, slide open the call, and put it on speaker phone. "Hey girl, hey."

"Hey girl, hey!" she volleys back. "What are you doing?"

"I'm working in the office."

Angie groans, "You're always working weekends. I miss you. I was going to ask if you wanted to come over for some hot totties and watch a Christmas movie."

"I know, I'm sorry. I'm just stressed over everything right now and I need to work like crazy. I think George is sick of being my only therapeutic outlet when I get home."

"Well, she's a cat, that's what God made them for I'm pretty sure."

I smile and huff a little laugh. "Yeah, I think you're right. That and bulldog puppies we find on the sidewalk."

She squeals over the line, and I can't help but think back on that night with fondness.

"Speaking of Jay... didn't you have your big event last night? How did that go? Was he there?"

"Oh my god, Ang. You're not going to believe this. Remember the massage that he set me up for? Well, I didn't know at the time, but his boyfriend, Marco, was my smoking hot massage therapist and I told that to Jay, but he didn't say anything. Flash forward to last night, I discovered Marco and Jay together at the party and I freaked out. I avoided them all night."

Angie laughs hysterically for what seems like minutes, but then calms herself down enough to say, "Wow, you've got yourself a proper mess, my girl. Oooh, but think of the mess the three of you could make..."

"Okay," I interject, cutting her off. "That's enough. It's just... I wish I kept my mouth shut about Marco."

Angie gasps, "Oh my god, this reminds me of an erotic audio I just listened to on the Quinn app..."

"Angie! You're such a perv," I giggle.

"Do you still have the app?" she asks.

"You mean since you took my phone and downloaded it against my will?"

"Yeah!" she cheers.

"Yeah," I grumble and search my apps, finding it tucked away on one of the last pages.

"Okay, I'm sending it to you."

"No! Angela Johanssen, I am not entertaining this idea. It's bad enough that I have the hots for both of them, one of which is my *friggin'* employee. Absolutely not."

Ding!

My phone chimes as a text message comes in from Angie.

"I'll just leave that there and you do with it what you will," she says, and I know she's smirking on the other side of this phone.

I roll my eyes and sigh. "Okay babe, I have to get back to work. I'm sorry I can't hang out today, but we will soon, alright?"

"Absolutely. Love you, Cora."

"Love you, too. Bye," I say, ending the call.

I immediately get back to working but after about thirty minutes, curiosity wins out and I pop my wireless earbuds in and hit play on the stupid audio.

The narrator has a low voice with a casual and slow cadence.

He's talking to his girlfriend, presumably me in this scenario, and says he wants his roommates to watch us together but under one condition: I have to do whatever he tells me.

Oh my god, Angie, what did you get me into?

The narrator goes on to tell me to take off my clothes and show them everything.

"Good girl," he purrs.

Ooh, praise? Yes, please. I close my eyes and lean back in my chair.

He has me sit on my knees and plant my face on the ground and play with myself. Then he tells his friend to take me from behind as he, my narrator boyfriend, jerks off.

"Take it baby," he commands.

Holy shit. I lift my hands and start to gently caress my nipples through my athleisure top. This is really hot.

"Watching you get taken by another man... you know what would make this so much better? If we open this up to another person," the narrator suggests, his voice like gravel. *"Take him in your mouth and I don't want you to let either of them out of you."*

He grunts and groans his pleasure in my ears and it's taking everything I have not to touch my actual pussy right now.

"Fill her up," he demands. *"Come on his cock, baby. Who's my good little whore?"*

Then, as the guys I'm being spit-roasted between come, and pull out, he says, "Now it's my turn. I'm going to lick the cum off you." Then I hear the most indecent licking sounds as he laps at my pussy.

The audio ends and I realize I'm now pinching my nipples. I release them and open my eyes.

"JAY!" I scream, panic coursing through my body like white water rapids. "Holy shit! What are you doing here? H-how long have you been sitting there?"

He's smirking and sitting with one foot resting on his knee, his hands clasped in his lap. "Would you like for me to pretend I didn't see... whatever *that* was?"

"Yes. Holy shit. Oh my god, I am so embarrassed," I stumble, barely able to form words at this point. My cheeks are burning hot. "Wh-why are you here?"

"I could ask you the same thing," he says with a quirk to his brow. "I was driving by the building and saw your car in the lot. I was confused as to why you would be here on a Sunday."

I let out a small huff. "Me working on a Sunday is not confusing. What's confusing is you not telling me I ogled your boyfriend."

I think about Marco's shocked face right next to Jay, sitting there in front of me last night. I press the palms of my hands into my eyes and throw the weight of my body back into the chair. "I am so sorry, Jay. Seriously, I feel like scum." I release my hands from my face and sit up to look him in the eyes. "I'm sorry. Please forgive me. I promise I won't go back to that spa—"

"Cora," he cuts me off. "It's okay, really. It's more my fault for not telling you he was my boyfriend ahead of time."

"Regardless, I am so... mortified and sorry, Jay."

"Don't worry about it. I'm serious. Marco and I were actually talking about the whole situation and we..." he stops, mid-sentence to contemplate his next words. "We'd like to be friends with you. Let's brush right past this and move on," he offers with a smile that puts me at ease a little bit.

They want to be friends with me?

I mean, I guess Jay and I have been getting closer over the last couple weeks. We work well together. He's nice company to have around. He's easy to talk to. From what I remember of Marco, he was very easy to have a conversation with, albeit I was trying to shut up while he massaged me, but he was nice. He had a calming presence to him.

Remembering Marco like that instantly puts my tension at bay, and I relax a bit before I give a small smile. "Uh, yeah. Yeah, I think that would be okay."

Jay beams that bright, perfect smile at me. "Yeah? Great. Maybe we can get together after work sometime soon. You guys can actually have a proper conversation since the three of us avoided each other last night."

I grimace. "Yeah... about that..."

"It's fine, Cora. The past is in the past," he says and nods his head. "But hey, speaking of last night." He pulls out his phone and scrolls through, looking for something. "I overheard a couple men talking in the hallway outside the ballroom. I was in another room that was vacant so they didn't see me, but I could hear them as they walked by. They said and I quote, *'The lawsuit is heating up, man. This is a lot more than everyone anticipated.'* And the other guy said, *'Relax. That bitch is going down.'*"

Jay keeps looking at his screen and says, "That was at 8:14 pm." He pockets his phone and looks back at me. "I wasn't sure who was saying that though, and by the time I opened the door to leave, they were already gone."

"Whoa. I guess that could go several different ways," I contemplate aloud and focus my eyes on the desk. "Maybe it's an employee just remarking that the lawsuit is more intense than we've let on? As the executive board, we decided to tell our staff that we had this under control and not to worry. That we would fight this and win. Maybe they're just seeing more of it and speculating or something."

Jay considers this and tilts his head to the side, propping his face against his fingers. "Maybe. But then why would the second person say *That bitch is going down?* No offense, but

I assume they were talking about you, since you're the only woman heavily involved in this case."

"None taken," I volley back. "There's also the possibility they were using the word bitch as a gender-neutral slang. I've heard guys call guys bitches."

"That's true, I guess," he contemplates. "Is there a possibility someone would want to sabotage the company?"

My eyes pop out and I explain, "If someone tried to sabotage that building, the legal ramifications for them would be astronomical. They'd lose any licensing they had, go to prison for falsifying documents, maybe coercion. God, if someone died... then involuntary manslaughter... the list goes on. Someone would have to be completely out of their minds to do something like that."

Jay takes in the information and nods his head, his face solemn. "You're right."

Both of us go silent for a couple minutes as we think to ourselves.

He breaks the silence and stands. "We will get to the bottom of this. I'm going to go, and I suggest you do the same. Have you seen your mom yet this weekend?"

Taken aback by his change in topic, I say, "Uh, not yet, actually. Saturday I spent preparing for the party. I was planning on going later today."

"Okay," he smiles, heading towards the door. "Tell her I said *hi*. See you tomorrow, boss."

Jay leaves, and I have the weirdest feeling of comfort come over me.

Chapter 11

Parental Support

Jay

After I leave the office, I go to the grocery store to pick up a few more items for tonight and head home. Marco and I are having my parents over for dinner, something we do every few weeks or so.

When Marco left the Army, he moved in with me right away. I had never lived with a partner before, but I was surprised at how smooth the transition was. Not only was living with him a new phase, but having an actual tangible relationship with him was brand new, too.

We had spent the last four years of his service messaging each other and talking whenever we could. Whenever it was safe for him to do so. Sometimes we'd go weeks without a single communication because he wasn't in a safe location and I would worry more than normal.

When he would come home for leave, we'd hang out almost the whole time, laughing, eating, playing soccer and basketball, going for runs together, and getting drunk. As time went on, we went from friends to... more. When he got out, there was no question in either of our minds that we had to be together.

Thankfully, Marco moving in with me, and us being together didn't phase my parents... much. When I first came out to them, as—well, not straight—it was a little bumpy at first, but they came around quickly. I think they sensed me pulling away and they couldn't stand it. Being their only child, they wanted to do whatever it took to keep me in their lives. I know I'm lucky to have loving and accepting parents. So many of my queer friends don't and because of that, some don't even talk to their parents anymore. I hate to imagine my life like that.

When I walk through our front door to our townhouse, I can already smell the intoxicating aromas wafting from the kitchen. Marco stands at the island, chopping some radishes while pans on the stove sizzle.

Walking over to him, I look through the bags and rattle off some of the items. "Alright, I got more scallions, ginger, sesame seeds, and I found some Korean beer!" I say excitedly, setting the bags on the counter. I peel off my coat, hang it and take off my boots.

As I make my way back to Marco, I give him a quick kiss and start to unpack the bags. He's wearing basically the same thing I am, jeans and an olive green t-shirt from his Army days. Mine's black.

"Did you find everything okay? You were gone for a little longer than I thought," he says, scooping up the cooked radish with his chef's knife and placing it in a bowl.

Remembering my little detour to the office, I give a little dramatic gasp, and place my hand on his chest as he continues to chop and scrape. "Oh, you are not going to believe this. I actually stopped in the office on the way to the store because I saw Cora's car outside. No one else was there obviously, but I walked into her office to ask why she was there, and I saw her sitting back in her chair, eyes closed, *rubbing her nipples over her shirt*," I beam, slowly enunciating each of the last words and staring at Marco with wide eyes.

He turns to face me, his body freezing and jaw dropping. "What?"

"I kid you not, man," I smile. "She had her ear buds in so she didn't hear me. I looked at her phone which was sitting on the desk between us, and she was listening to something titled *Threesome...* something or other, and it had these tag words like MDom, Praise, and Voyeurism." I waggle my eyebrows at him with a mischievous grin.

"*Fuck me,*" he bellows. "You're shitting me. No fucking way."

I chuckle, "I swear I'm not." I let go of him and fold up the bags and put them away in the cabinet. I grab two of the beers and open them, giving him one. "So, I sat down waiting for her to realize I was there."

He almost has his beer to his mouth before he stops and gasps, "Jay!"

"It was fine," I drawl. "She didn't do anything more than rub her breasts and pant the whole time. Five minutes, tops."

"Five minutes?" he exclaims.

Laughing, I say, "She opened her eyes, and I scared the shit out of her."

Marco sets his beer down and braces his arms on either side of the cutting board, jutting his ass out and sighing. "Great, you probably freaked her out so much she won't want to even consider our proposal, whenever that is," he mutters.

I lean my back against the island counter, crossing my ankles and tucking one hand under my other arm. I take a sip of beer using my other hand and with a cocksure attitude declare, "Oh, she's going to consider it. Are you kidding me? She was listening to a *threesome* audio, probably thinking about us."

He sighs and turns his head back to face me, still hunched over the counter. Resigned, he asks, "Was it hot?"

With a feral smile, I nod. "I wish you could have seen her, dude."

He lifts off the counter and grabs a metal bowl and a carton of eggs. "You're going to describe it to me later in great detail. Right now I need to make the *pajun*. Your parents are going to be here any minute and I don't want to have a boner when they arrive."

"How can I help?"

He gestures towards a bowl. "Can you hand me that bowl of flour and set the table?"

"Of course." I kiss him, hand him the bowl and gather the place settings.

When I'm almost done setting the table, I hear a knock at the door. Setting the rest of the silverware down, I cross the room to answer.

"Hi, Mom. Hi, Dad." I take the bottle of chardonnay from her grip, lean down and wrap my arms around her. "Thanks for coming."

"Of course, sweetie. We love these nights with you boys," Mom cheers, kissing my cheek. Then she hands her coat to Dad. She's a petite woman with straight blonde hair that bobs above her shoulder. It's getting a little whiter now, but it's hard to tell. She's wearing a cream colored turtleneck sweater dress and tall black equestrian boots. For a woman of seventy, she keeps herself in tip top health and very much cares about her appearance. She's been obsessed with skin care and staying out of the sun for as long as I've known her. Most people think she's about ten years younger than she actually is.

I stand up and Mom moves past me towards the kitchen and my dad steps up and gives me a tight hug and a pat on the back. "Good to see you, son." Dad, however, looks every bit of seventy-three that he is. He used to be about six feet tall, but he's shrunk an inch or two over the years. The man retired as a mechanical engineer five years ago, but his passion has always been gardening. He's outside working in their yard in Bryn Mawr any day there isn't snow on the ground. He has a trim salt and pepper beard, mostly salt these days and his hair is much the same, cut the same way it's been my whole life, short on the sides and a little longer on top. He tosses my mom's coat over the couch back and takes his own off. He's wearing a casual dark gray long sleeve button down, dark jeans and brown dress boots. "Good to see you, too, Dad." I take both of their coats and the bottle of wine and we head towards the kitchen.

As I hang up their outerwear, I head over to the counter and I hear Mom startle, "Oh, my. This is quite the... spread. What is that?" She points to one of the dishes.

"I'll explain everything in a minute. Have a seat at the table and I'll bring you a glass of wine, Mom. Dad, can I get you a beer?"

"Sure," he says and leads Mom to the table.

"Does this have something to do with you guys going to the Poconos for Christmas?" she asks, pulling out her chair and sitting.

"No, Mom. Just wait for me to explain, please."

I start to bring all the dishes over and Marco adds last minute garnishes. When we finally sit, each with a beer in our hands, we're across from my parents. The table is full of dishes and serving wear. Marco sits back with one arm draped over my chair, sipping his beer with a smile. I look at him with affection and grin, "Thank you for cooking. For doing this. It all looks wonderful."

"It was my pleasure, hon. Go on, tell your parents what's going on."

I look at them, both have a quizzical look in their eyes. "So, what we have here are all Korean dishes." I point to each one and describe it a little. "This is *pajun*, it's like a vegetable pancake. This is *japchae*, it's a sweet potato noodle dish with veggies. This is *dukbokki* which is little rice cakes in a sweet and spicy sauce, and this is *seolleontang*, ox bone soup. We've got rice over here for that and kimchi right there. That can go on basically anything you eat here." I get a little lost in my descriptions and when I finish, I look over at Marco and ask, "Did I get that all right?"

He nods. "Pretty much."

I look at my parents who are silent and a little stunned. This is absolutely out of their comfort zone, but I knew that going into this. Growing up with them, we never ate much in the world of Asian cuisine, save for the occasional Chinese takeout. Our home menu was a rotation of Italian, American, and bastardized Mexican fare. And being that they're both of European heritage, sometimes we'd have Polish, German, or French recipes that have passed down in the family for a long time.

I take a deep breath, calming my racing nerves before I continue, "Lately, I've been wrestling with my identity. I feel a strong disconnect between my Korean heritage and how I grew up. Obviously growing up in Bryn Mawr, I didn't see people like me."

My dad cuts me off, "Wait, what about the Patels?"

Jesus Christ, I want to faceplant into this table right now. I'm so glad no one else is around to hear him say that. "Dad, the Patels are Indian."

He pauses a moment. "Oh."

Needing desperately to leave this part of the conversation and get back to my point, I continue, "So, Marco has been kind enough to start cooking some Korean recipes to help me understand the food culture."

"You know we don't see color, Jay," Mom says, trying to defuse the situation.

I sigh. "Yeah, that's kind of, part of it all. You say you don't see color, but what I need... is for you *to* see color." She takes a sip of her wine and stares at me. "I want to feel a connection to Korean people and culture. I grew up in a mostly white town, with white parents who raised me... well, white."

Mom bristles in her chair and sets her glass down. "We raised you the best way we knew how," she snarls. "And here you are *blaming* us for giving you everything? You wanted for *nothing*, Jay Bishop." Her eyes are practically bugging out of her head at this point and my dad sits next to her quietly fuming.

"Mom, please don't misunderstand me, I'm not blaming you. I understand that you did the best you knew how, but sometimes I feel like a fraud. I look Korean but I don't feel like it."

"Oh my god," she cuts in. "I will not sit here and listen to you tell me that we failed you and how ungrateful you are." She stands up and pushes her chair to start to walk off. "We're leaving, Bill."

Marco stands up at the same time as my dad and interjects, "No, Kathleen, wait. Please hear him out," he pleads. "Jay's spent a lot of time thinking about this and wants to have an open and honest conversation."

But they're not listening anymore. When my mom gets like this, she shuts down all rational thought and I truly think her brain blacks out. I want them to stay and listen. To ask questions. To be supportive of this new chapter of my life, one I've wanted to explore for a long time.

"When *he* can learn to be grateful and appreciative for what he has, what we've given him, *then* we can have a conversation," she barks and marches off to grab their coats.

"Dad, please stay. I want to share this part of my life with you guys. Please—"

"Your mother is right, Jay." He grabs his coat from my mom as she surges past the table straight for the front door. He follows her and she whips it open.

She turns back to face us, Marco still standing and me sitting there with pleading eyes. "We probably won't see you before Christmas since you're going away instead of being with your terrible *white* family for the holiday. So *Merry Christmas*." Her words are laced with aggression and sarcasm. The door slams shut, and we're left there in shocked horror at what just happened.

Low instrumental Christmas music plays from the wireless speaker, taunting us. Marco falls down into his chair and we look at each other. "What on earth just happened there?" he asks.

Tears start to well in my eyes and my bottom lip trembles. "I don't know."

He immediately grabs me by the shoulders and hauls me into a tight embrace. "Hey, hey, it's okay, baby. It's going to be okay," he soothes.

Now I'm full on sobbing, leaning into his warm hard chest and he squeezes me. "But you worked so hard on tonight's meal and they just..."

"Hon, it's not about the meal right now," he says softly, stroking my hair, my face cradled in his neck. "I think they just need some time to think about this."

"What do they have to think about?" I sniffle. "They barely listened to me."

After a few moments, Marco asks, "Do you want a solution, or do you just want to feel your feelings?"

Knowing there's no way in hell a solution can be formed right now, I manage to sputter out, "I just wanna feel."

Marco stands, bringing me with him and he hoists me up, carrying me bridal style to the couch. He sits down and situates me on his lap, my side pressed into him, knees bent in a fetal position. I wrap my arms around his neck and bury my face deep in his scent. He keeps his arms wrapped tight around me. I'm soaking the collar of his shirt with my tears, but he simply holds me. This strong, gruff man is my lighthouse; he's calm in every storm, guiding me to safety. Anchoring me when my world is spinning.

Sure, I can anchor myself if need be. I know how to cope in situations like this by myself, but when Marco Borrelli is the center of your life, you let him take care of you.

I sit there in his lap and cry for I don't know how long. I can feel his erection growing and bulging beneath my ass. I chuckle through the tears, "Oh my god, really baby?"

"I'm sorry. I swear this is all about you and your feelings right now. I'm not going to act on... *this,*" he says, wiggling his lap ever so slightly.

But his words have already started to make me feel better. Him and his crying kink. I shake my head and smile as the last tears slide down my face. "You're such a pervert," I tease.

"But I'm *your* pervert," he whispers in my hair.

With a real laugh, I lift my head from his neck and look into his beautiful blue eyes. "Yes, you are. You're my favorite model of perv and I'm never trading you in."

He smiles and leans in to gently kiss me. Our lips connect and we both sigh into each other.

This man. Wow.

We break apart after a few moments, and he looks at me with a small smile and tenderness in his eyes. "When was the last time you went for a run?" he asks.

The question catches me off guard a bit and I think before saying, "Uh, I think it was the Turkey Trot about a month ago. Why?"

He tilts his head with a little sheepish grin. "Well, you've always found running to center you. You use it to both clear your mind and find answers. Why not give it a go? Maybe that can help you find some clarity with your parents. Or not. Who knows," he says casually.

"That's not a bad idea. It has been too long since I ran." Then an idea pops in my head. "Oh! I can use the gym at work in the morning."

"There you go, hon. Of course, I'm here to help center you, too," he offers, kissing me sweet and soft. "I love you, prince."

"I love you, too. And I know you are, but you know what I *really* need right now?" I ask rhetorically. "I need some of that soup and *japchae*. I'm starving."

Marco smiles wide and releases me. "Alright, hopefully everything is still warm enough," he says, and we both stand. He runs his hand down my back and guides me to the table, pulling out my chair and letting me sit as he scooches it in for me.

He serves each of us a little bit of everything, and explains the process of making each dish. We both look up the history of the ingredients on our phones and what they mean to Korean cuisine, explaining it to each other as we find out. I love this little discovery we're doing together. He's more than a lover; more than a boyfriend. He's truly a partner.

Chapter 12

Workout

Cora

It's almost 6:00 am when I walk into the office gym. As usual, no one is here. I don't love working out so early, but I really don't have the time other than now. And after a bad dream, exercising has always helped me calm down.

I have these dreams of my teeth falling out pretty often. Always in different situations. In last night's dream-scape, I was eating cereal and all my teeth fell out of my mouth into the bowl. I woke up in a panic, clutching my face and decided that going back to sleep was not in the cards for me.

So here I am, in my black leggings and lilac razorback athletic tank. My mess of curls is twisted up in a bun and I'm on day four of my hair washing cycle. I brought my shampoo, conditioner, and curling products so I could properly wash and style it after my workout.

After setting down my duffel in the locker room, I make my way to the front of the mirrored gym wall and turn on the television to My Lottery Dream Home on HGTV. I love this host so much. I can tell beneath that composed façade, he's really thinking, *this couple won eight million dollars and they want a condo in Miami that's facing the parking lot so they can save money by not having a view of the ocean?*

I set the remote down and roll out one of the yoga mats to start my stretching. I roll out my shoulders, pull my arms over my chest, pull my ankle into my hand to stretch my hamstrings, bend forward, and rest my hands on the floor. Then I finish off my warmup by getting on my knees, spreading them as far as I can, sitting my backside down to my ankles and stretching my hands forward on the ground, forehead to the floor. I love this pose so much. It feels amazing on my groin and back. I gently rock my hips back and forth, up and down, deepening the stretch.

"Am I always going to walk into work and find you in compromising positions?" I hear a familiar low voice announce.

I scramble out of my pose and look behind me at Jay, standing in the doorway with a gym bag over his shoulder, a hanging garment bag in his hand and a grin a mile wide.

I shake my head and roll my eyes. "I thought we agreed you would pretend yesterday's little surprise visit never happened?"

He walks away from me towards the men's locker room. "Well, that's the thing about pretending, Cora… it's just not real. And real things like that live rent free in my head," he says with a casual tone as he opens the door to the men's room to deposit his things.

I lay down on my mat, knees bent up and palm my eyes.
Is he flirting with me?
Why would he say that?
Does he think about me like that?
No, no way. He has a gorgeous boyfriend who lives with him.

He's not into me.

But then the memory of us in the back seat of his SUV races through my mind. God, that night! Unreal. Unmatched. This little crush of mine is unrequited, I'm sure. Is this even really a crush or am I just reliving the past?

Jay strolls out of the men's room wearing navy blue running shorts, a gray athletic t-shirt that's tight across his chest, and bright orange training shoes.

Heaven help me, he looks good.

Standing up, I do my best to avert my gaze and walk to the StairMaster. I'm just going to stay on this until my brain and muscles melt as punishment for having these thoughts about *my employee*.

Jay comes up next to me and places a water bottle in the cup holder of the treadmill on my right. There's very few machines here. A StairMaster, two treadmills, one stationary bike, and one recumbent bike. There's also a rack of free weights next to a couple yoga balls and mats. This space is akin to that of a hotel gym.

"Can I join you?" he asks, stepping on the treadmill and tapping the screen for settings.

My track of stairs starts to fall away and I begin climbing. "Sure," I say, focusing my attention back to the show on TV. "I hope you like reruns of dream home hunting because I'm not changing it."

The belt of his machine starts to cycle fast as he starts his jog. He chuckles. "I love this show. It's either totally wild what these people want or incredibly underwhelming."

"That's what *I'm* saying!"

"Oh, this part at the end is my favorite. When they visit the buyer after they've moved in and decorated the space, clearly showcasing these are just normal people and *not* HGTV designers." He pauses for a few moments while we watch the show. "*What?* No. She did *not* decorate her Miami condo with brown walls, red furniture and glass tables. No. Absolutely not. And the heavy drapes? Gold and red paisley? It's like she's trying to erase the fact that they live in sunshine."

I giggle and look over at him. "I think you're going to fit in at this firm just fine."

He looks over at me with that perfect smile, hair flopping from his movement. He looks back at his machine settings and increases the speed.

After about fifteen minutes, I realize Jay's a serious runner. He's not slowing down or showing any signs of fatigue. I do not understand those freaks. Running for pleasure? Ew.

But there's nothing gross about his lean, muscular body running next to me. Through the mirror in front of us, I can see his golden thighs and calf muscles tightening and releasing. His thin shorts skimming his groin. Sweat starts to soak his shirt around his neck and arms. His inky hair has begun to drip little sweat droplets on the track. He's composed. Agile. And I can smell his sweaty body from up here. It's a heady combination of salt and indescribable pheromones that are overtaking my senses and wrapping me in a beautiful haze.

The next thing I know, my machine slows, pulling me out of my own thoughts. Apparently it's already been thirty minutes and it's time for the cool down. I look to my side at the other wall of mirrors and see my reflection. My face is blotchy, and sweat is pouring from my hairline. I look down and see a river cascading down my cleavage.

Good. You know what? This is good. I look like shit right now and this will definitely deter any more flirtatious remarks from him.

I hop off my machine and make my way back to the yoga mat.

I sit down and chug my water bottle. Sighing, I situate myself for the last part of my workout. A quick circuit of planking, push ups, donkey kicks and wall sits. I turn my body so my side is to Jay and not my ass. He doesn't need to see me bent over in front of him again like when he walked in.

As I start my first plank, I look over at him and he's staring at me. "What?" I ask through a panted breath.

"Oh, uh, nothing. Your... form is perfect," he says with hitched eyebrows and huffing through his run. Most of his shirt is wet now and I can see streams of sweat going down his neck and legs.

My form is perfect? Does he mean my plank positioning or my... no. He can't be talking about my body. There's no double meaning there.

"Good to know. Thank you." I pause for a beat. "I don't know anything about running, so for all I know your form is shit."

He starts laughing hard, he falters and has to catch himself on the arm rests of the treadmill. He taps the screen and slows the speed down to a slow jog, still chuckling to himself.

He finishes his cool down laps after a few minutes and then hops off to join me on the floor with a mat. He's laying on his back right in front of me, a few feet away. His big chest rises and falls as he tries to slow his breathing. Then, like the tease that he is proving to be, he lifts the bottom of his shirt to his face to wipe sweat from his forehead, exposing his rippling stomach.

Holy shit. It looks like a riverbed of stones. I never got to see this part of him when we had our little tryst in his car.

Is he doing this on purpose? *Jesus*, I could reach my hand out and touch his abs, he's so close. I want to drag my tongue through every dip and bump on him. I want to taste his sweat.

I quickly look away before he brings his shirt back down and props himself up on his forearms. "Are you almost done? You wanna stretch with me?" he asks.

"S-sure. Let me finish this plank and I have one more wall sit."

"I'll join you," he offers, standing up as my phone timer goes off for my plank. We step over to the wall and lean against it, our bodies sliding down into a ninety-degree seated position. After only ten seconds he says through gritted teeth, "Fuck, how long are we supposed to sit here?"

I laugh, "A minute."

He groans and bobs his head down to his chest. "How can you do this after all those stairs?"

"Do you see my thighs?" I ask with a wry smile. "They're twice the size of yours. All my power comes from the bottom."

"That's not the way I remember it," he mutters to himself so low I can barely hear it.

I throw my hand over to playfully hit his chest and whisper, "Stop it."

With fifteen seconds left, Jay collapses to the floor, his legs splayed out in front of him. "You win," he winces.

When the timer goes off, I stand up and walk back to the mats, while Jay crawls. "Someone's a bit dramatic," I tease.

"Ugh, let's hurry up and stretch already. My legs are gonna seize."

I lead him through various stretches, focusing on our legs. He's nowhere near as flexible as I am. When we're sitting with our right legs jutting out at a forty-five-degree angle, I bend down with my face touching my knee, hands grabbing the heel of my foot. I peek over at him and he's hunched over, but can only bring his fingertips to his shins.

"You're not very flexible, are you?" I observe.

"What gave it away? The fact that I'm working up a sweat from just stretching?"

I lift up, and chuckling, I answer, "Yeah, something like that." I sigh, "Alright, that's it," I lean over to grab the disinfectant wipes and set them between us. "Let's clean up and hit the showers."

As we start to wipe down our areas, he asks, "Would you like to have lunch with me later?" He stops to look at me, grabs the back of his neck with a sheepish grin. "Marco kind of went overboard with my lunch today and I won't be able to eat it all. Not even after that workout."

"Um, sure. I think I have time around noon. Your office?"

"Perfect." We finish wiping everything down and he says, "See you later, boss."

We head to our respective locker rooms and I'm grateful for the solitude because working out next to Jay was mental torture. I turn on the shower, strip off my sweat-soaked clothes and release my mass of hair. I step in the shower and I sit on the ADA folding shower bench, thankful for the rest. Cool water pours over my hot body, and I breathe deep lungfuls of air, trying to calm down, but it's useless. All I can picture is Jay's hard body, glazed in sweat like a fucking donut I want to devour.

I wonder if he works out with Marco? If they get all sweaty together and lift weights? Maybe they wrestle... maybe they'd wrestle me...

I lift one foot up on the bench and expose my core to the water. My thoughts veer off into a yummy little gym time threesome with them as my fingertips find my clit.

They're both only wearing jock straps because—hello—*this is my fantasy world and things don't need to make sense.*

Jay's laying on a cushioned bench seat with his back slightly propped up and I climb on top of him, rubbing my hands all over his stomach and chest. I'm already naked, straddling him with my ass sticking out. Marco comes up from behind and pets my rear end and then slips his fingers in my wet pussy. He's breathing in my ear and tells me to relax. That he wants to make us feel good.

Marco rips off Jay's jock strap and guides his lover's weeping cock to my slit. With his other hand, he pushes down on my shoulder, forcing me to sheath myself on him. Jay and I both groan and start making out like teenagers as I ride him.

Then I feel the tip of Marco's cock at the tight little hole that's never been breached before. He's already lubed both of us up and because this is my fantasy, there's no need for prepping, he just slams into me and my breath hitches. I cry out in ecstasy as Marco and Jay thrust into me in tandem. Calling me a 'good girl' and grunting, telling me to 'take it all.' They each take turns slapping my ass relentlessly.

I can't take it anymore, and I come with all four fingers ferociously swiping over my clit and my other hand digging into my soft upper thigh. I do my best to silence my moan, but there's no stopping my jaw from dropping and squeezing my eyes closed, reveling in the after-orgasm bliss.

I remove my hands and slump over, allowing the water to rain over me.

Fuck, that was good.

It's then that I realize I can't fight this and I'm not going to. I'm going to allow myself to fantasize about us if I want to. I'm obviously not going to actually be with either of them. Ever. I would never cross that line. I would never be a homewrecker. I'm just going to allow myself to swim in the image of their love. Of their desire. The mind is a powerful tool and I'm going to keep them there.

By the time noon comes around I'm starving. The two protein

bars I had for breakfast definitely weren't enough. I'm actually looking forward to lunch with Jay now. If it was anything like the last one Marco packed for him, it's going to be delicious.

I leave my meeting with the Interior Design department and head for Jay's office. His door is open so I walk in and he has all the food laid out. It's already hot and plated, clearly set with extra sets of glass containers, chopsticks, spoons, and napkins. "Whoa, what's with the whole get-up? Did Marco think you were feeding the whole office today and provided the dishes for it, too?"

He smiles as he straightens one of the containers, shyly looking down at it. "Um, he actually packed enough so that I could share with you."

I take a seat across from him, staring at the buffet set in front of us. "Did you guys order too much takeout or something? That looks like kimchi. Mmm."

"Marco actually made all of this last night." My eyes widen for a brief moment and he continues, "He's been helping me learn about my Korean heritage through food. I don't think you knew this, but I was adopted into a white family when I was a baby. I've never really experienced what it means to be Korean, so this is where I'm starting—with ox bone soup and veggie pancakes," he grins.

I pick up my spoon and dig into the soup. Green onions whirl around a milky white colored broth with beef and some other veggies I can't immediately identify. Before I take a bite, I see Jay add rice to his, and I do the same. I take a big bite and fall in love.

"Oh my god," I groan. "I've had Korean food before, but I don't think I've had this. *Wow.*"

Jay nods, blowing on his next spoonful. "He's good, isn't he?"

"He can make me food whenever he wants," I proclaim,

breathing in the aroma.

He chuckles, "I'll let him know." He picks up his phone and fires a text.

"He's so sweet for doing this for you."

Jay finishes his mouthful. "He is. It's such a juxtaposition to other parts of him." It looks like he's just stopped himself from saying more and he goes still.

I worry for a moment and ask, "What do you mean? Is he... like... forgive me if I overstep and just tell me to shut up but..." I lower my voice to a whisper, "Is he abusive?"

"Oh no!" he exclaims and stands up to come around the desk, shutting the door. Sitting back down, he says, "Well, not in the way you're thinking." He grins and grabs a veggie pancake and loads some kimchi on it. "He's a total Dom in the bedroom," he announces flippantly.

I almost choke on my food when his phone dings and he reads the message aloud with a lewd smirk. "Marco says he's happy you like sharing with me. It brings him great *pleasure* to hear it." Jay emphasizes the word *pleasure* a little too much.

I want to speak, but the words aren't forming. I think my mouth opens and closes like a fish until I finally say, "Tell him thank you. This meal is a very," I clear my throat, "*pleasurable* experience. He seems like a very *giving* man."

Holy shit, you're playing with fire, Cora!

He bites his lower lip as he fails to hold back a smile, and his thumbs fly over his screen. "He is going to go nuts when he reads this."

"What do you mean?" I ask, still embarrassed that I even said those things. What happened to keeping this to myself and living only in my fantasy world?

"Oh, he has a big crush on you. He thinks you're really hot." He finishes his text, sets his phone down and looks up at me.

If I was drinking a beverage I would have spit it out at this moment. "Excuse me? Wha... are... are you okay with your boyfriend saying things like that?"

"Definitely," he says with confidence and ease.

"Wait, are you guys like... polyamorous or something?"

He considers this for a split second. "Well, no. Not—no," he stumbles. "But we have been talking about you—a lot."

"What about me?" I ask, not really understanding where this is going.

"About... sharing you." His boyish charm has vanished and it's been replaced with a slow, lust-filled stare. He's talking like he's not my employee. Like he's not my HR Director. Like he's not in a totally closed off relationship.

His phone dings again and he picks it up to read yet another message from Marco. "He says he would like to invite you to our home for dinner this Friday night." Jay looks up from his phone and into my eyes. "And I'd like for you to come, too."

What is happening right now? Am I being pranked?

"I don't know, Jay."

"Come on, Cora," he coaxes in a lowered voice. "You said the other day you wanted to be friends with us. Let's be... friendly."

I'm pretty sure my fantasy brain has taken over because that traitorous bitch answers, "Friendly. Okay. Friday night."

And just like that, his boyish grin returns. "Perfect. Here, try some of this *dukbokki*."

What did I get myself into?

Chapter 13

Indecent Proposal

Marco

"Hon, please stop adjusting the picture on the wall," I remark in an even tone. However, I'm anything but even and balanced right now.

Jay is fidgeting with a large black and white framed picture of us from one of the first nights we hung out.

He's changed his outfit four times since he came home from work. I think he's finally settled on a long-sleeve white Henley and fitted black jeans that make his ass look amazing. He was reading off a list he found on the internet called *The Sexiest Things a Man Can Wear According to the Female Gaze*. This sent him spiraling as he rummaged through our closet.

"I don't have a medieval linen shirt with ties down the chest!"

"I can't wear this chunky turtleneck sweater tonight, I'll cook myself alive with anticipation!"

He was ecstatic when he read that a Henley will make women swoon and he insisted that we both wear one. I opted for my favorite slacks and a dark green and cream colored vintage knit polo. It has buttons down the front and when I put it on and flipped the collar down, I turned to look at Jay and he groaned, "Fuck, you look good. I forgot I bought you that. Can I wear it?"

I just shook my head and told him to keep his Henley on. That was only an hour ago, and he hasn't relaxed since.

"I'm sorry. I'm just nervous and now super self-conscious that she's coming here and we don't have anything designy."

I'm also incredibly nervous for Cora's visit tonight. "De-signy?" I ask with a raised eyebrow as I unwrap the last sushi roll from my bamboo rolling mat.

"You know... artistic. Creative. *Aesthetically pleasing*. We have, like, zero interior design skills, apart from my ability to nitpick reality TV homes."

"What's your point?"

Jay steps back from the wall and turns to me, crossing his arms. "She's an architect, babe. She's used to like, the finer things when it comes to homes and décor." He juts his head forward a bit and mumbles, "What if she's not comfortable here?"

I narrow my eyes on him as I finish slicing the roll into eight pieces. I wipe my hands on the tea towel and toss it over my shoulder. Rounding the island corner, I stalk over to him and his eyes dart everywhere but my line of sight.

I take his elbows in my hands, and I look at his face and slowly say, "My prince, look around. Our home is clean, organized, and smells good. We have food and drinks and candles. We also have comfortable furniture. It might not be designer furniture—is designer furniture a thing?"

"Yes!" he exclaims softly with panic laced in his voice.

"But, that's okay," I soothe. "Do you really think she's that shallow?"

He looks into my eyes and then down at the floor between us. "No. She's fucking perfect," he mutters.

"Then she won't care that we don't have any fancy art or custom credenzas, okay?"

He sighs and falls into my chest. "Okay," he mumbles.

"Good boy," I praise, and I can feel him chuckle against me. "Now calm me down because I'm freaking out, too."

He stiffens up. "Why are *you* freaked out?"

"Maybe because we're about to proposition your boss to cameo in our bedroom?"

"Oh yeah. That," he winces and pauses for a moment. "You know I was thinking... What happens if this goes well?"

"I'm hoping that it does. What do you mean?"

"I mean, let's say, it goes really well. Everyone is pleased with the outcome. I know we said she'd be a unicorn; a one-time guest star, but..."

"But what if we all want more?" I ask, finishing his sentence. He nods, staring at me. I take his face in my hands and gently ask, "First of all, baby, thank you for being vulnerable and speaking your mind." I rub my thumbs over his high cheekbones and with a smile I continue, "If opening up our relationship to Cora is something you're interested in, then we can explore that."

"For real?"

"It's not something I've ever thought about. Hell, until I met you, I didn't know I'd ever be with a man either. But, there's something about her... and you... and us... that feels like we're supposed to be connected, ya know?"

"Yeah," he says, a little breathlessly. Jay leans in and brushes a soft kiss to my lips.

The doorbell rings and I swear a bolt of lightning rocks

through our bodies as we flinch and immediately head for the door in lockstep.

We both reach for the handle and he swats at my hand, but I hip check him into the wall and swing open the door to reveal a rosy-cheeked Cora, bundled up in a long red wool coat that's tied at the waist. She has a gold scarf wrapped around her neck and little snowflakes are falling on her long dark hair.

She looks like a damn Macy's advertisement personified.

Jay straightens himself and stands beside me. Together, we gaze down at her in awe, both of us letting out a quiet "Wow" at the same time. Cora smiles and I can't tell if the color on her face is from the winter air or if she's blushing.

Stepping aside, I remember my manners. "Please, come in. It's so good to see you again, Cora."

"You, too, Marco." She walks in and I shut the door. Jay steps over to her and leans in for a shared hug. "Thanks for coming over. It's nice to see you outside of work."

A hug? He gets to hug her? I want to hug her.

He releases Cora and asks, "Can I take your coat?"

"Please." She shimmies out of it and hands it to Jay, who takes it towards the back of the house where the hooks are by the back door. This leaves me with her, and I seize my opportunity. She's already looking at me and I step to her with open arms, wrapping them around her as she does the same. I don't care that the only time we've really spent together was thirty minutes in a massage room as client and therapist.

"Thank you for inviting me," she hums as we break apart. Jay comes back and eyes us. That's when I really take in what she's wearing. It's a tight black long-sleeve sheer top with a square-neck camisole underneath, or... maybe that's a bodysuit? Fuck if I know anything about women's fashion. She looks hot. She's also wearing a thick tan mini skirt and black tights that look like a starry night sky.

All of her curves are on display and she's absolutely beautiful. "You guys both smell really good," she says with a shy smile; and yes, she's definitely blushing now. "Thanks," Jay and I say in unison.

"Would you like to eat first or relax here in the living room?" I gesture.

She chews on her lip, stained a deep raspberry color. "I'm actually starving. I missed lunch today when I was out visiting a client."

Placing my hand in the middle of her back, I lead her towards the table. "Well, let's change that right away. Have a seat and I'll pull the sushi out of the fridge. Jay, can you get our friend a drink?"

When I walk back from the kitchen with the giant platter of sushi, I set it down on our table alongside the soy sauce dishes. Wasabi and ginger are already piled on the tray and each of us have matching rectangular sushi plates at our places. Those were a last minute buy from Jay when he panicked and said we didn't have the right dishes for dinner. He literally went to the closest Japanese restaurant and offered to buy three plates from them with matching soy sauce cups.

Jay hands Cora a glass of white wine and he pours one for himself. My beer already sits at my place setting.

"Thank you, Jay," she smiles, taking the glass from him. She's about to pull out her chair when Jay lunges toward her and does it for her.

"Let me get that!" he says eagerly. She huffs a small laugh and her smile grows wide. Jay pushes in her chair and from behind her, he looks across the table gives me a wild look of satisfaction.

So, it's going to be like that, huh?

Jay comes around to his usual spot, which is situated directly across from Cora, and sits down. I normally sit right where she's sitting, but we discussed this ahead of time, and I would sit next to Jay tonight, thigh to thigh. Wanting to win this little game we seem to be competing in, I pick up my place setting and move it to the head of the table, smack dab between Jay and Cora.

I don't have to look at Jay to know he's combusting inside. I chuckle to myself.

As I sit down, I look at Cora and say, "I wasn't sure what kind of sushi you prefer, so I made a bit of everything." Taking my chopsticks in hand, I point to each section. "This is spicy tuna. California roll. Salmon and avocado. Tofu and green onion. Asparagus avocado and cucumber. And this one is spicy shrimp tempura."

Her mouth drops. "You did not make all this."

"I did. You just need access to sushi grade fish and learn a proper rolling technique. Nothing YouTube can't teach," I wink.

"You guys spoil me. I feel so doted on," she laughs.

If only you knew how much we want to dote on you.

Gesturing to the spread in front of us, I say, "Please, help yourself. Ladies first."

She nods in appreciation, sets her wine glass down and takes her chopsticks in hand. She begins to serve herself as we watch her. I think she feels the building tension and speaks up. "Your home is very nice, guys. It feels inviting and warm," she offers with a smile. "How long have you been here?"

Jay chimes in, "About a year." He allows Cora to finish serving herself and then starts plating his own and mine. "Before Marco left the Army, we decided to move in together when he got back. So, I found this place about a month beforehand and... here we are."

"How did you guys meet?" Cora asks, dipping her sushi in

soy sauce and placing it in her mouth. Her full lips pursed around the chopsticks. I can tell she's being careful not to disturb her lip color.

I want to be the one to disturb her lip color.

Shoving the thought away, I speak up, "We met when I came home from one of my contracts. I was stationed in Afghanistan at the time." I don't typically love talking about my time in the Army, but I want Cora to see the real me. I want her to get a picture of what it would be like to be around me.

"I was home for a few months, staying with my sister, Rebecca, and her husband Vinny. In those days, I didn't really have a home, per se, so I floated around a lot. Anyway, after a while, I could tell my sister was getting annoyed with my attitude. I was a different person than what she had known growing up... *somehow* worse." I look over at Jay and reach for his hand on the table. Still talking to Cora, but looking at him, I continue, "So, I went to a bar that night, needing to escape myself, and I found him. He was vibrant and full of life. He had come there with a friend, but he and I somehow got to talking and the next thing I knew, the bar was almost empty and it was closing time. His friend had gone. I don't think I had laughed that hard—or felt that good—in a long time. Maybe ever.

"He asked me if I wanted to play basketball with him the next day and I agreed. We exchanged numbers and we kept hanging out every day I was on leave."

I turn back to Cora, "He had told me he was queer, but I didn't pay much mind to it. I didn't personally know anyone who was, but we had this instant friendship that felt like it had been cultivated over years, not days.

"We stayed in constant communication while I was away and I'd only come here on my leaves to hang out with him. It took me a while to recognize my feelings for him. I realized he was the only good thing in my life. He made me happy. Made me want to be a better man..." I trail off and look back at Jay, who's looking at me with such reverence. I narrow my eyes accusingly. "Made me question things about my sexuality."

I hear Cora giggle and Jay bristles. "Hey. I thought it was unrequited. You're the one who started it."

"I was not."

"Do you want me to pull up the messages from two years ago?" Jay threatens, pulling out his phone from his pocket.

"Not necessary! Put the phone away. Where are your manners?" I demand and then look back at Cora. "We're in the company of a beautiful woman."

Her cheeks blush the sweetest shade of pink and she grabs her wine to take a drink. "That's an incredible love story. I think I remember you telling me about leaving the Army and going into massage therapy because you wanted peace and to work in a relaxing environment, is that right?"

"Exactly. You have a good memory," I grin.

She sets her glass down and picks up a new piece of sushi before muttering, "I'm surprised I remember anything from that massage." And then pops it into her mouth.

"What do you mean?"

She finishes chewing as she shakes her hand side to side, non-verbally telling me to forget about it.

Hell, no. I want to talk about that night.

Cora swallows, and I'm staring at her, waiting for an answer. "It's nothing."

"It's not. You were a very memorable client, Cora. For several reasons."

Jay's foot starts to gently run up my calf, and I know he's pleased with how this conversation is going.

"The massage was, uh... it was very good, and I couldn't think straight."

"You found it pleasurable?" I ask, gently coaxing her to reveal more.

"It... was a massage," she says, still a little guarded. "Of course, it was pleasurable."

I tilt my head to the side and hum in contemplation. "Seemed to me you experienced a different kind of pleasure than most."

She then stashes two pieces of sushi in her mouth, essentially shutting herself up, and not denying my observation.

I lower my voice and grumble, "You like pain, don't you, Cora?"

Her whole face flushes bright red while she continues to chew slowly staring at me, still not denying my words.

My cock is swelling behind my zipper at the memory of her panting from the pain of that first encounter. I take a piece of sushi and bring it to my mouth and say, "Use your words, Cora," before taking the bite.

She swallows deep and timidly nods her head. With a soft voice, she finally answers, "Yes."

"Good girl."

She closes her eyes for much longer than a blink. It's like she's trying to collect herself. It's fucking adorable.

"You and Jay have some similar tastes it seems," I croon, turning my head to him with a smirk. I take his hand and kiss it. "Isn't that right, prince?"

"Yes, Sir," he says obediently, his eyes locked on mine.

Returning my gaze to Cora, I speak slowly. "So, Jay tells me you're a very important woman. Very in demand. You have a lot on your plate with work and your mother. Always in charge. Always in control. Is that right?"

She pushes her wasabi around with her chopsticks, her eyes fixated on the task. "I guess you could say that."

"Have you ever thought about giving up a little bit of control?" I ask, my erection now begging to be released.

"You mean like..." She looks at me and raises her eyebrows, "...in *that* way?" I nod in agreement. She darts her eyes down to her empty plate and bites at the corner of her lip. "I–I don't know," she stammers a little breathlessly.

"It can be quite freeing for some people. Especially those who control a lot in their life."

"I've never done anything like that before," she huffs.

Jay interjects, "Would you like to?"

Cora's eyes widen, and she stands up quickly and walks away from the table. Jay and I both stand, panic coursing through my veins.

Shit.

I glance over at him, and like me, he's tenting his pants. We both adjust ourselves as we move towards her, but she's pacing.

"Cora, wait. I'm sorry," Jay pleads. "We... I..."

"What is happening right now?" she exclaims.

I grab the back of my neck and squeeze. "I'm so sorry we made you uncomfortable."

She's still pacing the room with her hands on her hips, her eyes darting everywhere but to me and Jay, like she's trying to solve a mystery in her mind.

The both of us are standing close, but far enough away not to spook her. She's like a wild animal we're trying not to scare... anymore than we already have.

Fuck, we're idiots.

Just then when she's not looking, the toe of her ankle boot catches on the corner of the rug and she topples over onto her hands and knees. We both rush to her sides and pull her up to stand.

"Are you okay?" we both ask, concern heavy in our voices.

"I'm fine. Really. These shoes are just killing my feet."

"Here, have a seat on the couch," Jay says as we both lead her a couple steps over. She sits down and Jay sits on her right, his arm wrapping around her back and his hand holding her opposite arm. I kneel in front of her and lift one of her feet to place on my thigh and I unzip the heeled boot.

"You don't have to do that," Cora protests, but I slide the boot off and start on the next one.

"Nonsense," I whisper. I remove her second shoe and place them close by, still holding her ankle. I look at her feet and up to her knees. "Looks like your tights are still intact." I run a gentle thumb across her knee. "No rips."

I glide my hand down her leg, and both hands now cup her foot and ankle. I look up at her and ask, "May I rub your feet?"

"Um... okay? But can someone please explain to me what is happening here? I feel like I'm in an alternate universe."

I start to dig my thumbs into the arch of her foot, and she closes her eyes and breathes deep. I glance over at Jay and gesture for him to explain. He nods and starts, "Cora, I know you're my boss, and this is definitely crossing that professional line... but we're both really into you." She opens her eyes and looks at him, his hand now trailing over her shoulder and upper arm. Her eyes are round and her mouth is open. He takes his other hand and with his forefinger, he lifts her jaw to close her mouth.

He speaks slowly to her, "You're gorgeous and clever and fun. But you're stressed. We'd like to help you with that, if you'd let us." He pushes some of her curls behind her ear, but they fall back once he releases them. With a serious look, he declares his intentions. "We want you. We want to share our bed with you."

I keep massaging her foot, anxiously awaiting her response.

Is she going to flee again?

Is she into this?

Is she going to fire Jay on the spot?

She turns her head to look down at me. I lower my head and press a soft kiss to her knee, staring into her eyes. I move my hands and squeeze her calf. "Would you like that, Cora?" I murmur. "Would you like for me to bring you pain so pleasurable that you forget everything?"

She nods her head, her emerald eyes locked on mine, seemingly in a trance.

I kiss her knee again. "Use your words, beautiful," I command.

"Yes, please," she whispers.

"That's very good," I smirk and then lick the inside of her knee. "Jay, would you like to make Cora more comfortable? Perhaps she would like a kiss."

"Yes, Sir."

I look up to see him comb his hand through her hair at the base of her neck. Her eyes are glued on his. He leans in, his nose nuzzling hers, their lips only an inch apart. Her eyes gently close and he follows. "Please," he whispers.

Cora closes the gap and presses her lips to his; jealousy and pride mixing together in my body at the sight. They both breathe a deep sigh of relief.

How long have they both wanted this? I know Jay never really got over her, but the way she's kissing him tells me she's pined for this moment, too.

Cora's hands move to Jay's waist as their kiss deepens. I move my attention to her other foot and caress her leg, blowing hot breath over her skin.

Little moans escape her as she allows him to tilt her head back to kiss her jaw, her ear, and the column of her neck. "You smell so good, Cora," he groans, inhaling her scent. "*Fuck*, I've missed you."

"I've missed you, too," she replies breathlessly.

Jay returns to her lips and they're positively ravenous now. Their mouths open and wanting. Tongues searching for more. Her hands run up to his chest and she twists his shirt in her grasp.

I start to slowly massage past her knee, higher on her thick, luscious thigh. I kiss a trail behind my touch. "Cora, we need to discuss limits. What you like. What you're open to." My mouth is still focused on her leg; now it's only a few inches away from her center. I can smell her cunt, even through her tights, such a distinctive and decadent smell. I can feel her heat against my face. I want nothing more than to bury it deep in her pussy and suffocate myself, but I need to know her limits.

She unlocks her face from Jay, as he kisses her neck again. With her eyes closed, still floating in pleasure, she stammers, "I... I don't know. I've never done anything like this before. I've never had... never let..."

I can tell we're overwhelming her, which I love, but if she can't think straight, we can't move forward.

"Jay, pull away," I command.

"No," she whines.

Oh, what a needy little thing.

Jay exhales and slides his hands down her arms and holds her hands. She looks at me, concern in her expression. "Why are we stopping?"

I cup her calves and smooth my hands up her thighs and rest them there. Looking her in the eyes, I state, "Cora, as much as we want to continue this, you need to know what you want and what you don't. You've never experienced any form of BDSM before?"

"Um, I've been spanked before," she looks at Jay. "Once."

"Just me?"

She nods. "Yeah. I've thought about it before that, but never had the courage to ask for it."

He smiles. "I'm glad you felt comfortable enough with me to ask for it." He strokes his thumbs over her hands.

"So, you're not exactly sure what you like and don't like, is that right?" I ask her.

"Not really. I'm sorry. Is that... a deal breaker?" Her brows pinch together and a look of sadness spreads on her face.

"Oh, no, beautiful. Absolutely not. But I think it's best if you learn more about this. Do some research before diving in."

"Like... watch porn?"

"God, no," Jay interjects quickly. "Please don't watch porn about this. It's so rarely done right and honestly, it might freak you out."

"So, how am I supposed to research it?"

"Well, for one thing, there are excellent websites, articles, and forums you can find that can help you understand it better. I'd be happy to direct you towards them." Then I turn my gaze from her to Jay, "You could also... watch a real demonstration," I say with a devilish grin; Jay's face now mirroring mine.

Realization dawns on her face. "Y-you guys? In front of me?"

Jay lifts one of her hands to his mouth and kisses the inside of her wrist. "Yes."

"Right now," I add. "What do you think, beautiful?"

Cora gulps and gives me a tiny smirk. "That sounds really hot, actually. Yes. I'd like that."

I sit up straight on my knees, my legs flush against the couch, my body between hers. I grab hold of her ass and pull her towards me. Clutching the back of her neck, I stare into her forest green eyes. My heart rate picks up even more as my gaze dips to her parted lips. She moves her hands to my biceps and snakes them up my shoulders, neck, and face. She tentatively rubs her fingertips through my short beard as she bites her bottom lip.

Yeah, she's thinking about how it would feel against her skin.

I grip her chin, pulling her slowly until I can feel her breath mix with mine. I graze my lips against hers, feather light, until I can hear her breath hitch.

When I simply cannot hold back any longer, I seal us together. She tastes better than I imagined. She tastes like Jay, too, and if my dick wasn't already hard as fuck, it sure as hell would be now.

"I've wanted to kiss you since the moment I saw you."

"Me, too," she whispers, and then pulls on my lip.

I guide her legs to wrap around my waist and say in between kisses, "Hold on to me." She obeys and squeezes her thighs tight, and wraps her arms around my neck. I lift her up and start to carry her to the stairs.

"Stop, I'm too heavy. It's okay, I can walk."

I growl in her ear as Jay trails us and chuckles, "Oh, Cora. Lesson number one is you don't argue with him."

We make our way up the stairs as I quickly walk past the other doors. "Guest room, guest bath, massage studio." She laughs at my crude house tour, and we enter the bedroom. I walk to the soft leather arm chair in the corner of the room and call over, "Prince, turn the bedside lamps on, undress and wait for me on the floor."

"Yes, Sir."

I sit Cora down in the chair, kneeling once again between her legs. I slide my hands under her skirt, which is mostly rucked past her hips at this point. I rest my thumbs in the warm crevice between her belly and thighs, my fingertips caressing her lush hips.

"I want you to watch, but if at any point you're uncomfortable, you have the power to leave without warning, do you understand?"

"Yes," she nods.

"I want you to make mental notes on what intrigues you. What turns you off. I need you to know that what Jay and I do together is not necessarily what we would do with you. These are the things he likes—that I like—and there are numerous other things that we won't get into this evening that we would enjoy, so *do not* leave here tonight thinking this is our only speed. Do you understand me?"

"Yes... Sir." She hesitates, the look on her face tells me she's not quite sure if she should have said that or not.

I lean in and kiss her, digging my fingers into her thighs. "You're a quick study, Cora. Very good."

She smiles as I watch the blush spread across her face. I trail more kisses down her neck and whisper against her nape, "Now you're going to sit here and watch. You will not touch yourself. If I give you direction, you will listen to me. Do I make myself clear?"

"Yes, Sir," she says with more confidence now, but I can tell she's distracted from my tongue lapping at her delicate skin.

"Is he ready for me?"

"I think so, Sir. He's on his knees."

"Perfect," I grumble and stand up. I look her in the eyes and narrow mine, "Be good."

Turning my back to her, I can see Jay mere feet away. He's done exactly what I asked, his clothes folded neatly on the dresser. He's on both knees, spread apart, arms crossed behind his back and clasping his elbows, and his head bowed. He's so fucking perfect like this. I can tell he's flexing his muscles though. Is he doing that to show off to Cora? Is he trying to put up a wall? That simply won't do.

I take a couple steps forward and lean down to his ear. Quietly, so she can't hear, I ask, "Are you okay with this, prince? You may speak freely."

With his head still bowed, he simply says, "Yes, Sir."

I'm not buying it. "Don't lie to me. You're flexing your muscles when you should be nothing but obedient right now. Tell me what's going on."

"I–She's never seen me like this," he stammers.

"Submissive?" I whisper in the shell of his ear.

"Yes. Well, not entirely, Sir."

Ah, I think I know where this is going. He wants to appear like he has control, too. Really, he has all the control when we have a scene. When we switch occasionally, that dynamic changes. I know it's been a long time since he was with a woman; I think he's worried she won't see him as manly or something. Ludicrous.

"Prince, you know being submissive doesn't make you any less manly."

"Yes," he exhales softly.

"We can talk more about this later, but I need you to trust me. Submit to me. I promise I'll take care of you."

"Yes, Sir. I trust you."

"Good. Now relax and be a good boy," I growl.

I stand up and see his abdominals relax and his arm muscles release. That's it. My mind has already adjusted for the situation and I know what I need to do. As I walk to the en suite bathroom, I call over my shoulder, "Get the chest and wait for me on the bed."

I walk into the bathroom, do what I need to do, and walk back out. I'm still wearing my clothes, but my feet are bare. I pad over to the bed to find Jay has set out the wooden chest of toys we keep and placed it next to one of the nightstands. He's again in the box position, his feet dangling off the end of the bed.

He's also put a bottle of lube on a coaster for me and I smile at that. I walk over and grab it, tossing it between my hands. I chuckle and ask, "And what makes you think this will be necessary tonight? You're very presumptuous, my prince. Is it your job to direct a scene?"

"No, Sir."

"That's right. If I don't tell you to do something, you don't do it. Seems like someone needs a reminder. Lean forward and plant your face in the bed. Ass up," I seethe.

"Yes, Sir." Jay does as I command, keeping his arms locked behind him. He's completely exposed to me and Cora. I take my time finding the right leather paddle in the chest. It's my favorite one. Slightly flexible, it's rectangular and about six inches long after the handle.

I go to stand behind him and gently caress his tight, round ass and strong legs. Then I pinch the inside of one thigh and command him. "Spread them more."

Still watching him, I call back, "Cora, pick a number between one and twenty."

"Um, twenty?"

He groans and curses into the bed. I don't think she knows what she just sentenced Jay to.

I chuckle. "Twenty. It. Is." I glide the paddle against his golden skin. "Count for me, pet." I swat his right cheek hard.

His body tenses and he releases a breath. "One."

Crack!

"Two," he breathes.

Then I quickly get through five more in rapid succession while Jay counts along. His voice is growing tight.

When I get to ten, he's already starting to whimper and I run the paddle along his balls and taint. "I think I'll give your ass a little break. Wouldn't that be nice of me?"

"Yes! Thank you, Sir," he exclaims.

But then I immediately swat his taint and watch his balls contract as I hit them, too. He lets out a low scream, but his body is shaking. He's laughing from the pain. I know it's involuntary when he gets like this, but I egg him on regardless.

"Oh, that's funny is it?" With more force, I go back to his ass. *Crack. Crack. Crack.*

Through tears he tries to say, "Ten?"

Fuck, my cock is so hard right now. "Nope. Start over."

"Oh my god," I hear Cora whisper in the corner.

"Cora will count for you now, since you can't seem to handle this one little thing I ask of you."

"What?" she gasps.

Crack. Crack. Crack. Crack.

She obeys, counting each strike. When we get to twenty, Jay is heaving breaths, his skin slick with sweat. I hunch down and kneel behind him, peppering his red skin with soft kisses. "You're so beautiful, prince," I murmur into him. I flatten my tongue over his taint and drag it to his quivering hole, gently circling it.

"Do you think you can take a little more for me? Can you be a good boy and do this for your sir?"

"Yes, Sir."

"What do you say?"

"*Please.* I want more, Sir. Please," he begs. And *fuck me,* do I love it when he begs.

I go back to the chest and pull out the flogger and then dangle it over his body. It gently skims his back and shoulders, his ass, thighs, calves, and feet.

"Count, Cora," I demand.

I give a few hard blows on each ass cheek as she counts. I can't look at her right now because I'm focusing all my attention on

Jay's body language. If he's not counting, I want to ensure he's still responsive and willing.

When she gets to six, I stop. I gently cup his balls and palm his leaking erection. Jay whimpers, and I ask, "Are you still with me?"

"Yes, Sir," he rasps. I can tell he's well on his way to subspace at this point, and I can't wait to see it.

I take a step back and position my feet in a striking stance and then start to flog him in a circular motion, rapid-firing, until I hear Cora exclaim, "Twenty!"

I drop the flogger and push him face-down on the bed and crawl over his legs. My face dives in as I spread his beaten red ass with my hands, hitching one of his legs up ninety degrees. I lick and suck and lap at his tight hole, rewarding him for a job well done. He moans and squirms as I nose my way between his perfectly suffocating crevice. He's rutting into the mattress at this point, and I can't wait any longer.

I push myself off him and growl, "Turn around and sit in the middle of the bed." With no hesitation, he does as I command. I open my belt and pull down the zipper. With my dick finally released from the confines of my boxer briefs, I step up on the bed and stand in front of him. "Take it and cry for me," I grit out.

Jay eagerly grabs hold of my shaft and sheaths his mouth over every inch he can take. There are no warm-ups or gentle licks. This is pure lust taking shape. His hot, wet mouth bobs back and forth, going deeper with every inch. My hands fist his hair, and I thrust without mercy. He gags, and tears stream down his face. "Yes, pet. That's it. *That's fucking it.*" One of his hands moves to my balls and cups them. "That's a good boy. You're doing so well, my love. Would you like for your sir to reward you?"

He nods his head frantically, his big brown doe eyes fixated on mine. I pull his head back, and his mouth pops off, saliva trailing in its wake. "Lay down on your back." He does, eyes never leaving mine. Standing over him, I unbutton my polo and shrug it off, dropping it on his chest. He swiftly folds it as I pull down my pants, allowing him to take and fold them as well, stacking together and placing them at the edge of the bed.

I squat down and straddle his lap, our cocks rubbing against each other as I lean down and suck hard on his nipples. My hands grip his pecs, causing him to moan and hiss simultaneously. "You may touch me," I tell him.

His hands fly to my back, fingers searching for purchase. I take his mouth in a punishing kiss, and I can taste myself on his lips. I run my tongue over his tear-streaked face and praise him. "You did so well, prince. Take it out."

His face screws up, and he whispers, "What do you mean, Sir?" I grab one of his hands and lead it to the plug I put inside me earlier. He gasps, "Really? I–I can? Sir?"

"Yes, prince. Come on. Let's show her what she's missing."

I close my eyes and breathe as he pulls out my plug slowly. I take it from him and lean over to grab the lube, and set the plug on the nightstand. I pump a generous amount into my hands and bring it around to my hole. I then rub the rest down Jay's thick erection as he shudders.

His hands are on my hips, and I can feel his fingers twitching in anticipation. I guide his cock to my entrance as I watch his eyes fixate on me sinking down, enveloping him slowly, tortuously. His wide crown breaches that first ring of tight muscle, and I can't help but close my eyes and breathe deeply, allowing my body to accept his.

Once fully seated, I plant my hands on his chest and start to rock. "Such a good little whore; letting me use you like this."

"Uh-huh. Thank you, Sir," he whines.

"Grab my cock and stroke it. Don't stop."

He grabs the lube and takes a quick squirt before taking my dick in one hand and deftly moving in tight constricting pulls. With his other hand, he anchors onto my hip.

I lean down, grab hold of both his shoulders, and growl, "Take it, Jay. Give me everything you have. Do not hold back." He then shifts himself, so his knees are bent, and he thrusts hard and fast into me. *Fuck*, the way he hits that spot inside me is electrifying. The pressure is so strong, but the pleasure outweighs it.

He keeps stroking and pumping into me at the same time, and my hands tighten around his neck. "Fuck, you're big. You're gonna make me come. I need you to follow me, prince."

Jay bites his bottom lip, and it's such a beautiful sight to see him like this. He is chasing his release, obeying my every word, submitting to me. Watching him beneath my hold, I can feel my release coming.

"Come for me, prince." I release my grip on his neck, cup his square jaw and kiss him hard. Our teeth, lips, and tongues are in a fight for survival. "Come for me. Right... fucking... now," I grit out as I grunt through my release. Jay's thrusts have faltered and become sporadic as I feel him unload everything he has inside me.

As our bodies pant in unison, our hearts beat together for each other. His arms slide around to hold me tight to him, and I bury my face in his neck, kissing him.

"Thank you, Sir. I love you so much."

"I love you, too. Would you like for Cora to come over and help me take care of you?"

He nods his head and hums in agreement.

I lift off and extract myself from him. "Turn over." I steady my feet on the ground and look over at Cora as I make my way to the dresser she sits next to. She's frozen with her hands over her mouth, and her legs pressed together tight. Her eyes find mine as I open a drawer and pull out a pair of comfortable gray sweatpants and pull them on. I smile at her and ask, "Would you like to help me? He needs a little TLC right now."

She removes her hands and nods.

I hold out one of mine for her to take and lead her to sit on the bed by his head. She starts to stroke his hair and praise him while I open the nightstand and find the arnica oil. "You did so well, Jay," she coos.

"Can I kiss you?" he asks her as I start to slowly rub the oil all over his inflamed backside. She lowers herself to lay next to him and gently kisses his lips. It's soft and delicate, and they're both smiling. As I lightly massage his back and shoulders, my heart swells with emotion too strong and blurry to describe.

"Are you in any pain?" she asks him, her expression curious.

His eyes are still closed, their faces only an inch apart. "The best kind," he whispers.

I lean my head down and kiss his hair. "I'll be right back," I tell him and go to the bathroom for some water, aspirin, and a warm wet cloth. When I return, I have him roll on his back, Cora scooting over a little to accommodate. He sits up, and I give him the water and pills to swallow. I take it back when he's done and begin to wash his hands and groin.

Cora places her hand on his stomach and looks up at him. "You were incredible." She looks at me, "Both of you."

I slip into bed next to Jay and hold him, his back cradled in my chest, my arms wrapped around him. "So, you stayed," I observe.

"I did. It was so intense, but I couldn't look away."

"Is it still something that interests you?" Jay asks, hope lacing his words.

Cora props her elbow and rests her head on her hand. "I think so. I need to process this more, though."

"Of course," I nod. "We'll send you some information you should look into."

"I appreciate it," she says with a smile. Then she rolls over to her back and covers her eyes with her palms. "I can't believe this just happened! Who am I?"

Both Jay and I chuckle, and he answers, "Hey, we've never had an audience before. Lots of new stuff happened here tonight."

She rolls back towards us and gets to her knees, kisses Jay, then me before saying, "Thank you for sharing this with me."

"You're welcome," we say together.

She sighs, "I think I need to go home, though. Think this through. Talk to George about it."

My entire body tenses, and I can feel Jay's do the same thing.

"Who's George?" Jay asks, his voice tentative as his legs curl up.

"My cat. She's a real bitch, but she's my sounding board."

The air rushes back to my lungs, and I loosen my hold on Jay. *Thank god George is a cat.*

"Well, let me walk you to your car," I offer, and Jay tries to get up. "No, no, mister. You stay put and relax. Your head is still in the clouds anyway." He gives me a little pout and then lunges for Cora before she can get off the bed and pins her down. She giggles as he cups the back of her neck and proceeds to make out with her. His other hand runs down the side of her body along her curves, and he hitches her leg around his naked waist. I lean over and lightly spank him.

He jolts back as she keeps giggling. "She said she needed to go. Let's respect her wishes," I smirk.

He winces and exhales. "Fine. Have a good night, Cora. We'll talk soon." He kisses her one more time. "Sweet dreams."

"Goodnight, Jay. You, too." She gets up and takes my waiting hand to lead her downstairs.

Once I gather her things, press her remote start button, and bundle her up, I walk her to her car just outside our front steps. I'm still only wearing sweatpants at this point, but my body is radiating heat. Before I open her car door for her, I bring her close to me and tilt her chin up with my finger. "I hope you'll consider this, Cora. I think it could be really good for you. Good for us. But while we wait for your answer, don't you dare come without me. If you want this, then I'm in charge of your pleasure. Do I make myself clear?"

She looks stunned, but she slowly nods. I give her a warning look, and she quickly recovers. "Yes, Sir."

I bring my face to hers and give her a chaste kiss. "Good. Text Jay when you get home." I open her door and guide her in. "Goodnight, Cora. Thank you for everything."

"Goodnight, Marco."

I shut her door and step back onto the sidewalk, watching her drive off. I miss her already.

Chapter 14

Brunch

Cora

I wake up the next morning, positive I had been dreaming about what happened with Marco and Jay last night. They wanted to have a threesome with me? They let me watch them?

Unbelievable.

I want to replay every single second. The way Marco was so direct with his words made me want to melt into a puddle at his feet. His hands all over me, his tongue licking my knee... I wanted to curse those tights I wore for being such a fucking cockblock. Marco has these complex layers I want to crawl inside and explore. He was so dominant yet soothing.

Then Jay... when we finally kissed, the night we met came flooding back into my memory. Not that I ever forgot about it. Quite the opposite. It was like our kiss opened this hidden door to my brain, and a secret garden of desire and longing bloomed wild and vibrant. All I could think was, *why did I ever stop kissing this man in the first place?*

Watching both of them, though? That was the hottest thing I've ever seen. The trust Jay had in Marco was incredible. To be so exposed and compliant, believing your partner will take care of you—it was inspiring and thrilling.

When I got home last night, I was soaked and I wanted nothing more than to get myself off, but Marco's warning words rang through me and sent chills down my spine. I don't think I have ever done so many involuntary Kegels in my life.

Sex with Theo was never like *this*. Our lovemaking was always pretty vanilla and tender. It was good, don't get me wrong. I usually came, but I secretly wanted it to be rougher—I just didn't know how to bring it up. But when I was alone in bed, I would experiment a little here and there while masturbating. Pinching myself was how far it got.

I wasn't a virgin when Theo and I started dating in college, but my sexual partners before him weren't exactly experienced or memorable. Once Theo and I got together, we found a rhythm that was good for both of us, and we kind of stuck to it until the end.

The bitter fucking end.

My phone rings on my nightstand, and I see it's Angie. "Well, good morning. It's a bit early, isn't it?"

"Good morning, sunshine! I'm at the Italian Market right now, and that one place has your favorite stinky cheese back in stock! Do you want me to pick some up for you?"

"Please and thank you!"

"I'll come over when I'm finished here. I assume you're going to see your mom later, so I'll be at your place around ten, okay?"

"Okay, that sounds good. Ooh! Do you think you could stop by that bakery and get some little treats, too? Let's make this a proper brunch. I, uh... I have some things I want to talk to you about, and I think sweets are necessary."

"Hell yes. I'll see you soon."

I hang up with her and get out of bed with a gust of excitement and get ready for the day.

When Angie arrives, she strides right in, using the key she has for my place. The girl is my emergency contact, after all.

"I brought champs and orange juice, too!" she hollers, carrying several bags and closing the door with her hip. She's wearing a casual tan cashmere sweater and boyfriend jeans. Her shoulder-length brown hair is tied back.

She walks through my front sitting room and into my galley kitchen. It's a little tight, but this townhouse was built in 1850. My father did everything in his power to maximize the space while staying true to the history of the home.

She sets her bags on the white marble counter, and I give her a big hug. "I missed you!"

"It's been too long, babe. Is that hazelnut coffee I smell?"

We let go of each other, and I open the cupboard to grab mugs. "Yes, it is."

"*This* has turned out to be a surprising little morning. It's like the stars have aligned. Usually, you're working or already at your mom's."

I pour our coffees, adding creamer to both, and head towards the dining room table, where I set them down. "Yes, well... something strange happened last night, and it kind of threw me off kilter."

Angie's already grabbing champagne flutes and unwrapping the bottle. "What happened?"

I open the bakery bag and pull out an assortment of fruit tarts, tiramisu, and cream puffs. "I sort of went over to Jay and Marco's house last night for dinner."

"Whoa. How was that?" she asks, adding a tea towel to the top of the champagne bottle.

"They asked me to have a threesome with them."

POP!

Angie's eyes bug out, and her jaw drops, the sound of the bottle popping not even registering with her. She stares at me for too long, so I take the bottle from her and pour the flutes with bubbly and orange juice.

She's still standing there, utterly transfixed. So, I take the glasses to the table and come back.

Still there.

Still in shock.

I then take the container of baked goods and gesture to the dining room. "Are you coming?"

"Did you?" she blurts, and I chuckle as she follows me. "Oh my god, Cora! Can I manifest, or can I manifest?"

I can feel my cheeks blush as I smile and nod. "You can manifest."

We sit down, and she's positively beaming. "I hate to crush your dreams, but we didn't exactly have a threesome last night. I watched them."

I go on to explain everything that happened, sparing some of the more intimate details in the bedroom.

Once she finally composes herself enough to speak again, she asks, "So, is this something you're interested in? Being a sub?"

"I think so? But I think I need to understand it more."

"Cora, I think this is great for you. You're the most stressed-out person I know, and *I know* a lot has happened in the last few years. You've lost a lot, gained this CEO role unexpectedly, and the lawsuit is eating you alive, not to mention you're a workaholic. *Imagine* relinquishing control in this one aspect of your life."

"It's not like this is a large aspect of my life, Ang," I counter, rolling my eyes.

"It doesn't have to be for this to make a difference. Maybe this will awaken something great in you."

"I don't know. With Theo, I did most of the initiating. I was mostly in control, and it worked fine."

"But you shouldn't settle for *fine*. You should have world-shattering sex, babe! You actually have all the control when you're the sub."

I screw up my brow. "Huh?"

"As a sub, you need to lay out all the things that are off limits, things you want, and things you're open to trying. It's the Dom's responsibility to direct you based on your requests. With trust in them, this allows you to stop thinking and accept the pleasure that they give you."

"How do you know so much about this?"

"I read a shit ton of spicy romance," she smirks.

We spend the rest of the morning chatting about her life and the miserable dates she's been having lately. The most recent guy actually told her that her breasts were too small and asked if she'd consider getting them done. She obviously cut him loose.

I wish she would have actually *cut him.*

I truly don't understand how such a genuine, kind, and beautiful woman can keep a steady line of fuckboys knocking at her door.

When she leaves, I clean up the rest of brunch and prepare to head out to the assisted living home for the rest of the day. I sling my laptop bag over my shoulder when I hear my phone trill with a text message. I look to see it's from Jay, and I smile like an idiot.

> Jay: Hello, beautiful. I hope u slept well. Here is some info we talked about last night. Read thru it and let us know if u have any questions. Think about what

> u want and what u don't. I can't wait to see u. <kiss emoji> <two eggplant emojis>

I click the first link he sent, and it's a website about BDSM, all kinds of kinks, and a very thorough explanation of a Dominant/submissive relationship. The site doesn't seem shady in the least. It's very descriptive and answers questions I didn't even know to ask.

The next link is a form I can fill out about different BDSM aspects and kinks. I'm supposed to rate each one with my interest level. There's a ton of stuff I've never heard of—terms I need to look up.

I realize then that I've been sitting on this chair with my coat, bags, and shoes on for thirty minutes, reading everything.

I shake myself out of it and remind myself I need to go. I'll have to continue this research after I get back tonight. I shoot a quick text back.

> Cora: Hello to you both. I'll be sure to do my homework. <blushing emoji>

CHAPTER 15

The Nightmare

CORA

I sit on a stool in a photography studio. A white backdrop hangs behind me. I'm dressed in a tailored navy blue suit. The photographer in front of me peers into his camera. I can't see his face fully. He snaps a few and then calls from behind the lens, "Okay, but can you smile for the next few? You may want professional photos of you smiling, too."

I do as he says, parting my lips and smiling bright. Suddenly I feel my teeth crumble and fall out of my head. My hands reach up to catch them and I look at my palms, horrified to see the bloody mess. I swipe my tongue along my gums and feel nothing there.

"No!" I cry.

"Perfect, Cora! These are great!" the photographer cheers. I look up to see him pull his camera away from his face, revealing my ex-husband.

What the fuck?

Theo takes a step toward a table behind him. "They're already printed and ready to view. Come see."

I stand and warily walk to where he's standing. I look down at the large prints. It's me, in my suit, on the stool. The first images are of me looking stoic. Poised. Guarded.

The next images I see myself smile and then my teeth are falling out. I gasp as I witness what happens to those images.

Black ink seeps from my mouth in all of them, spreading across my face and body, ruining the prints. He collects the pictures of me looking stoic and hands them to me and says, "You know the cost."

The room then disappears and I'm standing at an open grave. I sob into my bloody hands and collapse.

"Fuck you, Theo!"

I wake up in a panic, my hands clutching my heaving chest and then my mouth. I touch all my teeth and exhale. George scurries away from my sudden wake up.

The sun hasn't come up yet and it's still dark in my room. The lingering effects of my dream are weighing on me. I feel heavy. I feel like this blanket is filled with sadness, weighing me down in the best and worst way. I want to bury my face and never see the light of day.

I lay there for several more minutes and the moment gets the best of me. I begin to sob ugly, unruly tears.

How could he do this to me?

Why can't I let this go?

Will this ever get better?

I can't stay here as badly as I want to; I can't stay in bed and wallow. I need to be stronger than this.

Fake it till you make it, girl.

I reluctantly swing my legs out of bed and make my way to my dresser where I grab a sports bra. I take off my top and put the bra on. I can't be bothered changing out of my pajama bottoms at this point. It's taking all the energy I have to put this bra on.

I slip on some socks and training shoes and head down to the basement where I have a small workout space. Just a treadmill, yoga ball, mat, and some hand weights. I get on the treadmill and press play on my sound system remote nearby.

You can't be sad and listen to Lady Gaga.

Well, you can, depending on the song. But I'll only be listening to her party bangers at this point.

As her lyrics fill the room, I run as fast as I can, punishing myself.

I will *get rid of this.*
I am in charge of my life.
Fuck Theo.
Fuck gross and vicarious negligence.

When I'm done, I'm not really sure how far or how long I ran, I barely make it off the treadmill without collapsing. I'm sweating head to toe, but I feel a little bit better.

With wobbly legs, I head up the three flights of stairs to my bathroom and strip down to shower. I can't be bothered to give my curls the attention they need, so I throw my hair up in a tight twisted bun.

I finish getting ready, putting on a comfortable outfit that barely passes as presentable for the public.

My stomach gurgles and I roll my eyes. *Yeah, yeah, yeah.* Yet another part of me with its own fucking agenda.

I grab my laptop bag, a granola bar and head out the door to see Mom; the fog of this morning's episode still lingering inside me.

When I arrive, I see she's already up and ready for the day and doing her sudoku. Her shoulder length dark brown hair is wavy and her gray roots are starting to show. She's wearing a beautiful beige loungewear set with a matching long cardigan I got for her birthday last year.

THE NIGHTMARE

I stand near her table in the common area. "Good morning." I wait for her to reply to see if she remembers me or not. It can come and go, but I don't ever want to freak her out and call her Mom when she doesn't think she has a daughter.

She looks up at me with a smile. "Good morning."

"May I sit down with you?"

"Oh, sure. Have a seat. I'm Connie."

I inwardly sigh my disappointment. I know this is part of the disease, but it doesn't make it any less depressing.

"Hi, Connie. I'm Cora. It's nice to meet you. Is it okay if I work on my computer?"

"Of course. I'm just trying to figure out this sudoku."

Ha. *Figure out.*

The woman goes through books and books of the hardest sudokus you've ever seen with a pen. Never one mistake.

I start to open my bag and haul out my giant PC. "Oh my," Mom says. "That's a very large laptop you have."

"I'm an architect. I have to have a big computer with lots of power."

"Oh, wow! An architect. You know, I'm married to an architect."

"Oh yeah?" I know better than to ask what his name is or how long they've been married, or any other prying questions. She might not know and wrack her brain over and over, then panic that she can't remember. So, as much as I want to hear her talk about Dad, to talk to me like her daughter and not a stranger, I keep things surface level.

"Oh yes; he is quite handsome."

I smile and hold back the emotion the best that I can. "I bet he is," I choke out, barely able to fight back the tears. She nods and returns to her book, writing the numbers she can so easily find in her mind.

Needing to space myself from all the emotional strife this morning, I bury myself in work. Reviewing new proposals from my team, changing them and editing minor errors I find on drawings, I find myself lost until a notification pops up.

10% Battery Life. Consider charging soon.

Holy cow, I've been working for six hours straight.

As I pull my charger out of my bag, I hold it in my hand and look at it for a long time. Frozen.

Fuck me... I'm the computer, aren't I?

I can work and perform the functions everyone needs me to perform until I'm at the end of my life. But if I just allowed something else to help me, to power me for a little bit, I could operate efficiently again.

It's then that I make my decision.

I'm going to do this.

Chapter 16

Piping Hot Tea

Jay

When I get to the office Monday morning, I'm nervous. I haven't heard back from Cora over the weekend after our short text exchange. Marco and I tried to distract each other from fixating on calling and texting her. We went to the gym to play basketball for hours on end; we went over to his sister Rebecca's house for a visit, anything that would distract us. She said she would do research, and that's what she was probably doing, right?

But walking into work has me itching to be near her. I have to see her and read her. Is she okay? Is she retreating? Is she scared? Have I ruined our working relationship? Are things going to be awkward now?

My mind races as I set my things down in my office and prepare for the morning meeting with the department heads. When I get to the conference room, she's already there at her spot at the head of the table. Jennifer, our Marketing Director, and Katie are also sitting there, talking to each other. "Good morning, everyone," I say, unbuttoning my gray herringbone suit jacket and sitting down. Jennifer and Katie quickly stop and look at me with smiles, repeat the greeting and go back to their conversation.

I look at Cora. "Good morning," she smirks. Just that little smile... just that little eye contact puts me at ease. She's so beautiful today wearing a dark teal knit top and a black blazer with no lapels. Her sleeves are rolled up a little bit, revealing most of her forearms. Gold jewelry adorns her wrist and ears. Her hair is in a loose bun, and she looks every bit the confident and cool woman I know she is. She looks like everything she does has a purpose.

All I want to do is go up to her and kiss her. I want to lay her on this conference room table and feel her supple curves as I run my hands all over her body. I want to kiss every last inch of her. I want to taste her.

Calm down, Jay. Do not get a boner at work—again.

Everyone else files in, and Cora starts the meeting. She's a damn boss. Watching her ask for the status of every department and delegating tasks, she's an absolute vision. I know she said she wasn't ready to take on CEO, but she looks every bit like a seasoned professional to me. I'd follow her anywhere.

"Alright, and that leads us to HR," Cora says. "Mr. Bishop, how did the new benefits package fare this open enrollment season?"

"It actually went very well. We had more people sign up this year than last, and based on the survey results I collected, people are the most pleased with the added mental health support and increased parental leave. Honestly, I'm impressed. Can I ask... what made Define want to expand the maternity leave from twelve weeks partially paid to eight months fully paid?"

Cora rolls in her lips, and a slightly somber look appears. She looks down at her notepad, where she's idly smoothing the length of her pen against the paper. "Parents should not have to worry about money or losing their job when their life abruptly changes." She looks up at me. "They should be able to focus on their new baby and healing."

"And I couldn't be happier about this new change!" Katie chirps, sitting across from me and rubbing her big belly. "Just in time for this little one. I'm due at the end of January," she beams.

The meeting continues after a couple of colleagues ask Katie about her plans for the baby. By the end, Cora's sad look is gone and replaced with her collected and in-charge self.

When the meeting ends, Cora takes off first, clearly not wanting to stay and chat. As I walk back to my office, I take a look at my phone and see a text from Marco.

> Marco: Good morning hun. How are you?

> Jay: Good morning, my stallion <horse emoji> <wink emoji> I'm fine. Just got done with the morning mtg.

> Marco: Was Cora there? What's she wearing today?

> Jay: A silk nightie with fuzzy trim and fuzzy high heels.

Marco: Damn... You guys have a pretty casual dress code. You should follow her around and wait for her to bend over. Maybe bump into her and knock her off her feet and have to catch her in your arms.

Jay: Ur such a scheming romantic.

Marco: It's not scheming. It's directing. And also a little stalking.

Jay: Lol u think that's one of her kinks? Stalking? I could be into that...

Marco: For her... for you... I can be into anything.

Jay: I know one thing we haven't tried...

Marco: For the last time, I'm not doing horse play with you. You will not be sticking a horse tail butt plug inside me and saddling me.

Jay: But ur my stallion! Think about it! We could have *My Pony by Ginuwine* playing in the background... So hot. <panting emoji> <biting lip emoji>

Marco: <Cry laughing emoji> Good Lord.

As I wipe a laughing tear from the corner of my eye, I hear someone ask, "Can I come in?" Cora stands there with a smile and two mugs. She raises a quick, perfectly shaped eyebrow, "I heard you like tea."

Fuck yeah. I can feel the tension I built by worrying all weekend melt away instantly. She still wants to be friendly and talk to me. I'll take it. I'll take anything she gives me at this point.

God, I'm pathetic. I don't care.

She sets the cups down on my desk and closes the door.

Oooh, she's closing the door!

She passes me a steaming mug of green tea and takes a seat on the edge of the chair, her hands molded to hers. Cora's eyes lift from the cup to my gaze. "I think I'm ready. No, I know I am. I'm ready. I did a ton of research last night. I want to do this with you guys."

Holy fucking shit, it's really going to happen!

I think I'm smiling, but I can't be totally sure. My brain is misfiring. She could have said an entire monologue just now, and I wouldn't have heard a thing because Cora The-Sex-Goddess Dalton wants to fuck me and my boyfriend. My *boss* wants to fuck me and my boyfriend.

"Oh my god, yes!" I exclaim with a whisper. I abruptly stand from my chair and pace towards the windows. Clenching my fists and swinging them up to my head, I give myself a tight victory cheer. "Yes!"

I hear Cora chuckle and turn to see her sitting back with her tea, legs crossed, watching me with an amused look. "My thoughts exactly."

I'm too wound up. "I need to kiss you right now," I whisper and step toward her. She sets her tea on my desk, and I pull her up against me and immediately fuse our lips together. I feel weightless and invincible right now. Her hands wrap around me, and I gently hold the back of her neck, trying not to disturb her hair. My other hand at her back slowly slides down to her round ass as I deepen the kiss. But before I can go further, she pulls away and chides, "I'm wearing lipstick! It's going to smear all over us."

"What? Is berry not my color?" I ask with a sarcastic grin.

She giggles, "Smeared lipstick is not a good look, Jay."

"Oh, I beg to differ. It looks *very good* in certain situations." I give her a lewd look and a wink.

Her cheeks blush, and she shakes her head. "I filled out that form you sent. Do you want to see it?"

"I've been dying to see that list."

She releases me and pushes me toward my chair as she rounds my desk to sit back down in her seat. She pulls out her phone and taps a few times. "Sent."

I look at my phone and see her text come in with a link to a shared private file. I begin to scan it, unable to hide my intrigue. "Ooh, open to stalking, I see..." I mutter.

"How should we tell Marco?"

Just then, I get a text message. "Speak, and he shall appear." I read his text to myself.

> Marco: My last client for 6 pm canceled, so I'll be home early today if no one books last minute.

"I know exactly how we can tell him."

Chapter 17

Let's Get Wet

Marco

"Have a great night, Judy. Make sure you drink lots of water when you get home. I'll see you next time." I watch my last client walk to the reception area and wave. She's a hoot. She sees me every two weeks, and I always give her light pressure, but she says she loves my deep tissue massages. I think she would break if I gave her even a medium pressure.

I head back to my massage room to clean up and restock so I can head home for the night. I strip the table of its sheets and blanket, put them in the dirty bin in the laundry room, and head back to put new linens on. I start to wipe down the half-moon leg bolster with a disinfecting wipe when I hear a knock at the open door.

"Think you could squeeze in one more?" I look up to see Jay leaning against the frame. With his finger, he holds his suit jacket over his shoulder, his white shirt collar open at the top revealing golden skin that contrasts so beautifully.

I walk towards him. "Hey, what a nice surprise." I kiss him, putting my hand on his back and pulling him into me. "Yeah, I could do that. Did you talk to Cheryl already?"

"Yeah, she said it was fine and already left. I made sure to lock the door behind her."

I smile against his lips. "So, it's just us here?"

"It would appear so, wouldn't it?"

I slap his butt playfully. "Get undressed, prince." He starts to hang up his suit jacket, and I ask, "Did Cora talk to you today?"

"She did..." I turn my head to stare at him. "And she wants to do this."

"She does?" I exclaim.

Cora steps into the room from the hallway and whispers, "She does."

Excitement pummels through my body. Electricity firing from the soles of my feet to the hairs on my head. I can't believe it. My cock twitches behind my zipper even more now that I have both Cora *and* Jay here with me.

Here.

Here?

I take her in my arms and ask them, "You wanna do this here? You know I have a massage room at home, right?"

"We thought it might be fun if you're okay with it," Jay smirks and closes the door.

Cora slides her hands up my chest and gently draws circles with the pads of her fingers. She looks up at me with those soft emerald eyes and long dark lashes. I—*we* are going to devour her.

"Did you do your homework, beautiful?"

Jay comes to stand behind her, his torso bare. He wraps his hands around her waist and untucks her top from her pants, sliding his hands over her stomach and leaning down to kiss her neck.

She closes her eyes. "Yes, Sir."

"I just sent it to you," Jay murmurs. "Check your phone."

I pull away slightly from this Cora sandwich we've made to take out my phone and start reading her list of limits and interests.

"Alright, you're into a little bondage... a good amount of impact play... oral... double penetration... orgasm control... all kinds of sensation play... *Oooh*, dirty talk, degradation, yes."

Jay interjects, "Stalking..." still kissing along her neck and removing her blazer.

Cora giggles. "What is with you and stalking? I think I'm regretting that one now."

"What's this? No golden showers?" I feign a hurt expression.

She keeps laughing and tugs on my black polo. "Absolutely not."

I have a good idea of Cora's limits now, and hopefully, if we continue this, I'll study them further to get really good scenes from both of them. But for right now, I have enough to go on.

I pocket my phone and turn my attention back to Cora and Jay. They're both looking at me as he fondles her with slow, sensual touches. I step closer to press my now rock-hard cock against her. I gently lay one palm on her collarbone and stroke up her neck. With my other hand, I grab hold of the back of Jay's head and pull his lips to mine. "You were a very good boy for bringing her here. Thank you, prince."

Jay hums in our kiss. "You're welcome, Sir."

I turn my attention to Cora, and she's biting her bottom lip, her eyes begging for me. Her hands are on my chest, but not moving any further as I rest my forehead on hers. "I want you both to speak freely tonight, but you will still address me as 'Sir'. I want to know exactly where your head is at as we go, Cora. Are you comfortable with that?"

"Yes, Sir," they both reply.

"Good. Do you want a safe word?"

"I don't know. What one do you guys use?"

"*No* and *stop*," Jay murmurs, his hands now massaging her shoulders. "No need to get fancy about it."

"I'll just stick with that then."

"I would like to employ the stop light system as well. If I ask you about your tolerance levels, I need you to tell me green for *yes, more*. Yellow to *slow down* or you need to take a moment to collect yourself. And red will obviously be *stop, no more*." I lift my head off hers and nuzzle her ear. "Is that clear, princess?"

"Yes, Sir."

"Good girl." I lower my hands to the waist of her pants and start to unbutton them. "Now, let's get you undressed to *my* comfort level, shall we?" I unzip them, shimmy them down her hips and let them fall. I step back and pull her with me, allowing space for her to step out of them. Jay quickly crouches down to pick up and fold them, laying them on the chair in the corner. He does the same with her knit top once I pull it over her head. And there she stands, in only her black panties and light pink bra.

"I... I didn't anticipate we'd do this tonight. So, I didn't wear a matching set."

The bra and panties she's wearing are beautiful on their own, but I really don't give a shit. "You know what the best thing about a bra is?"

"What?" she whispers as Jay unhooks it and slides his fingers under the straps.

"Taking it off," I growl as her breasts release. Absolutely stunning. Her chest is a work of art. Her whole body is. This is the kind of body built for carrying babies. For feeding them.

Lush, ripe curves that I want to sink my teeth into.

My mouth parts as I look in awe at this woman. I turn her and push her back against the wall and immediately dive into her cleavage. Jay comes up next to me, and I move to one breast so he can devour the other. Her tits are so large that even my huge hand looks small against it. We lap at her nipples and suck and nibble until I hear her moaning, and I can feel her breathing start to deepen, quicken.

"You're so beautiful, princess."

"*Fuck*, I want to live in these tits."

My hands move to her ass, and I pull down her panties tortuously slow. Just looking at her pussy like this is making my mouth water. When I lower myself to the floor to collect her underwear, I see she's still wearing her heels. I pocket her panties and command her, "Sit on the table, Cora." Jay pulls away from her and lets her obey. She sits at the foot end, her legs hanging down. I remove her shoes and set them aside. Looking up at her, I ask, "Would you like to continue our last massage? Perhaps the same pressure and this time... we can both live out the fantasy we played in our minds that first time, yeah?"

She nods eagerly. "Yes, please. Yes, Sir."

"Lay on your stomach. Face in the cradle." She twists around and does as I say, laying down on the soft navy blue blanket. "Lucky for you, Miss Dalton, I have an assistant. He's very skilled, and I think you're really going to enjoy your session today." Jay and I exchange mutual grins. "Allow us a moment to discuss our approach."

The two of us stand as far away from her as we can and whisper to each other what our plan of attack will be. When we're done a couple of minutes later, I stand at the head of the table, her face down in the headrest. "Are you comfortable, ma'am?" I ask, pumping oil into my hands.

"Very. Thanks for fitting me in on such short notice."

Oh yes, she's playing along so well.

"Ma'am, it's *you* who will be fitting *me* in tonight." I watch her body shiver as goosebumps pebble every inch. I look up at Jay, who's rocking his head and mouthing *nice*.

I lower my hands to her shoulders and slowly slide them down her back. Starting with moderate pressure, I steadily increase it to the level I know she craves. I kneed my knuckles into her back and shoulders, and I hear her let out a sexy moan that's not at all quiet.

"Jay, would you please start massaging her feet and calves?"

He pumps the oil into his hands, and as he starts to grip her, I press my thumbs hard into the muscle along her spine. She's already starting to sweat from the pain.

"You know, I've never had a client get totally naked and lay on top of the sheets before. It's quite unprofessional, Miss Dalton. Are you trying to tell me you want more than just a massage?"

"Yes, Sir," she purrs.

"Are you a needy little slut?" I whisper in her ear, squeezing, pinching her traps.

Her breath catches as she tries to talk through the sensation. "Yes... I am... Sir."

I gesture at Jay to start massaging her thighs and plump backside. "You need two strong men to take care of you? To take care of that ache in your pussy?" She whimpers in agreement. I indicate to Jay to spank her hard, and he does, startling her.

"Use. Your. Words," I growl.

"Yes, Sir!"

I drag the side of my thumb under her shoulder blade, digging deep. "That's a good slut." I look at Jay, whose fingers are getting dangerously close to her center. His eyes are laser-focused on her as he clenches his jaw. I watch as she wiggles her butt slightly, trying to chase his touch.

"Do you think if we spread your legs, we'd find just how desperate you are, ma'am? We'd find how needy you are?"

"I am, Sir. Please."

"Spread her knees to the edges of the table," I direct. "Would you like to taste her, Jay?"

"More than anything, Sir."

"You've wanted this for a long time, haven't you, prince?"

"Yes, I have, Sir. I've dreamt about it. I've jerked off to the thought of it."

"Then you better get to it and *thank me* for letting you."

His mouth plunges right for her core. "Thank you, Sir," he gasps between kisses on her inner thigh. "Thank you so much." He trails his tongue straight to her pussy, his nose nestled between her cheeks.

Cora moans, "Yes. Oh my god."

I move my hands from her back to the globes of her ass and spread it, giving Jay more access. His hands grip the back of her thighs tight, and his fingertips dig in so deep I know she's going to bruise.

I let him eat her out, listening to them moan in pleasure.

"Fuck," he pants, coming up for air. "Ma'am, you taste so good. You're so soft and wet," he dives back in. "I love it. Thank you, Sir."

"Bring your ass up, ma'am. All the way." I release my grip on her, and Jay undocks his face from her pussy long enough for her to do as I say. "Now, prince, I want you to lay on your back and let her straddle your face. Plant your feet on the end of the table to balance yourself." He does so, allowing Cora enough space to place her hands at the head of the table, her knees bracing on either side of his shoulders.

I see his erection tenting his gray dress pants. "Hold her thighs and pleasure her," I command him.

"Yes, Sir," he says eagerly and gets back to his duty, Cora's moans getting louder as she rides his face.

I then unbuckle Jay's belt, unbutton and unzip him, shucking his pants and black briefs off quickly. I set them aside, along with his socks. His cock is so big and beautiful, standing so proud, precum dripping at the tip.

The sounds he's making against her wet pussy are just as erotic to listen to as it is to watch. He's slurping, sucking, and growling into her. He's making a whole fucking meal out of it. I can't stand it anymore; I need to eat.

I stand at the side of the table facing Cora as my hands fly to her hips, and my head lowers to her ass. I circle that forbidden little rosebud with my tongue, and she gasps. "Yes!" she cries.

I flatten my tongue and drag it up and down, alternating between a hardened tip and a flat lazy stroke. I take my sweet time with her, savoring her taste, swimming in her sounds. "You're such a wanton little whore, aren't you?"

"Yes, Sir. Oh my god. Fuck, I'm gonna come."

"Come for us, Cora. Do it. Now," I seethe.

I can feel her body tense up, her ass clenching together as we keep our assault. "Yeeeeees!" she sings. "Fuck, fuck, fuck!"

"I might be the one with my tongue in your ass, but you're the one with a dirty mouth, princess."

She sighs and whimpers as she tries to come down from her orgasm, but we aren't stopping. "Okay, okay!" she exclaims. "I came. You can stop now."

"Absolutely not. You're giving us another one. And another one after that." *Whack!* I slap her ass hard, and growl, "I'll be the one to say when you've had enough, understood?"

Whack!

"Yes, Sir."

I then start to trace my finger gently between her folds as Jay continues to nibble and suck her clit. "Good girl," I croon and slowly insert my index finger inside her warm, soaking-wet pussy. This angle is absolutely perfect for me to stroke her G-spot.

She moans deeply, "Yes, right there. Thank you, Sir. That feels so good, you guys."

I'm eating up this praise she's giving us like I'm eating her ass, with abandon. I'm living for this.

I insert a second finger and start to pump, still stroking that rough little spot on her inside wall. I can feel those walls starting to convulse, to contract, and I double down my efforts. Right before I think she's about to come for the second time, I growl, "Bite her clit and use both hands to pinch her labia, prince. Right now."

I add a third finger, pumping hard as Jay's arms wrap around her thighs, and he pinches her lips between his forefingers and thumbs as she shrieks.

Just then, she surprises me with the most glorious gift I could ever receive. As her pussy contracts like a vice around my fingers, she squirts all over our hands, down Jay's face, and across his naked body.

"Holy shit! Yes, Cora!" Jay cheers as we both lap it all up, greedy for more. "Thank you, ma'am."

"Oh my god, I'm so sorry!" she cries, but she can't turn it off.

"More princess. Keep going," I demand. "Give us more." Jay and I are fighting for this unexpected prize, our tongues meeting, eager for the last drop.

As her body finally ends this Super Soaker of an orgasm, Jay and I find ourselves making out, both of us rubbing Cora everywhere we can.

Her legs are trembling, but she tries to get up. Jay and I stop as we hold her in place, and I ask, "Where do you think you're going, princess?"

"I'm so sorry. That was so embarrassing. Please don't look at me," she whispers.

"First of all, princess, you will never apologize to me in a scene unless I tell you to. And second, what are you talking about? Haven't you squirted before?"

She props herself up on her hands so she's on all fours and looks back at me. "No." I narrow my eyes at her, and she adds a demure "...Sir."

"That was the hottest thing I've ever seen, Cora." My tone is serious.

Jay chimes in from below, "Boss, that is going to be a core memory for me for the rest of my life. In the best... way... possible."

"You guys liked that?"

"Yes!" Jay groans.

"Now that we know you can do that, it's going to be our mission to get it every time. Buckle up, princess."

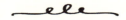

Cora

That was the most intense orgasm I've ever had. I mean, two tongues, two mouths eating me out? And Marco's fingers—so strong and precise.

What happened to my body?

There are a lot of firsts happening right now. My first threesome. My first time... squirting? Good Lord, I didn't know I was capable of that.

But I'd be lying if I said I'm not having an incredible experience. I may be embarrassed at what my body just did, but I'm not regretting this one bit. They put me in one of the most vulnerable positions, spread me open, and ate me like a buffet.

Of course, I've fantasized about two men before, but even in my wildest dreams, I didn't imagine this level of orgasm. This level of raw sexual desire. This level of *man*.

Men.

I must be zoning out because Marco, *my sir*, asks me, "Where's your head, Cora? What's your traffic light color right now?"

I love that he's checking in like this. It makes me feel safe. It makes me trust him more. "I feel really good. Green, Sir."

"Good," he looks down at Jay, who's stroking his hands over my smooth legs. "And you, my prince?"

"Green, Sir."

"Good. Now princess, grab my hand and get down slowly." I obey wordlessly and look to see Jay lying there, glistening in my cum from his face to his stomach. He looks positively blissed out, even with a raging erection. Seeing both of them so visibly turned on is turning me on even more. The horny little engine inside me is revving, and desire is racing through my body.

"Move up, prince. Head at the top of the table. That's it. Cora, why don't you go thank Jay for making you come so hard you lost control of your body, hmm?"

Jay sits up, and I whisper, "Yes, Sir."

I step towards him and take his head in my hands, fingers sifting through his gorgeous raven hair and kiss him deeply. He puts one hand at the back of my neck and the other at the small of my back, pressing me close to him. Our tongues dance against one another, and I can taste myself on him. It's earthy, a little sweet, a little salty.

I can hear Marco wrestling with Jay's pants. I don't dare open my eyes to see, though.

"My turn," my sir purrs.

Jay reluctantly lets me go, and I open my eyes to see Marco drop a couple of condoms on the table next to Jay's hip, then stalk toward me, his eyes dark and intense. His dark hair curling so perfectly that I just want to muss it up with my hands.

"I'm gonna kiss you the way I needed to the moment I saw you." He roughly takes hold of me, scooping me up though my toes stay on the ground. Our mouths part, and our kiss is frantic. Our lips are a tangled, beautiful mess. My mind is completely blank save for the unconscious mantra I play: *More. Yes. More. Yes.*

Marco pulls his mouth away quickly to command, "Stroke yourself, prince." He immediately resumes our hot and heavy make-out session.

His thick erection pushes into my stomach, and I realize he's still fully clothed. With one arm wrapped around my back, his other hand slides down my ass crack, and he cups my wet pussy from behind. I'm well aware of the flood that has occurred down there because my legs are dripping wet now.

As he strokes me there, I move my hands to his belt and start to untuck his shirt. I've been dying to get my hands on his chiseled chest with all its tats and hair.

"No," he warns in a deep, authoritative voice that scares and arouses me.

I stop touching him right away. "I'm so sorry, Sir."

"I told you, you don't apologize unless I tell you to."

"You're right, Sir. I just thought—"

"Absolutely not, princess. Your job is not to think. Your job is to do as I say. That's how this works."

Fuck me; he's so hot like this. So dominant. So controlling. "Yes, Sir."

"Good girl. Now *kiss* me," he growls, and I swear I might be melting.

With our bodies pressed against each other, I feel my need expanding. He must sense it and commands me to rub myself against his hard, muscular thigh, bending his leg out for me. I find myself thinking I must look ridiculous, humping his leg like this, but then I remember what he told me. I need to stop thinking and trust him.

I give myself over to him and clear my mind. The only things that exist are his words and my desires.

"That's it. Use me, Cora. You like that? You like riding my leg, you needy little whore? Can you feel the fabric of my pants against your clit?"

"Yes, I like it. Thank you, Sir." And I *am* thankful. I'm chasing that next wave that's approaching way faster than I thought.

"Encourage her, Jay. She needs your help, too."

I grab hold of Marco, my arms tight around his torso as I hear Jay's words of praise. "That's it, ma'am. Ride him and take what you need. Yes... yes... You're doing so well. Come for us. Come on, that's it!"

And then I'm crashing right there, my legs seizing as I clamp my thighs tight around his and contract over and over.

My brain is gone. All I know is pleasure.

If they're talking, I can't hear them. All my senses are either missing or heightened. I can't even tell which ones are which.

The next thing I know, I'm straddling Jay on the table, not really knowing how I got here. I feel a pair of hands cup my jaw, and through a sound fog, I hear a low voice crescendo, "Where are you, Cora? What's your color?"

Marco. *Mmmmarco.*

"Green, please," I say lazily.

I can feel the body beneath me shaking a bit. "I think she

might be in subspace already, Sir."

"Princess, I would like for you to ride my prince. Can you do that for me?"

"It would be my pleasure, Sir," I whisper with a blissful smile.

"That's my girl. You're going to ride him, and I'm going to belt you. You'll start with five hits and then a little surprise. If you can't handle the belt at any point, you must tell me. Do you understand?"

"Yes, Sir."

"Good. Now lower yourself on that perfect princely cock."

I might be in the clouds right now, I really might be, because with Jay's thickness inching inside of my wet channel, it feels like heaven.

Jay's hands are on my hips, and he groans a deep, guttural sound. "Yes, ma'am. It's so wet and warm."

Once I'm fully seated, I feel Marco push me down on Jay's chest, my hands connect with his pecs, and I touch my forehead to his collarbone and breathe deeply.

"You two are so beautiful like this." Marco's words fill me with pride.

I start to feel Jay thrust from below, and so I match him, grinding myself against him.

"That's it, you two. Keep going."

Crack!

I gasp at the sudden pain scorching my backside.

"Oh my god, that felt good, ma'am," Jay moans as our rhythm picks up intensity. "I can feel you squeeze me from inside."

Crack!

Crack!

I can't believe how good this feels. This is exactly what I've always wanted.

"Yes," I cry. "Thank you, Sir."

Crack!

He hits me harder now as Jay pumps into me, our bodies slick against each other, his hands moving to my breasts to guide them into his mouth to play with—to bite. His face is lost beneath me, branding me with his teeth and the strong suction of his hot mouth.

Crack!

The hardest hit by far. The stinging radiates through my flesh for several moments, and then I feel a warm liquid pour down my backside.

Jay stops all movement rather abruptly as Marco presses one of his large fingertips to my back entrance and slowly pulses in and out in shallow thrusts.

"That's a good girl," he says in a low, soothing voice. "Just relax and know that I'm in charge. I promise to make you feel good."

"I trust you, Sir."

I can feel a little movement from Jay, and I open my eyes to see his locked on mine. He gives me a soft smile and whispers, "You're perfect, Cora."

And, *fuck me,* if that isn't the sweetest and most tender thing to hear right now.

I lean in, and his lips meet mine in a delicious, all-consuming kiss. I can feel Marco work himself into me slowly, really taking his time. With this drugging kiss and his hands still caressing my breasts, I start to feel Marco add a second finger.

"Talk to me, princess."

"It feels good, Sir. It's tight, but it's feeling better. Green light."

Marco hums his appreciation but takes his time opening me—preparing me. "You are such a treat, my dear. And you are doing such a wonderful job with her, prince. You're such a good boy. I'm so proud of you both. Princess, are you ready for more?"

"Yes, Sir."

"Then get after it."

Jay starts his pace back up. The sensation of a cock and fingers inside me at the same time is unreal. This is too much in the best way.

I moan for them, for me, for us. "More, please," I beg. Marco starts to actually thrust his fingers in conjunction with Jay's movements, and the two of us pant and whimper and grunt together.

"Yes, that's it, ma'am. Oh my god, this is incredible. You're incredible."

"You feel so good, Jay. You're so big."

"Are you ready for a third finger, princess? Can you take it?"

"Yes, I want that," I beg him. "Please, Sir."

When he does, it feels impossibly large, but I feel like a sex goddess! I feel free and powerful and perfect. Everything feels so intense.

Crack! Crack! Crack!

I cry out in pleasure as Marco spanks me repeatedly. And then, out of nowhere, my orgasm makes a grand fucking entrance, and yup—there it is—another waterfall between my legs.

"Yes!" Marco bellows. "That's my fucking girl! More."

Crack! Crack! Crack!

I can't even make a sound at this point. My mouth is wide open as I silently cry out.

Jay squeezes my nipples hard as he grunts out, "Sir, I can't last much longer like this."

"You *will* hold off. Don't you dare come until I say so."

Before I even feel my orgasm leave, Marco's standing in front of me, his pants undone just enough to free his huge, leaking erection—veins snaking all around it. The wide crown is dark and angry looking—and I can't wait to swallow it.

Jay

This is the best night of my life. I could have come without a single touch several times at this point. It's been torture watching Cora get off again and again. Watching the man I love control not only me but this extraordinary woman is blowing my mind.

I can feel Marco's crotch pressed against the crown of my head, and I watch Cora look up at him, waiting for his instruction. She's a quick learner.

He guides his massive cock to her waiting mouth, smearing the precum like lip gloss. "Take it, princess." As I watch her take him in, sucking his fat head, I can't help but marvel. I can't help but love the way he calls us his prince and princess. It makes me feel like she and I are a complementary pair designed for Marco and each other.

I keep my hips thrusting hard into her. She's so wet, the table we're on is wet from her fucking pussy dam bursting, and our bodies are covered in sweat and her juices. The sound of skin-on-skin slapping echoes in the small room, overpowering the gentle spa music, and the erotic sound of her taking my lover's cock deeper, deeper until she gags and—

"Oh fuck," I groan, her cunt squeezing around me as she chokes.

"Play with my balls and spank her hard," he instructs me. "Princess, use your hand, too. That's it. Very good."

I tilt my head back to allow his sac to rest in my mouth as I suck each one of his testicles inside me. With both hands, I waste no time and slap her perfect ass as hard as I can, every spank causing her to contract. She moans as she sucks, her cheeks hollowing out and her hand pumping the base of his dick, the other bracing herself on me.

I add a bit of teeth and tug on his balls. He groans, encouraging us, "You're both fucking whores; you know that?" He grabs a fistful of Cora's hair behind her bun. "What kind of sick freaks are you two?" he grits out as he thrusts into her mouth. Then he pulls away without warning. "Keep spanking, prince. She needs to feel it in her bones. That ass is so thick it's gonna take a while before the pain reaches her there."

She cries out as I mercilessly slap her. The next thing I know, Marco is behind her. "Both of you hold it." He rolls on his condom and asks, "Princess, I *need* to enter you. What's your color?"

"Green! *Fuck!* Please, Sir. Please fuck my ass. I've been so bad. I'm so desperate for you," she pleads. As if nothing else could surprise me tonight, her desperately begging to be fucked in the ass has been added to the list.

"I love it when you talk like that," he says with a devilish smirk as he takes the oil from his pocket and pumps it on her, and rubs it all over himself.

"Nice and slow. That's it, princess... just gotta get the head in first. Mmm, that's it, you dirty girl."

Cora's face is twisted up as she tries to let him inside her. I cup her cheeks and bring her head down to my chest, holding her, kissing her forehead, and whispering, "You're doing so well. Relax, and let him ease in. I know it's tight. It's okay. We'll make you feel so good, I promise. You're perfect, Cora."

"Okay, princess. I'm as far in as it will go. I'm going to wait here and let you start at the pace you need, alright?"

She takes a deep breath in. "Yes, Sir." She gives a couple of experimental hip movements. "Oh... god," she moans. "I feel so full. I've never... This is... Oh my god."

Her hips move faster now as she sets into a steady rhythm. She turns her head to meet mine, and she passionately kisses me. I want to lose myself in her. I love that she's owning this side of her. She's magnificent like this.

"That's a good girl. Are you ready for me to take over?"

"I am, Sir. I trust you. I trust you," she whispers into our kiss, unable to detach from each other. Well, in more ways than one.

Marco starts shallow thrusts, and he slaps her ass so hard I swear I can feel the sting transfer to me. She cries out, and I can feel our dicks rubbing against each other inside her, with just a thin wall between us. God dammit, I can't even think anymore. All I know is I need to rut and never stop.

As I shut off my brain, only allowing for the occasional direction to guide me, I can faintly hear words of praise and cries of pleasure, spanking, and grunts. I'm not even certain who they're coming from.

I am not me.

I am Marco's.

I am Cora's.

"Yes, Cora. That's it!" I hear, as warm liquid splashes everywhere. "Come for us, princess! Come on our big... fat... cocks!" We keep working her, an endless stream of cum trickling down.

"Now, prince. Come now," he commands.

I've been holding it back for so long it takes absolutely no more waiting. I hold her tight to my body and release myself, my hips jerking uncontrollably. I think I might cry tears of relief as I choke out, "*Fuuuuuck!*"

And before my hips can settle down, Marco is coming, too.

His hands gripping her ass so tight her flesh spills out between his fingers. His whole body is clenching as he is barely able to speak. "Yes. Yes. Yes!" he grits out and collapses over us.

Then all time stops. There is nothing but heaving chests and breath. I don't know where my body is.

I feel a big hand touch my head, pushing my hair out of my face, and then a soft kiss. I open my eyes to then see Marco kissing Cora and his other hand brushing strands of curls away.

How long have I been out?

When did Marco get off the table?

"I brought you both water and fresh sheets to wrap up in. Come on, Cora. Can you dismount?"

Her eyes are closed, but she nods slowly, and he helps her off me. He sits her up and wraps a sheet loosely around her, and hands her a water bottle after unscrewing the cap for her. Once he's satisfied that she'll stay upright, he does the same to me, removing my condom and tossing it in the trash, and having me sit right next to her. Her head falls to my shoulder, and I wrap an arm around her lower back, nestling her in.

Marco squats down in front of us and gently rubs our legs. "Princess, how are you? Can you tell me how you're feeling?"

She gives a satiated smile. "Amazing. Incredible. Floating."

"That's what I like to hear. Do you feel any pain? Are you sore?"

"I don't really know. I can't feel my body."

"And you, prince?"

"I feel spent. Out-of-body. I feel really good."

"You both did so well. I'm so proud of you. And Cora, you're a natural submissive. You were so brave. It was an honor to have your trust. I hope I didn't disappoint."

"Oh, no, no, no. You—you both exceeded my expectations. Thank you."

"You're very welcome, princess. Now, you're both driving home with me because you're out of your mind, and I'm going to take care of you, feed you, and wash you. I will not hear otherwise, understood?" We both nod at him. "Good."

Chapter 18

Smile for the Camera

Cora

I walk into my office the next morning, and the entire world around me is blurred and out of focus because nothing exists except the memory of last night. It was better than any fantasy I've ever had. I was used, bruised, spanked, bitten, cherished, praised, degraded, and out of my mind with pleasure.

I loved every second of it.

When Marco drove us to their home, he took us to the shower right away, stripping our clothes and guiding us in, where he proceeded to wash every inch of our bodies with slow, gentle strokes. When I protested that I could do this myself, he gave me a stern look and shushed me, telling me this was his job to take care of us.

It was the first time I was able to see his bare chest up close. He let me trace his geometric tattoos over his pecs and shoulders and down his strong arms. Let me run my fingers through his tight chest hair. But when my hands wandered down his muscled stomach, he caught them before I could go any lower. When I gave him a little pout, he told me this moment was about our care and then called me an insatiable she-devil.

He gave us sweet little kisses and whispered affectionate words in our ears as he washed our hair—which by the way, they had brand new bottles of curly hair shampoo and conditioner for me. Apparently, they had put a lot of hope in this working out between us.

When Marco was finished washing us, he wrapped us in towels, gave us mild painkillers, and rubbed arnica oil on my backside, which I was very thankful for. Marco told Jay to find us some comfy clothes while he went downstairs to make dinner. Jay dressed in a pair of sweats and long sleeve t-shirt and gave me a pair of sweats as well and a big hoodie. The pants didn't fit because—hello—these are slim-waisted men, and I'm the complete opposite of that. He kept looking for other options but couldn't find any that would fit. I laughed and tried to reassure him that it was okay. So, I just put on a pair of big warm socks, my panties, and Marco's hoodie that didn't quite cover my rear end. Jay just smiled and said, "Yeah, I like this look better anyway."

Marco made us linguini that we ate on their couch, and we talked about our evening, recounting our favorite parts. It was so easy talking to them. We just shared this intensely intimate evening together, and yet... I didn't want to shy away. I felt emboldened. I felt confident.

When it was time to go, I had to put my work clothes back on, which felt utterly wrong, but a girl needs pants at eleven at night in the city in December.

Marco drove us to our cars back at the spa, and Jay hopped

out to warm them up. When he got back in, Marco was kissing my hand. "I know I said this several times already, but you were perfect tonight, princess." Marco looked at Jay and then back to me. "I think I speak for both of us when I say we'd love to do this again with you. We'd love to spend more time with you."

My heart was beating out of my chest at his words. Wasn't this supposed to be a one-time thing? That's what I thought, at least. Before we had sex, yes, that's what I thought. But now... now that I've tasted this forbidden fruit, I want more. I need more.

As he continued to kiss my hand, I said, "I would like that, too. But why don't you guys take a little time to talk about this with each other? This is your relationship I'm... stepping into? I don't know what to call it," I look at Jay sitting in the middle of the back seat. "Just make sure you guys are on the same page. I would hate to cause any strife between you two." He nodded and promised they would talk.

They walked me to my car, both of them giving me a tight, warm hug and kissing me. When I drove away, I couldn't wipe the smile from my face.

As the morning goes on, I can't help but feel lighter. It's like this unconscious burden has been lifted from my shoulders. I'm breezing through my work, responding to emails with a positive attitude, talking to colleagues, and asking about their families. Not that I didn't do that before, but today just feels... better. Everything is better. Even Jonathan's scowl can't bring me down.

I get a text message from Jay and see that it's already noon.

> Jay: Come over to my office for lunch. I checked ur calendar and I know u don't have any meetings <raised eyebrow emoji> <smile emoji>

I bite my lip and amble to his office. When I stop in the doorway, he stands up from behind his desk, his outfit a little more casual than his normal suits. He's wearing a thin black wool sweater and a collared shirt underneath. With his dark green slacks and black belt, he looks so damn fine I could climb him like a jungle gym right here.

Not taking my eyes off his, I close the door, and he raises an eyebrow with a devilish smirk. He walks around the desk, takes one of his guest chairs and brings it around to his side, and plants it facing his seat. "Come. Marco made us lunch."

I stroll over to his side and see two containers and two cans of sparkling water. "Us? He made me lunch?"

Jay sets one container in front of me as I take a seat. "Well, after I told him you don't always eat a proper lunch and after last night... he apparently has taken it upon himself to make sure you're fed well."

His words cause me a moment of worry, and I lower my brows. "*Fed well?*" I repeat. "Wait, does he have a feeding kink or like—" I gulp, "a fat fetish or something?" Oh my god, how could I have let this happen? I don't want to be someone's fucking fetish! I am more than just a beautiful body, and I won't stand for it.

Jay's eyes bug out, and panic spreads across his face. Before I can finish my internal rage monologue, he quietly exclaims. "No! I'm so sorry. I didn't mean it like that. *He* doesn't mean it like that, I swear. I mean, yes, we love curvy women, but," he stumbles over his words. "But, I–I swear it's not like that. And he's like this with me," he quickly adds, gesturing to the food. "He wants to make sure I'm taken care of. This is just one way he likes to show his affection. He loves to cook. I swear, that's it."

He takes my hands in his and rubs my knuckles with his

thumbs. "I swear," he repeats with a pained expression.

If there's one thing I know about Jay Bishop, it's that he's honest. Well, except for the fact he didn't tell me his boyfriend was my massage therapist. I guess I can look past that one now.

My lip curls up ever so slightly, and I nod once. "Okay."

"Yeah?" He brings my hands to his lips and kisses them. "Good. Now please, help yourself. And he left a little note for you."

He releases my hands, and I turn to see a yellow sticky note attached to the container lid that says *Text me* with a phone number. I open my lunch to see it's a hearty Greek pasta salad, a tangerine, a bag of roasted cashews, and two Ferrero Rocher chocolates.

I grab my phone and give Jay a knowing side-eye as he opens his lunch. I enter the number, save it and text him.

> Cora: Thank you for lunch. Maybe next time send the whole package of chocolates?

I set my phone down and start to dig in when I get a text back from Marco right away.

> Marco: Now why would I do that? I have to keep you coming back for more <smirk emoji>

I hope that means what I think it means. I smile at my phone and look at Jay. "Did you guys talk about last night?"

He looks like the cat that got the cream. "We did. And we very much want to continue this with you."

I'm so relieved I could scream. Butterflies are fluttering through my body at the thought of regular sex with these delicious men. These sweet, dominant, fun men. Right? That's why I have butterflies. It's just my horny little brain going nuts.

Our phones go off simultaneously, and it's a new group message from Marco.

> Marco: I can't stop smiling today. It's messing with my tough guy look.

> Jay: We both know ur only a tough guy in the sheets. Ur a marshmallow everywhere else <kissy face emoji>

> Marco: Don't tell anybody <shushing emoji>

> Cora: I can't stop smiling either. Jay said you guys talked about it last night and... you want to keep doing this? I drank the Kool Aid, I'm in.

> Marco: Fuck yes! Good dick will do that to you.

> Marco: *Dicks <two eggplant emojis>

> Jay: Babe, u should see what she's wearing today <drool emoji>

I'm wearing a tight but stretchy dark blue, mid-calf length skirt with a simple cream-colored crop sweater. My hair is up in a loose bun, and I have my favorite black pointed-toe pumps on. It's perfectly professional, in my opinion.

I give Jay a rueful smile and shake my head, but he sits back in his chair with his phone and says, "Stand up. Sit against the desk—yeah, like that—turn slightly towards me. Put this front hand on the desk but don't put all your weight on it. Put the other hand behind your neck and arch your back. Now bite your lip."

I purposefully bite my top lip, jutting out my chin. He throws his head back and laughs that beautiful, infectious laugh I love. "Your bottom lip, you dork."

Changing my lip-biting pose from dork to minx, I hear several camera clicks and watch him review the images for a few seconds, his eyes alight and smile broad. "Oh my god, boss. This is so hot," he growls. "Wait, one more before you sit down. Turn around, hands on the back of the chair, one knee on the seat, lean forward a bit, and turn your head to look back at me. Yes. Arch an eyebrow. Perfect. Okay, okay! Can I send these to Marco?"

Sighing and sitting back down, I can't stop grinning at this goofball. "Yes, thank you for asking."

He fires the pictures off, and I see them pop up on my phone. Not bad. "Where did you learn to pose like this?"

"Girl, I was on gay dating apps for years," he says sternly. "You have to have top-tier photos. It's the law."

I chuckle and hear the new message from Marco. Except it isn't a text message. It's a video call from him. I show the screen to Jay, and he swipes it from me, answering the call.

"Let me see her," Marco demands. Jay props the phone against his monitor so Marco can see me in the frame. He runs a hand over his face and rubs his stubbled jaw. "Are you kidding me with that outfit, princess? Fuck me."

With a confused face, I look over at Jay and then back at the screen. "What do you mean? It's fine for work. The only skin I'm showing is a little collarbone and some leg. It's perfectly appropriate."

Jay places his hand on my knee and starts to slide it up my thigh. I can feel the electricity coursing through my veins at his simple touch. I can feel the heat of his hand radiating through me. And the thought of messing around like this here in the office... here with my employee... oh, god.

"Oh, it is," Marco replies. "But I know what lies beneath now. That skirt is nothing more than a second skin. All I can picture is that plump ass slamming into me. When I see that soft top, all I can think about is releasing those sweater puppies."

That last phrase throws me out of it, and I laugh hard. "You did not just call my breasts *sweater puppies*."

"Oh, yes, I did. And you're going to let Jay touch them right now. Stand up. Jay, lean your back against the cabinet and hold Cora's back against your chest. I want to see both of your faces. Is your door locked?"

He eagerly starts to move us in position. "Yes, Sir."

My blood starts to heat up. This is going to be more than just a stolen kiss and a gentle caress...

When we settle, Marco praises him, "Good boy. Now kiss her neck. Does she smell good?"

"Yes, Sir. Like our shower from last night, and—what is that? It's like spicy vanilla."

My eyes are closed as I get lost in his kisses. "It's called Black Opium by Yves Saint Laurent."

He nuzzles me, inhaling deeply. "I love it."

"Now touch her. Move your hands under her sweater. She needs to know she can't get away with wearing these tempting outfits."

I know deep down, neither of them actually attributes a person's clothes to their willingness for sex. But dammit, if being objectified doesn't turn me on. Clearly, feminism does not belong in the bedroom for me—or in this case, the office.

Oh god, am I really doing this here? The forbidden aspect of fooling around with my employee mixed with the terror of being caught—why is that turning me on so much?

Jay obeys his words, and I let him. *God, do I let him.* Thankfully Jay's office is in a corner, and it's not next to anyone else because I can't and won't stop this train.

His hands snake up my body, and he cups my breasts. "They're so soft, Sir," he breathes into my neck. "So warm and full."

"Show me what she's wearing underneath."

Jay lifts the front of my sweater, exposing my light blue balconette bra that's pretty much sheer. I open my eyes to see Marco on the small screen in front of us. He's very clearly stroking himself, but his dick is hidden from view. He looks like he's at home on the couch.

"Fuck, princess. You're so sexy."

"I want to see all of you, Sir. Please?" I ask, giving my best sad girl eyes.

"Me, too, Sir."

"Hmm... Will you do everything I say?"

"Yes," we say in unison.

"Okay." He adjusts and sets the phone on the coffee table, then sits back with his feet propped up on it, giving us a front-row seat to his thick erection jutting proudly from his unbuttoned jeans. Lifting his shirt off, he sits back and starts to stroke himself again. "Now, be a good girl and play with yourself. Jay, unzip her but do not take off her clothes."

When he does, I reach my hand in as fast as I can to play with my clit. Part of me is so thankful he's letting me keep my clothes on. I know Jay's office is locked, and the windows are opaque, but it does make me feel safer.

"Thank you, Sir," I pant. Watching him stroke that big cock

has my mouth watering. And with Jay's hands roaming my body, tweaking my nipples through the thin material, his full lips caressing the shell of my ear, nipping at my lobe... I could combust right here. I can feel how hard he is behind me, slowly undulating enough for me to feel but not enough to register on the video.

"Good girl," Jay whispers in my ear.

"Who's the boss now, Cora?" Marco growls.

Without hesitation, I say, "You, Sir."

"That's right. I'm going to count down from ten, and you're going to come when we get to one. Do you understand?"

"Yes, Sir."

"Good. Ten... that's it. Keep playing with yourself," he grunts. "*Ungh*, nine... Yes, princess. Ohhh, yes. Eight... faster now. Come on, make me proud. Seven... Jay, take her tits out and pinch them. You know how our girl craves pain."

Our girl. *I'm theirs?* The thought scares me, turns me on, and comforts me all at once.

Jay pulls the cup lining down, and he is in no way gentle. He pinches my nipples so hard the entire bottom half of my body clenches.

"Six... Yes, that's it. I can see your thighs squeezing together. God, I want to put my face between them and wear you like earmuffs. Five... *Ungh*, oh fuck. That's it you two. My prince, you're doing so well. She's getting so close. Four... Tell me you're close, Cora."

"I'm so close, Sir," I whine, leaning all my weight into Jay, who's holding me steady, because I'm sure I'd be on the ground by now if he wasn't there.

"Faster, faster, come on. *Ungh!* Three... Yes, yes, yes. Almost there, princess. Tell me what you're thinking about."

I close my eyes and turn my head into the crook of Jay's

neck. "Both of you. Filling me up. Stretching me. Spanking me. Pounding into me so hard that my body shakes." I can feel my orgasm almost cresting, and I want it so bad.

"You filthy little whore. You want to be used?"

"Yes, Sir."

"That's it... Two. Two. Two..." he growls so ferociously I swear I could come by his voice alone. Just when I feel the wave start, I hear him say, "Stop."

Jay lets go of my breasts, and my fingers halt.

What the hell?

Then in a completely friendly, calm voice, Marco smirks, "You know what? I think we've been neglecting our prince. Don't you, Cora?"

Breathlessly, I give a little pout. "But... Sir, I didn't finish."

"Oh, don't worry, beautiful. There will be time later. Jay, why don't you have a seat and let Cora give you some attention, hmm?"

Okay, if he says I'll get there, then I will do as he says. Not that this is in any way a punishment. I literally can't wait to put him in my mouth.

"Unzip his pants and take him out, princess," his commanding voice returning. "Jay, take the phone and switch the camera view so I can see what you see."

"Yes, Sir."

"Now suck his cock like it's gonna save your life."

I obey and eagerly grab his thick, heavy cock with both hands and lick from his balls underneath his shaft, all the way to the wide tip. I watch him and the camera as Jay groans and bites his lower lip—a painfully beautiful expression adorning his face. But the way he's looking at *me*—with such desire and reverence—it's enough to spur me on even more.

I make a pool of saliva in my mouth before guiding the fat

head between my closed lips and slowly parting them as I push my mouth down.

Jay's eyes round in disbelief as he pants, his breath hitching. "Oh my god, Cora. Holy fucking shit."

"What a nasty little slut you are."

Jesus Christ, when he says things like that, a shiver of shameful delight washes over me. It makes me even more hungry for them.

I lower myself on his length, letting him hit the back of my throat. There's still a little more to go, so I add my hand to make up the distance.

I take a second to examine my situation. Look at me—the CEO on her knees sucking off the Director of Human Resources during business hours at the office. My pussy pulses in appreciation of this twisted and completely inappropriate scenario.

"Tell me what it feels like, prince."

"It's so hot and wet, Sir. *Fuck*, she's dripping everywhere. I can feel the back of her throat."

"Suck him hard, princess. Play with his balls. He likes it when you push your palm against his sac between his balls and shaft." Jay groans but tries to muffle himself when I follow the orders. "Yeah, that's it. Good. Now keep stroking him and bite his sac. Nip it. Keep doing that."

Jay whimpers as I bite him, and I have to laugh to myself. Weren't we always told never to use teeth in a blowjob? But here he is, squirming and breathing hard, unable to take his eyes off me. I might be one of two submissives in this scenario right now, but I've never felt more powerful.

"Do you like her mouth on your balls, prince? Do you like her little hand stroking you?"

"I do, Sir. Yes. *Fuck*, it's good."

"What should you tell me for letting *her* use you like this? Because she is. She's *using you*, prince. She's just as turned on as you are." I nod, staring at the camera. "What do you say?"

"Thank you, Sir. Thank you for letting me have her mouth. It's so good. I'm almost there. Can I please come?"

"Princess, back to his shaft. Suck him hard and stroke him fast. Good girl," he growls. "Fuck, you're so sexy. Yeah, yeah. Ohhhh, that's it!" And then I hear a long string of grunts from Marco.

Jay's eyes are on the screen and his mouth is open. "Sir, that was so hot. I can't keep it... please let me come."

"Stop."

No! No, not again!

Reluctantly I listen and lift away from Jay, and he whines, "No, please, Sir! Please, I was *so* close."

Marco returns to his calm, friendly voice. "Oh gosh, I have a client coming over to the house in five minutes. I have to go get the room ready for them."

"What? Well... can we finish ourselves?" Jay asks, puppy dog eyes on full display.

Back in his Dom voice, Marco chides, "Absolutely not. You will go about your days, and you *won't* touch each other until you come home tonight, and *I* will finish what we started." We both sigh, and Marco continues, returning to his calm voice, "Have a wonderful day you two. Enjoy your lunch."

CHAPTER 19

Wise Advice

CORA

I think if Marco knew the kind of day I was about to have, he wouldn't have left me hanging like that. Not only was I left on edge from our little lunchtime tryst, but now I have a meeting with Horatio about the lawsuit.

"You ready?" Jay asks, stepping into my doorway, laptop in hand. I nod and get up, undocking my computer and following him. We're in lockstep as we head to the small conference room in silence. Horatio is already there, and he displays his computer screen on the giant monitor above the table on the wall.

Horatio is wearing his standard, perfectly tailored, expensive navy blue suit. His dark hair slicked back, and wristwatch shining. "Hey, Cora. Hey, Jay. Thanks for coming."

We both take a seat across from him. "No problem. This is absolutely our number one priority, so we are at your disposal," I say.

"Good. Let's start with what's happening right now. As you

know, we provided the prosecution with all the documents in regards to the soil inspection reports done by Define. They're stating those reports clearly show the acceptance of the findings, proving the soil was suitable for building a structure of this magnitude." He gestures his head to the monitor and zooms in on the signature field. "As you can see, this was signed off not only by Chris Francis, the Lead Soil Engineer assigned to this project, but also the third party city inspector, and both signatures are dated."

"Yeah. What are you getting at?" I ask, not really sure where this is going. I've read this document a hundred times since the building fell.

Horatio continues, "Look at the inspector's signature. It's nothing more than a dip and a long line." He's right. It kind of looks like a long division symbol. "As we know from our investigation thus far, the inspector that day was Bob Sabin. Cora, could you please bring up other soil reports and look for Bob's signature? I want to compare them."

"Sure," I say, opening my computer and digging through our old soil reports. It will take a minute, so I'm relieved to hear Jay speak up while I hunt this information down.

"While Cora's doing that, I wanted to bring up what I heard at the holiday party. I overheard two men talking outside an empty banquet room I was in. I couldn't really make out their voices to discern who was talking, but I heard one man say, 'The lawsuit is really heating up. This is more than everyone anticipated.' And the other man said, 'Don't worry, that bitch is going down.'" Jay turns his phone over to Horatio and shows him. "I wrote this down and time-stamped it."

Our Legal Counsel reads the note. "Please send this to me. Screenshot this with nothing cut out. I need that time stamp."

"Of course." Jay nods and takes his phone back; sreenshotting right then.

"And you didn't see who it was?"

"No. I tried, but when I exited the room to see, they were already gone."

Horatio thinks for a long moment, furrowing his brow. "Jay, do you think you could call the hotel and ask for security footage from that night. Be as specific as possible about the location. If they give you any pushback, let me know and I'll write up a legal document requesting it."

Jay writes a note to himself. "Of course."

"Alright, I found some of Bob's old reports," I chime in, taking control of the large monitor to display my screen. I have four different reports from over the past six years signed by Bob. "His signature clearly looks like his name." It's jerky and angular, but you can clearly make out *Bob Sabin.*

Horatio interjects, "And it's consistent. Each one looks more or less the same. So, why not this one? I think this could be the new direction I want to work in."

"I agree. And look at these signatures of other inspectors we've had. No other signature looks like this one."

He sits back in his chair, his arm folded over his chest and his other hand holding his dimpled chin as I show file after file of different signatures. "Okay, I'm going to pay the city inspector office a visit and request all previous soil reports from the past five years be sent to us. I want to see if I find any other signatures that match this one."

An email notification pops up in the corner of my screen, reading *Request For Quote - Philadelphia Art Center Auditorium from Maureen Hansel,* and my heart pounds. I *just* sent this quote package to her a few days ago. I open it up, not caring that this is rude to be doing work while I'm in this meeting, but I can't help myself. It takes no time to read the short email.

"Are you kidding me?" I exclaim, rage burning like a fire inside me.

"What's wrong?" Jay asks, looking up at the monitor to see what I'm seeing.

"They rejected our proposal! That quote was airtight; I worked those numbers myself—and they're not even going to counter? No negotiation, no questions? This is bullshit!"

"When did you send the quote?" Horatio asks.

"It's only been three business days. Usually, for a project this size, there are several rounds of fine-tuning, questions, and negotiation before the client makes a final decision. A *quick* answer would be like two weeks after submission."

Horatio leans forward, his elbows planted on the table, and stares at me. "And you've worked with this client before, right?"

"Yeah, for a couple of other projects in recent years. They loved our work. It's literally documented in a couple different architectural magazines how much they loved our design."

"Can you send me those articles and that email?"

"You think this was rejected based on the lawsuit?" I ask.

"I absolutely do. When we win this, we're going to use this as evidence for defamation."

His confidence in winning sets me at ease for the briefest of moments before I put my guard back up and I sigh, "Alright."

"We're going to get through this, Cora." Horatio says. "We have a few promising leads to go off of right now. The battle has not been won."

I nod in agreement, but I don't feel that way. Regardless of the new leads in this case, it feels like the end has already come, and everything my father built is going to sink with me at the helm.

When the meeting ends, I book it out of the conference room. I'm so pissed about the rejected quote that I can't be

WISE ADVICE

around anyone right now. All I want to do is curl up and pull a blanket over my head and never surface again.

Instead, I dial Maureen's number when I get back to my office and close the door. The call goes to voicemail, and I roll my eyes. I present my best collected professional voice and speak once I hear the beep. "Hi Maureen, it's Cora Dalton from Define. I just got your email, and I wanted to talk about it. If you could share your thought process behind your decision, it would really help me. I'd like to know where we can improve. Please give me a call back when you can. Thanks."

I hang up and slump into my chair.

After I broke the news to my staff that we lost the nomination for the auditorium project, I did my best to keep busy the rest of the day. I was too embarrassed to see anyone for longer than necessary.

I left the office early to avoid seeing Jay. I know we had plans tonight, but I can't shake this awful feeling.

When I walk through the doors of the assisted living home, I can already see Aunt Shelly sitting with Mom at one of the tables playing Scrabble. I walk up to them, and Aunt Shelly greets me with an endearing look. "Hi honey. Cora, this is Connie. Connie, this is my niece, Cora. Would it be okay if she sat down with us?"

Mom nods with a big smile, "Certainly. Would you like to play with us? We just started another game."

"I'd love to." I grab a wooden Scrabble rack and a handful of letters from the bag.

I set everything up, and Mom says, "We've already gone, so you can go."

I set my first word down and Mom records the score. "Cora is such a pretty name," she says while looking at her tiles, shifting her focus to me. "It's very fitting for you."

All I can muster out is a small, "Thank you."

Aunt Shelly starts to arrange some tiles on her rack, contemplating her next move. "How's work, darling?"

Her question is simple, but the answer is daunting.

Gross and vicarious negligence.

I don't think I have the ability to talk about my day or the shit storm that's happening right now without breaking down. I sigh, "I'd rather not talk about it to be honest."

"Okay." Her voice has that same soft tone that reminds me so much of my mom's. They share so many features and mannerisms that it's easy to tell they're sisters.

"So, have you been seeing anyone?" she quirks a brow. Not an uncommon question coming from her. She's incredibly nosey but in the sweetest way. She asks me this question at least once a week.

I hesitate, fidgeting with my tiles. I don't really know what to say to this for the first time in a long time. "Uh, not really."

Her eyes light up, and she turns her head towards me. "What do you mean? There *is* someone? Who is it? How is this the first I'm hearing of this?"

Wow, this woman can really read into nothing more than *look* sometimes.

"Don't get excited. It's probably nothing. I don't have time and—" God, I cannot tell my aunt and my mom that it's a friends-with-benefits situation with two men, and I can't emotionally commit to anyone after my divorce... after everything. "—and I just don't think I'm there yet." I give her a knowing look.

She knows why.

She plays her word, counts the score, and writes it down. "I understand, but honey, you need to get out there and enjoy your life while you're still young. I'm not saying you need to settle down with someone, but you need to live your life. Work cannot be your life. Look at your father. He always made sure he made time for you and—" She looks at my mom, who's engrossed in her tiles, and then she looks back at me. "—your mom. You girls were his life. Yes, he loved his job, and he worked hard, but nothing gave him more pride than his family."

"*Decant.* Double word score," Mom says, oblivious to our conversation's meaning.

"I'm just saying, try and let loose once in a while. Go fuck around."

A small laugh bursts out of me, and I cover my shocked mouth. Mom even looks at her with color blushing her cheeks.

"What?" Aunt Shelly sneers. "You're in your early thirties, own your own home, and run your own company. You're not some twenty-year-old with no experience and your whole life to fuck up in front of you. You're a smart woman who can have careless fun if she chooses and it won't ruin your life. So do it."

Can I do this? The three of us are flirting dangerously close to something that feels... binding. I think friends-with-benefits is the most accurate term for us, but is it? The way they flirt, the way they listen, the way they care—I don't know. It's not so clear cut.

Maybe I'm reading too far into this aftercare stuff Marco is so fond of. Honestly, I love it, too. Aftercare is the fucking best. He's supposed to care for me—for us—after a scene. I have no frame of reference outside of them. Is this normal aftercare for a friends-with-benefits situation? Is it more?

But it's *so* tender, and they're *so* affectionate that it's hard to tell if they're just doing this because it's an integral part of the

BDSM agenda, or if they're hoping for more.

It's the *more* part that worries me. I already feel like I have the *most* going on in my life. How am I supposed to make room for more?

Bringing myself back to focus on the ludicrous words of my aunt, I remove my hand from my mouth and chuckle. "Okay. We were supposed to meet up tonight, but—"

"Oh, you're going, young lady," she cuts me off sternly. "You're going to text him and tell him you're coming, finish this game with us, and then leave and have a great time. And I demand you keep doing that if it brings you happiness."

I roll my eyes and smile, pulling out my phone. I see there are already texts from both of them.

> Jay: Hey I can't find u. Did u leave the office already? Are we still on for tonight? I know the meeting this afternoon was hard but we want to help.

> Marco: I do believe I owe you both some relief <wink emoji>

> Cora: Sorry. I'm visiting my mom right now, but I'll be there in about an hour, ok?

> Jay: <big smile emoji> <two eggplant emojis>

> Marco: We'll see you soon, princess <crown emoji>

Chapter 20

Inspection

Cora

When I arrive outside Marco and Jay's townhouse, I sit in my car for a few more moments to collect myself. I know I want this. I need this. I need to feel like someone else has the reins for a little while.

Aunt Shelly is right—if this brings me happiness, I should indulge. My feelings about what this all means with them, be damned.

I take a couple deep breaths and walk up to their door. It swings open before I can even knock, and Jay pulls me inside by grabbing the fabric belt to my coat and tugging me into him. His smile radiates and warms me from the inside out. He's still in his work clothes like me, but he's lost his sweater, and his black dress shirt is almost completely unbuttoned.

He cradles my back as he slams the front door closed with his foot. He gently pushes me with his body to the wall, and I feel like prey the way he's looking at me.

"Good evening, ma'am." My body vibrates with desire at his words. "I've been on edge all day thinking about you." And *I* can very much feel that edge poking me right now.

He grinds into me, and my hands glide up his bare chest to his neck. "Good evening Mr. Bishop," I smirk.

He lowers his mouth to kiss my neck, and I close my eyes. He starts to untie my coat while murmuring against my skin, "May I take your coat?" Wordlessly, I agree, and he smooths his hands over my collarbone and shoulders, letting it slide off, and then tosses it behind him to lay over the couch back.

When he turns to me, I pull him in for a scorching kiss. He feels so good pressed against me. He tastes like the distraction I need.

"Where's Marco?" I pant.

"He's upstairs," he hums, kissing me between his words. "I'm in charge of making you comfortable and escorting you to the bedroom."

I chuckle and drag my hands to his ass. "Oh, you're an escort now? Do I not pay you well enough?"

"Ma'am, I will be anything you want."

I think about his words and answer him honestly. "I want to be used. I want to escape."

He lowers himself to one knee, picks up each foot, and removes my heels. He stares at me, his eyes darkening. "*That* we can do for you."

When he stands back up, he grips my hips and drags his body against mine, then tugs me towards the staircase. With his hand clasped in mine, he leads me up to the top landing but stops in front of the bedroom door. "Do you need to freshen up or use the bathroom before we go in? Because he's in full Dom mode right now, and once we go in, I don't think we're leaving for a while."

I really should try and pee before I go in there. Maybe then I won't soak the sheets this time. "Yeah. Where is the bathroom? You guys didn't exactly give me a grand tour last time I was here."

Jay chuckles and shows me a simple but warm guest room, Marco's home massage studio, fully outfitted with a proper table, a shelf with a Himalayan sea salt lamp, a diffuser, a hot fridge, and various oils. I definitely want to come back here at some point.

Then he shows me to the guest bathroom. It's a standard three-piece bathroom with masculine energy. Dark gray towels neatly hang from the bar, and everything is pristinely clean.

I turn to face Jay. "Thank you. I'll just be a minute."

"Take your time."

When he closes the door, I do my business and wash my hands while staring at myself in the mirror. Somehow, the feelings Jay had just worked into me have already faded, and I can't help but see the failure that I am. I've been denied that auditorium project, failing my company. The lawsuit looms over me like a storm cloud that never dissipates.

I don't deserve to be here. What was I thinking? I can't escape my responsibilities to this firm. I need to be thinking of ways to get us out of this mess, not fucking my subordinate and his boyfriend.

I'm shaken out of my thoughts by a soft knock on the door. "Cora? Are you okay?" Jay whispers through the door. It's then I realize I've been in here far longer than I thought, lost to my own self-loathing. I swipe away at an errant tear.

When did I start crying?

"I'm fine." My words are curt, and I steel myself to walk out there. I open the door to see Jay standing against the wall, and his smile falters. "I need to go. I'm sorry."

I start to move past him, but he blocks me, moving his hands to my shoulders and ducking his head to meet my eyes. "Hey, what's wrong? What happened?"

"It's nothing. It's just something I need to deal with."

A look of realization crosses his face. "Oh. You know, Marco and I don't care if you're on your period. Also, there are tampons under the sink in there if you need them."

I smile and drop my head. Sickos. "No, it's not that. I just... don't think I should be here when there's so much work to do."

He takes my chin in his fingers and lifts it tenderly. "I'm not trying to pressure you, and if you really want to leave, you can, but I really think you need to let off some steam." When I don't respond, he tucks me under his arm and leads me to his bedroom. "Let's just have a talk, okay?"

"Okay," I sigh.

He opens the door, and I see Marco sitting in the corner of the room in the armchair. His jean-clad legs look powerful and spread wide, his feet bare and his gaze stern. His dark curly hair is so shiny in the low lamp light that it reflects off it. But as soon as he sees us, he can tell something is wrong and his features shift. He furrows his brow and stands up. "What's wrong, princess?"

Jay leads me to the foot of the bed, where Marco joins us. He sits down, his large tattooed arms wrap around me, and he pulls me to his chest so I can still see Jay sitting next to us. Marco puts my head on his shoulder, his short beard rubbing against my hair, and I feel like I have a weighted blanket wrapped around me. Without even speaking yet, he's calmed me down.

"Talk to us. What's going on?" Marco asks, his chest filling with air and releasing slowly.

"I have work to do. I need to go," I mumble, defeated.

"It can't wait until tomorrow?" he asks softly. "Also, how much more work needs to get done? Isn't tomorrow your last day in office for the rest of the year? People are already leaving for their vacations and checking out."

"I found out today we didn't get this big job, and it's probably because the lawsuit is making us look bad. I need to figure out how we're going to recover from this. I need to make sure all our other proposals are tight. I need to make sure all our current projects are on schedule."

Jay speaks next. "Cora, you know the other projects are on track. They give you a status update three times a week—and don't tell me you don't review those other proposals every day, looking for areas to improve. I'd like to point out that it's literally *not* your job to do that. You have a top-notch design and estimating team that does this." He raises an eyebrow. "Am I wrong?"

I pause. "No," I mutter.

"Don't you remember why we're doing this, princess? Other than the fact that you're gorgeous and smart and wonderful," Marco adds with a smile.

I sigh, knowing what he wants me to say. "Because I need to give up some control."

"That's right," his voice shifts a little into that lower register, his tone more demanding. "So, you are going to listen and obey, do you understand, princess?"

Even though he's wrapped around me like a boa constrictor, I know I have the option to say stop, to say no, and get out of here, but my aunt's words ring in my ear.

"You know, I saw my Aunt Shelly tonight when I went to visit my mom." I softly giggle and continue, "She pretty much told me to fuck around if it brought me happiness."

Marco chuckles, and the rumble in his chest reverberates through me. Then Jay brings my hand to his mouth, kisses it, and asks, "And do we?"

"Very much."

Jay leans in and gives me a soft kiss. "So, you'll stay?"

"I will."

Marco grabs my neck and squeezes lightly. "Good girl," he purrs into my ear. He stands, taking me with him. "Now why don't we resume, hmm?" Jay stands and presses against me as Marco continues. "I'm going to sit down and watch you undress each other."

He steps away, and we both say, "Yes, Sir."

Marco sits back down, his hands lying on each rounded leather armrest. "Shirts," he says simply.

My hands quickly find the last two buttons of Jay's dress shirt, and I slide it off his shoulders slowly, staring into his eyes. I have a feeling Marco wants us to take our time with this.

He grabs the shirt before it hits the floor and folds it, placing it on the dresser a couple feet away. When he steps back, he helps me out of my sweater, folds it, and places it on his shirt.

"Skirt."

Jay leans in, his hands sliding over my waist to my back, where he unzips it and slowly pulls it down as he kneels. His face is mere inches away from my panties, and I can feel his breath as he looks at me. I place my hands on his strong shoulders and step out of my skirt, allowing him to take it and add it to the pile. I stand there in my light blue lace panties and bra.

"Pants."

I unbuckle his belt and let the dark green slacks drop, exposing Jay's tight black briefs. His erection is prominent. I bend over, giving Marco a very clear view of my backside, and pick up the pants to fold and set aside.

"Showing off, princess? Why don't you show me more. Let's get a *really* good look," he says with the most sinister tone. "Take off her bra and panties and give them to me. Then position her on the bed for inspection, prince."

"Yes, Sir." Jay obeys his commands, giving him the last pieces of my clothing, then he moves me to the bed and positions me on all fours. I'm completely exposed to both of them, but it thrills me to no end to be objectified like this.

"Touch her, prince. Describe her. Is she of good breeding?"

Jay runs a smooth hand up my spine and purrs, "Beautiful structure." He sifts through my hair and grabs a tight hold, making me moan softly. "Lush, thick curls of hair," he rumbles, desire thick in his words.

Then he runs his hands to hold each breast and weighs them. "Large, heavy tits. Enough for both of us, Sir."

"And what about her sex, prince?"

Jay takes one hand, and with a feather-light touch, he cups my pussy. "I can feel her heat; she's radiating warmth." He presses his hand in and slides his fingers through my lower lips. "And she's soaking wet for you, Sir. Absolutely drenched."

"Based on how wet her panties are, I'd say she's been like this all day." Marco clicks his tongue. "Poor, needy little thing. Open her wide," he commands, and I feel Jay use both hands to spread my ass open for Marco's viewing pleasure.

Oh my god, this is so degrading—shame and lust fight for dominance in my body. I want more.

"Perfect holes for whatever you desire, Sir."

"Do you think we should keep her, prince?"

Jay squeezes me and breathes deep. "Please, Sir. We can take good care of her."

Suddenly, I'm not positive that this scenario only has *one* pretend meaning anymore. It feels like what they're saying is something real. Maybe that's just my submissive brain taking over. I *do* feel lost in Marco's commands.

"She does appear to be in excellent condition. An exceptional form. It's settled then, my prince. We can keep her."

"Thank you, Sir."

I hear Marco lift off the leather chair. "But you know what?" he asks and grabs my jaw, yanking me up onto my knees and staring at me with that serious look. Then he rubs his bearded cheek against mine and growls, "She needs to be trained. She needs to be *branded*."

He releases me, and the loss of his touch is like an ache. He steps away and goes to the chest to open it, and leans down to gather some rope. "Get naked and mirror her position, prince." Jay quickly does as he says as Marco continues talking and pulling ropes out. "Face to face and hold each other's hands."

When he steps back over to us, Marco asks me, "You're okay with being tied up, beautiful? I remember seeing that you were on your questionnaire... I just want to make sure that's still the case."

I nod, "Yes, Sir. No changes in my answers."

"And if you don't like what's happening, what do you say?"

"Stop or no, Sir."

"Good girl."

He makes quick but assured work of tying our wrists together. I meet Jay's eyes, and we both smile. It's hard not to with him. How can someone be so sweet and goofy and yet so sexy? I want to laugh with him as much as I want to fuck him.

And with Marco... he has such a commanding presence. He can soothe me and dominate me. He has this way of centering me, allowing me to focus once again.

Marco tugs on the ropes. "How does it feel?"

"Good. Not too tight," Jay says.

I flex my fingers and can feel decent blood flow. "Good, Sir."

Marco then pulls a condom out of his pocket, opens it, and rolls it on Jay's hard-on, all the way to the base, where he gives his balls a firm tug. Jay lets out a haggard breath, but Marco releases him and moves his hand to my sex, sliding two fingers through my slit. He hums in appreciation. "You weren't lying, prince. *Fuck*, she's ready." He removes his hand and sucks his fingers clean of my arousal. "On your back, princess. Hands above your head."

A wave of excitement crashes over me as Jay steers me down to the bed, his eyes never looking away from mine. I can feel his massive erection nestle between my thighs as I spread my legs for him. His warmth mixing with mine has me pulsing my hips ever so slightly. His thick, yet silky black hair falling forward.

And as if he was reading our thoughts, Marco commands us, "Kiss."

Oh, thank god.

Our mouths crash in a desperate tangle of lust; our tongues dance together, and I want more of him. I want to devour him. I feel the bed shift, most likely Marco kneeling behind Jay.

He groans into my mouth, "Yes. Thank you, Sir."

"You like it when I lick your asshole, prince?"

Jay sighs against my lips, "Yes, Daddy."

Oh my god. I've always thought the term Daddy was cringy, but hearing Jay say it makes my stomach drop and my pussy throb. Holy shit, that's hot.

Then I can feel Jay's crown slide up and down against my clit, Marco clearly in control of his lover's cock. "Enter her slowly." He holds him still as Jay pushes inside, stretching me, filling me with every glorious inch of himself.

"Now, hold still," our sir commands, and it's so difficult not to move my hips, but then I see him in the corner of my vision, and he picks up the flogger.

Jay

All I want to do is move inside Cora. She's so warm and tight that it's borderline impossible not to jerk my hips. And her kiss... *Jesus Christ*, how am I holding it together right now?

Marco comes back to me, his strong hands bracing my hips as he dives his face between my ass and then adds a finger. We've been doing this long enough that it doesn't take much prep for me anymore, but I still appreciate it.

He pulls away and grips my backside hard. "We'll use the traffic light system, okay?"

"Yes, Sir."

Then I can feel the flogger graze over my back, and a chill runs over me. The thin leather strips trail down my body, and I realize he's waiting for my next answer. "Green light, Sir."

He starts to gently smack me, but it's a tease more than anything. I want him to be ruthless. I want to quiver from the pain.

"Please, Sir. I need it. I need you."

"And what about your princess? Do you need her?"

I can feel her soft body beneath me, her scent filling my head as I nip at her neck. "I do, Sir."

Just then, he lets go, the flogger stinging my thighs. It's not the hardest hit, I know he's warming me up, but that doesn't take away from that initial jolt of pain.

Cora gasps, and I look at her as she whispers, "That felt good." And I realize I just thrust into her without purposefully doing so.

Marco keeps going, and I can't help but jerk each time. "You only thrust when the pain tells you you need to, do you understand?"

I'm frantically kissing Cora's neck and collarbone when I

murmur, "Yes, Sir. Thank you."

Marco keeps going. Each hit in a different spot. Each hit getting a little stronger than the last. If I could see my ass and thighs, I would be able to see them glowing red. Thank god he's letting me move inside her because I don't think I could hold back at this point. Each slap of that flogger creates this urge to bury myself deeper in her.

"Light?" Marco asks

"Green, Sir," I pant.

"Green!" Cora exclaims quickly, and Marco chuckles.

But now Marco really lets me have it. I can't even be sure how long he's been doing this, but I know he's hitting hard and fast and I can't help but whimper countless *Thank You*'s as I rut into this goddess below me—and that's exactly what I'm doing because as he stops his assault, I *can't* stop myself from this primal state I'm in.

He growls from behind me, "I thought I said you only thrust when the pain tells you to."

"I'm sorry, Sir. I can't stop. I need... I need..."

Crack!

I yelp and throw my hips in one deep, clenching motion as he slaps my ass *hard* with his bare hand.

"Then it looks like your turn is over. Get on top of him, princess. Show him what restraint looks like. Show him what a good girl you can be."

She squeezes her legs around me and without pulling out, I roll us over, our hands still bound together above our heads. As she straddles me, she gives me a smile and silently mouths the word *smooth* as I return her remark with a kiss.

Just as it starts to deepen, I see Marco sit beside us, lean down and kiss the arch of Cora's foot. He murmurs against it, "Sweetheart, are you comfortable if I use a plug in you?"

She pauses for a moment. "Um... yes?"

"You don't sound certain," he assesses, his nose tracing up and down the sole of her foot.

"I like the idea of it, I just... I think I would want my own, is all. No offense. I'm sure you guys clean your gear well, it's just—"

"Well, it's a good thing I got you your own today, isn't it?"

"You what?"

He leaves our side and goes to the chest to pull out a black silk bag with a ribbon drawstring. He opens it and pulls out a black silicone butt plug. It looks to be an appropriate size for a novice like herself—well, a novice who's about to take a big cock afterward.

A smirk crosses his beautifully gruff face. "So, what will it be, princess? My fingers or this?" he croons casually.

"I'd like to try the toy, Sir."

"Yeah, you would. Good."

As Marco gets ready, I look Cora in the eyes and whisper, "You're positive?"

"I had his cock in my ass yesterday, Jay," she whispers back, "I think a little plug will be fine."

I smile and kiss her, "As long as you're sure. Tell us to stop if you want to."

She nods, "I know."

"Alright, princess—now breathe for me. Relax." Marco pauses, and I watch Cora's face scrunch up, and I feel her pussy tighten around my dick. "Tell me where you are, Cora."

"Yellow, Sir. Can you just keep it there for a little bit?"

"Of course," he replies. "Do you need more lube?"

"No, Sir. I just need a minute."

"You're doing great, ma'am," I soothe. I wish I could touch her with my hands right now. I want to hold her and pet her to get through this.

After about five more minutes gradually going deeper, allowing Cora to adjust, Marco grins behind her. "It's all the way in, sweetheart. Look at you. You're perfect. Are you ready for more?"

"Yes, Sir," she whines, and Marco reaches into his pocket and pulls out a little black disc of some kind. It looks like a car key fob, and presses it with his thumb. "Whoa!" Cora jolts, and my cock is rewarded with her squeezing me as I feel... "It vibrates?" she pants.

Marco smirks, leans down, and kisses her butt. "It vibrates," he purrs.

"Oh my god, it vibrates," I groan.

Without him even asking, she smiles, "Thank you, Sir. Green light. Green, green, green."

Marco chuckles and picks up the flogger. He does the same thing to her and drags it over her body. She relaxes into me, and I tell her how beautiful she is. How strong she is. How much she's going to love the pain. Her cheek rests against mine, and I look at my boyfriend. He gives me a look that says *it's time,* and I nod.

Cora gasps at the first impact, and I feel that tight squeeze from her. Fuck it's good. Marco pauses, waiting for any signs of distress, but she gives none and confirms, "Green, Sir."

With every strike to her backside, I feel her pussy like a vise grip, and the rare moments she's not contracting around me, I feel the vibrations from the toy lodged inside her—so no matter what, I feel an intense sensation. I can't imagine what she's going through then. I'm trying my best not to move, but my patience is running thin.

"That's it, you fucking pain slut. You want more?" Marco bellows.

"Please, Sir."

He strikes her hard. "Then tell me who's in charge."

"You are, Sir," she whimpers.

"That's right." Another hit. "I'm in charge. I'm in charge of your pain." Another hit. "Your pleasure." Another hit. "Your burdens." Another hit. "You *will* give them to me, and you will *not* fight it, do you understand me?" Another hit.

"Yes, Sir!" she cries out. *Really* cries. Tears are falling down her face and I kiss them.

"Who takes care of you, princess?"

"You do, Sir."

Marco drops the flogger and takes his t-shirt off, exposing that chiseled chest and stomach, tattoos covering his pecs and arms, tendrils of curls dusting his entire torso and converging in a line down to his groin. He slides his belt out of the loop. And it's impossible not to notice his enormous erection begging to be let out. How does he have this kind of restraint?

I bite my lip as I see him quickly take himself out of his boxers and jeans and place them on the side of the bed. He grabs the belt, folds it in half, and it cracks over her skin. She lets out a scream as her arms clench around my head, and she lifts off of me slightly before settling back in my lap.

"Color," Marco demands.

"Green, Sir," she sobs.

He hits her again and again and again, each one intensifying what I feel and her cries.

"Fuck her, prince."

He doesn't have to tell me twice. I bend my legs and thrust up into her tight channel. She moans and I lose my mind. Her head rests in my neck, and I hear the crack of the belt a few more times before Cora floods me with her orgasm.

"Oh shit," she cries out as I continue to pump into her, her ejaculate splashing everywhere.

I close my eyes and revel in her wet, quivering pussy, but never let up.

"That's my girl," Marco purrs. "God, I love it when you do that. And my prince... you are doing so well, but I need you to stop."

Marco

He listens like the good boy he is, and I move to untie their hands. As I finish, I lean down to kiss each of them. Cora's in a daze already and Jay is barely keeping it together.

I take a condom from the nightstand, quickly roll it down my shaft, make my way to the other side of the king bed, and lay down. With both hands, I tap my thighs, "Come join me, princess. She slides off Jay, and I grab her by the waist, guiding her to a reverse cowgirl position. She tries to lower herself, but I stop her. "Ah, ah, ah. Wrong hole, honey." I grab the lube from the nightstand by me, and apply a generous amount to my cock. Yes, we have lube in both nightstands. And the shower. And hidden in the couch cushions. And in the laundry room. And the kitchen.

I grab hold of the vibrating toy in her ass and start to work it in and out for a couple of minutes before I bring it all the way out and hear the sloppy *pop* sound. She moans from the loss, and I hand it to Jay, who's lying next to us and watching intently. He takes it, and puts it on the nightstand for now.

I apply more lube to her asshole and start to rub the head of my throbbing cock against it. "Do you want this, princess?"

"Yes, Sir. I want this."

"Good. I'm going to ease you in slowly. You tell me when you're ready for more." She begins to lower herself but stops before the head is even halfway in.

"Fuck, you're big."

"Jay, help her feel more comfortable."

He sits up and kneels in front of her, taking her mouth with his and wrapping an arm around her waist, the other behind her head.

She sinks a fraction of an inch lower. "Take her hair down," I command. And when he does, her hair falling out from her bun, he fluffs it out for her, and I'm mesmerized by how long it is. It reminds me of ivy spreading over the side of a country home.

Jay begins to kiss her neck and moves lower to hold her breasts and suck on her nipples. She must enjoy it because she lowers herself enough that my whole crown finally goes in, and my breath hitches.

"Good girl," I muster out and slide my hands everywhere I can touch. "You're doing so well, princess."

After a few more minutes, she finally does it. She's completely seated on me as she moans and whimpers. She gives a few exploratory bounces. "I'm ready, Sir."

"You feel good?" I give a little flex of my hips. "There's no pain?"

"There's no pain right now. It feels good. But I could do with more, Sir."

A smile crosses my face. She's perfect.

"But—" she begins to argue, and I know she's going to try and tell me she's too heavy, so I want to shut it down before she can utter those ridiculous words.

"No buts. Do it. Your job is to obey me and that is it."

"Yes, Sir," she hesitantly agrees, and starts to lean back from her straddling position. Jay helps her down, and just when I think she's going to untuck her legs to straighten them out, she sighs and nuzzles herself into my neck. Content.

Puzzled, I ask, "Are you comfortable with your legs like that?"

"Yes, Sir. Very. I've always been flexible."

I move my gaze to Jay's, and we exchange a lewd smirk. I grab hold of Cora's neck and whisper in the lowest tone I have, "*This* is valuable information, princess. Put your hands behind my head." I feel her skin prickle over mine at my words as I begin to thrust into her slowly. "Put your mouth to good use, prince."

He eagerly descends on the both of us, alternating between her and I, between his mouth and fingers as I feel him lick my taint and fondle my balls. Between him and my drive into Cora's tight heat, I'm in ecstasy. Cora moans and I feel the vibrations in her neck under my hand. "That's it. Let yourself go. We've got you."

With my other hand, I squeeze her ample breast and pinch her stiff nipples. "You need more, princess?"

"Please, Sir," she whimpers.

"Get inside her, prince."

He sits up and kneels on one leg, touching my inner thigh, the other over our opposite hips. "Absolutely, Sir." He obeys, lining himself up. I slow my pace and watch his face crumble when he enters her again. "Oh, ma'am... Thank you, Sir," he whispers and grabs her waist. He starts to thrust deep and I love feeling his cock inside her next to mine. I'm not sure why, but somehow this woman makes me feel even more connected to Jay than I already am. She feels like the solder between two interlocking rings. The rings were always made for each other, but the solder binds them together forever. I wonder if Jay feels that, too. I wonder if Cora even *wants* to be the solder. *I pray she does.*

Cora's cries pull me out of my fantasy daydream and back to

the very real fantasy happening before me. I can tell she's as close as I am, and I want to push her over the edge. I slap my hand against her tit and tell Jay, "Keep slapping her here. Pinch her hard." When he moves his hands to do so, I bring mine down to her cunt and dig my fingers into her soft flesh, pulling and pinching without mercy.

"Oh, fuck! I'm gonna come, Sir." She pulls at the back of my head and I feel her whole body start to clench. Our bodies sliding against one another is sweat-slick bliss.

I keep my pace and coax her, "That's it, princess. Come for us. *Come* on our dicks right now," I growl.

"Yes!" she shouts, and I can't help but erupt inside her as she constricts around me.

I then furiously rub her clit, and she releases that dam once again. "Good fucking girl." I watch Jay's face as he locks his eyes on the show beneath him. His mouth agape, and eyes lit up like fireworks. Like he's never seen anything more spectacular in his life.

But then that expression quickly changes as his hips lose their rhythm, and he grunts out, "*Fuck, yes. Goddammit.*"

The three of us are silent and motionless, save for the heavy breathing. I turn my head to Cora's and kiss her with such reverence, unable to believe how perfect she is. "You did beautifully, my dear." Without releasing her, I take my hand and run it up Jay's calf muscle at my side. "You, too, prince. Come on—both of you lay down and relax."

When we ease out of her, she groans, and Jay pulls her up. She looks at the wreckage beneath us and says in a daze, "*Shit*, I'm so sorry. Your mattress is soaked."

Guiding her to the middle, I have Jay spoon her, and I turn on my side to face her, rubbing my toes against theirs. She places her hand on my chest and I shake my head. "Don't worry about it. I got a waterproof mattress liner today."

She giggles through her daze and rubs her face. "Wow, a waterproof sheet *and* a butt plug? You spoil me."

I nip at her nose and playfully add, "If you'd let us, we'd never stop."

Her brows furrow, as much as they can based on her blissed-out state. "What?"

Jay murmurs against her shoulder, "Cora, we know it's fast, but we want to be with you. We want to take care of you. We want to be your partners... or boyfriends, or whatever you want to call us."

She stares at me, her face a little shocked, and I nod, taking her cheek in my hand. "It's true."

"I–I don't know," she whispers. "Guys, you don't know that much about me. I don't really know all that much about you. I have baggage."

"So do we," I say, resting my hand next to Jay's on her hip. "But we'd like to learn about every single piece of you."

She sighs and looks over her shoulder to Jay. "This is kind of unexpected. I sort of resigned myself to being single because I don't exactly have the time to dedicate to a relationship."

Jay kisses her shoulder again. "Well, it's a good thing I work with you and get to see you all the time."

She looks back at me. "I think you need to understand that we're not fair-weather men. When we say we want to take care of you, *know* that we mean it. We want to make your life easier."

I kiss her lips. "Better." Another kiss. "Just as we know you can make ours."

"Guys, I'm divorced," she blurts.

"Sounds like you're trying to scare us off," Jay muses. "That's not gonna work."

"Do you still love him?" I ask.

"Hell no," she answers quickly.

I grin. "Then we see no issue."

She inhales a deep breath, and I'm inwardly thankful she isn't bolting with this discussion. "Can I think about it?"

"Absolutely, sweetheart," I say, brushing the stray curls away from her face. "What would you say to joining us on our little vacation to the Poconos tomorrow after work?"

Her body goes rigid. "Tomorrow?"

"Yeah," I smirk. "We'll be there for a week and come back the morning of New Year's Eve. Unless you have plans already?"

"Well, not exactly." She considers. "I was going to spend more time at the assisted living home with my mom." I keep quiet and let her think it over. "But Aunt Shelly did tell me to live a little—and all my cousins *are* coming to visit her throughout the week." I can practically see the gears turning in her brain, making this scenario work.

Jay speaks up, "We can play house and get to know each other on a deeper level. We can pretend we're really together so you can get a sense of what it would be like."

When she closes her eyes and smiles, I know we've hooked her. She sighs, "Okay." Jay raises his hand, and I high-five it, both of us grinning like idiots. "I can't believe you're springing a vacation on me, and I have, like, zero time to pack."

I kiss her, humming into her mouth, "Mmm, this is a clothing optional trip." She chuckles, and I add, "We have some wardrobe options here for you if you want to take them."

"What do you mean?" she asks.

I get up off the bed and make my way to the dresser where I pull out brand-new leggings, sweatpants, and warm winter socks.

"They're cut for women, and just in case they don't fit, I have other sizes, too."

She sits up to get a better look. "Why did you buy me these?"

"Because we didn't have any pants for you to wear home last time, and you had to wear your work clothes. We wanted you to be warm and comfy. Oh, that reminds me, I also got you these slipper boot things. They're downstairs."

She gapes at me and then at Jay, who has a smug look on his face. "Just let us take care of you, okay?"

She looks back at me and feels the soft fabric of the socks. "This is... very thoughtful, you guys. Thank you."

I lean down and crawl to her, pushing her back down into Jay's arms and rubbing my cheek against hers. "Now stay right here and let me get you some pain relievers. Then we're all going to shower, get in our soft clothes, and eat. Is that understood?"

"Yes, Sir," they both smile.

I'm a lucky man.

Chapter 21

Oh, She's Rich

Jay

When I hang up the phone with the hotel, I shoot an email to Horatio to let him know that they've agreed to send over the security camera footage from that night. Relieved I got them to agree to this without hesitation sets me at ease, and puts me in an even better mood to leave the office today for our vacation.

There's barely anyone here, and it's not even 10:00 am when a new company-wide email comes across my inbox from our fearless leader herself telling everyone to have a happy holiday break and leave the office by lunch time. She herself is working from home today, and I have a feeling it's because we sprung a last-minute trip on her, and she's panic-packing.

Our plan is to pick her up at her place in the afternoon and then make the two-hour drive to our rental cabin in the mountains. To say I'm excited is an understatement. I'm positively giddy. Marco and Cora all to myself for an entire week sounds like perfection.

After Cora left last night, Marco and I talked about our strategy to woo her. If we're going to do this poly thing, then we really need to make it seem possible and worth the judgmental remarks from others. I'm sure my parents are going to be weirded out by this, not to mention the firm's confusion.

But I can't think about everyone else; I have to focus on what both of them mean to me—and that's everything. I want to be everything to them. I want to provide for them, care for them, love them. I want to make them happy and feel safe. But more than anything, I want their trust. I know I have Marco's, but I need Cora's, too. She obviously trusts us with her body, which is truly a gift I will not squander, but if this relationship is really going to work, we need to show her she can trust us with her heart and mind.

And that's exactly what we plan to do on this trip.

My phone dings, and it's a text from one of my many cousins. My favorite.

> **Isabelle:** WTF Jay! I just heard you guys aren't going to be at xmas this year. Who's going to chug wine in grandma's dank basement and play family phrase bingo with me if you're not there?

> **Jay:** LOL. I'm sorry! Let's do it at Easter. Nothing says Christ is Risen like getting shwasted and listening to Uncle Chuck explain his newest "lucrative" business endeavor and try to get the family to invest.

> Isabelle: How he's still allowed to be in the family after the marijuana farm went bust and the SEC is on his ass is beyond me.

> Isabelle: Why aren't you going to be there? Mom said you guys weren't coming but didn't know why.

I sigh, trying to decide if I want to tell her the other reason I won't be there. Honestly, if I wasn't going on this trip, I wonder if I would even want to come this year after what happened with my parents. Ultimately, I decide I should tell her. I know she'll understand.

> Jay: Marco and I are going to the Poconos for the week as a gift to each other. Also, I'm not sure I'd feel comfortable around my parents right now. Mom kinda blew up at me recently. I told her I was trying to connect to my Korean heritage, to learn more about it because I feel like a significant part of my identity is missing. She got angry at me for "being ungrateful" for my childhood. We haven't spoken since then <sad face emoji>

I decide to leave out the bit about Cora coming with us because it's too new, and as much as I trust Isabelle, I don't need her accidentally letting it slip that Marco and I are trying to form a throuple.

Isabelle: Whoa, I'm so sorry that happened. Why is it that our parents think they have a right to treat us like this just because they raised us? Like, you were just trying to explain your feelings and this new development in your life and now they're going to punish you for it? Rude <eye roll emoji>

Jay: Yeah. It's been really hard not talking to them. I don't really know how to approach the subject again. She said not to talk to her until I can be grateful and appreciate what they gave me.

Isabelle: That's BS. Your feelings are valid and they're seriously delusional to tell you your relationship with them depends wholly on their terms. That's not how a loving relationship works. I'm sorry. Let me know if I can help you in any way. <heart emoji>

Jay: Thanks, cuz. Ur a real one. I hope u still manage to have a good xmas without me. Maybe start a rumor that Aunt Pam has a secret prison boyfriend in Florida.

> Isabelle: LMAO Yes! Great idea. I love you, dude. Merry Christmas.

> Jay: Love u, too.

I set my phone down on the desk as Chris Francis walks into my office. He's wearing what appears to be a slight variation of his standard work attire: a thin black puffer vest, light blue checkered dress shirt, and khakis.

He steps in a few feet and leans against the open door, crossing his arms, and smiles. "Hey Jay, how's it going?"

"Good, Chris," I reply, a little confused as to why he's here. He's not really someone I've spoken to much since starting. That's not to say he doesn't have some kind of HR question he needs answered, though. "Are you packing up your stuff to get out of here soon? Cora just sent that email letting us know to start our vacations early. Don't know if you saw it or not."

He huffs a small, humorless laugh, "Uh, no. I didn't read her email."

Okay... Where is he going with this?

"I was wondering if you can tell me anything about the lawsuit," he casually asks.

"Well, you know as much as everyone else. Cora and Horatio have been sending updates as they develop," I tell him. As a whole, the executive team decides what information we tell our staff, and we've been forthright with that, but we certainly don't divulge any leads or strategies we're taking.

He shrugs. "Yeah, but like... you're in the mix, right? You can see where this case is headed."

Putting on my best neutral expression, I place my forearms on the desk and lean forward. "I'm sorry, Chris. I can't discuss the case with you more than your contribution as the project's

Soil Engineer. Do you have any new information you need to discuss?"

"No. I just thought maybe you could—" he hesitates and seems to search for something to say. "Never mind, actually. I just find the whole thing so interesting, you know? I'm just being nosey." He pushes off his lean and gives a quick wave before leaving. "Anyway, have a good one."

"You, too, Chris," I call after him.

I replay his words: *I just find the whole thing so interesting?* The man is the Lead Soil Engineer for a major building failure resulting in a lawsuit. I wouldn't be so cavalier about that.

I document the interaction I had with Chris, save it, and send it to Horatio. It could very well be nothing, but it just seemed suspicious.

A couple hours later, Marco and I pull up in my SUV to the curb in front of Cora's townhouse, and both of us stare in silence. This is not your typical Philadelphia townhouse. This is stunning. The façade looks to be huge slabs of pale granite with decorative historic windows and a large archway over a set of tall arched wooden doors with large glass windows and wrought iron door knobs. There is a placard on one of the doors with the house number and street, clearly indicating this is a historic home.

I look over at Marco in the driver's seat. "I mean, I figured she had money, but I didn't know she had *this* kind of money."

He unbuckles his seat belt. "Well, let's not jump to any conclusions. Come on, let's go get her."

Getting out of the car, we walk up the stone steps and knock using the lion's head door knocker. We can see all her bags in the foyer—*yes, a full foyer*—with another set of solid wood doors about five feet from the front ones. She opens the interior doors and upon seeing us, she gives a big smile. Her hair flows down her shoulders and she's wearing a matching oat-colored athleisure outfit. The fitted long-sleeve shirt tucks into her high-waisted sweats, and every curve of her body is on display.

"Hi, guys," she beams, and gestures to the numerous bags sitting in the foyer. "Sorry, I know it seems like I'm bringing a lot, but you weren't clear on what we'd be doing, so I may have over packed. Also, I hope the owners of the rental don't mind having a cat because I can't find a sitter for George at the last minute so she's coming with us." She's clearly worked up because she's rambling, and it's adorable.

The pair of us wrap her up in a hug, and before she can say any more, I give her a long, drugging kiss, and she sighs in relief. When I pull away, Marco brushes his thumb over her cheek. "Relax, sweetheart. Vacation starts now." He gives her a chaste kiss. "Why don't you show your boyfriends your home, and then we'll pack up the car."

She gives a silent giggle, "Plural. Okay, yes. Follow me."

If we were stunned outside her place, we're even more so inside. She shows us the main floor, with a sitting room in front, and moving back, there's a gorgeous kitchen on the left with white marble counters, open railing wood stairs on the right, dining and then living room towards the back. The basement has a guest room, bathroom, and workout studio. When she takes us up to the second floor, I can't help but notice all the artwork. She explains it's a mix of her father's work, real artists, thrifted finds, and *her own*. God, she blows me away.

When we reach the second floor, it's another living room/library and an art studio, bathroom, and laundry room. Everything in this place looks to be original except the furniture, which she said is mostly her own. Gorgeous wood casings, high ceilings, ornate fireplaces in almost every room, all beautifully decorated.

Yup, we're dating an architect all right. This woman has *style*.

She tells us this house was designed by a famous architect named Frank Furness in 1850 and it was her childhood home. When her father passed away last year, he left it to her knowing Cora's mom wouldn't be able to take care of it.

We keep going up and she shows us her bedroom. It looks so soft and light. Pale blue walls mix with fluffy white bedding and a sand colored fabric headboard. It reminds me of a beach or watching the clouds on a summer day. She shows us three more guest rooms, two bathrooms and another level. *Five* levels in all.

As we make our way back to the foyer, I ask, "You don't have any siblings? What did you do with such a big house with just a family of three?"

"My cousins were over all the time. Believe it or not, it was a madhouse. Laughter and chaos everywhere," she says with a longing smile.

"I love that," I say, picking up her large duffel and a bag of cat food. "I had a similar childhood actually. We can talk more about this in the car, but let's load up. Is this everything?"

She looks behind in the sitting room and grabs the cat carrier housing an angry George. She huffs a laugh and with an amused expression shakes her head. "She's gonna hate you guys."

Marco and I chuckle and load up her things in my SUV. She heads back to the door to lock up, but then I see her come back out with a laptop bag slung over her shoulder. When she gets in the front seat next to me, I give her a quizzical look. "You're not working on this trip are you?"

She gives me a sassy side eye. "Don't. I'm the CEO; I never stop working."

I pull away from the curb as she buckles in. "How much were you planning on working?"

"Mmm... maybe five or six hours each day."

"What?" Marco and I both exclaim.

"Absolutely not ma'am," I say. "*One* hour each day, and that's it."

"Four," she counters.

"Thirty minutes."

She groans, "Fine. One hour."

"You're going to be too busy with us anyway," Marco says, leaning forward from the back seat to squeeze her shoulders.

She leans into it. "I promise not to work at all if you keep touching me."

"Deal."

Halfway through our trip, I realize Cora is a huge K-Pop fan and has a degree in BTS. I had her connect a playlist so we could get a sense of her music preferences, and wow. She calls this her Boy Band playlist and it has everything from The Backstreet Boys and N*sync, to The Jonas Brothers and BTS. She sings along to every lyric as I cranked the volume and hold her hand tight.

"You know more Korean than I do," I tell her with a self deprecating grin.

She turns the volume down a bit. "I only know lyrics and names of food. You don't know any Korean?"

I shake my head with a little guilt. "No. Wasn't really given the opportunity to growing up. Guess I don't have an excuse now. Maybe I should learn."

She smiles at me and squeezes my hand. "I can replay these songs for days on end, and you can learn the lyrics that way."

"Let's do it."

"Did I ever tell you I have a half-Korean aunt?" I shake my head, but a huge smile spreads on my face. "Her name is Rose and she's married to my Uncle Robert, my father's brother. They live in New York and have two grown kids. I don't see them as often as I should, but Aunt Rose is awesome. She's always making us great food and sharing her culture with anyone that will listen."

"I'd love to meet her. I'd love to meet your whole family."

"Me, too," Marco chimes in from the back seat. "Maybe she can share some recipes and techniques with me."

"Oh god, she would *love* that."

My heart leaps at the idea that not only does she want us to meet her family, but there are other Korean people in her life. People I can meet and hopefully connect with. This is so cool!

"What are your parents doing for Christmas?" Cora asks me, her other hand gently stroking mine.

My heart sinks. "They're having Christmas at my grandma's house, where it always is with the whole big extended family."

"Are you going to miss seeing everyone?" she asks, unknowingly.

"I am," I answer honestly. "Though my parents aren't talking to me right now." I go on to tell her about the dinner we had with them, where they stormed out on us.

Cora's face turns sorrowful. "That's awful. I'm sorry that happened to you. But before that, you were close with them?"

"Very."

"They'll come around. Something will change. You're too sweet to stay away from," she says with a wink.

"Uh, you did for two years," I counter.

"Touché," Marco adds. "But now I want to hear all about the night you two met. From both of your perspectives. Start from the beginning and give me all the horny details."

Cora giggles and looks back at Marco. "Well, he was holding a puppy, so naturally, I melted. I didn't stand a chance."

Chapter 22

The Cottage

Marco

Once we've unpacked everything, including the groceries we stopped for on the drive here, I start to make dinner while Cora introduces George to her new surroundings. The cottage itself is small, with two bedrooms and one bathroom. I could tell Jay was a little nervous about whether or not she would like the place, but when she set her eyes on it, she beamed. She told us this was the cutest A-frame mountain home she'd ever seen and gushed about the architectural details—the stone fireplace, the large picture windows overlooking the mountain view, and the knotted wood paneling seemed to turn her on. No joke—she was flushed and would pat her own cheeks with the pads of her fingers each time she found a new little treasure to tell us about. She lives in a stunning historical gem of a home, and she's freaking out over a rustic cottage. This woman keeps surprising me.

As I slide the homemade lasagna into the oven and set the

timer, I see a box sitting next to the butcher block island. Pulling up the box and opening it, a big grin falls across my face, and I call towards the living room where Jay and Cora are lounging and drinking wine. "Darling, what did you bring us?"

They both turn to peer over the sofa at me and she stands up. "Oh no! Part of that is your Christmas gift." She pads over to me with Jay close behind her. She takes the box, pulls out the two wrapped presents, and sets them in front of us. "You may as well open them now." Then she takes two cards over to the small Christmas tree and places them in the branches. When she saunters back to us, Jay looks at her and asks, "When did you have time to get us presents?"

"I honestly don't know. I've barely slept since I left your house last night."

I don't love hearing that she hasn't had any rest. "You didn't need to do that. Your sleep is more important than gifts. Also, Christmas isn't for another two days."

"It's better if you open them now. Trust me."

I do as she requests and open the small box to reveal a tin-foil-wrapped loaf of banana bread. I look up at Jay, and his mouth is wide open, a smile plastered to his face. I then turn my attention back to Cora. "This smells amazing. You can bake?"

She gives me a knowing look. "You're not the only one with kitchen skills. My mom taught me how to bake from a young age. This is her recipe."

Jay grabs her by the waist and tugs her into a hug. "I *love* banana bread. Thank you. This is so nice."

When he releases her, I round the butcher block and do the same. "How you found the time, I don't know, but I very much appreciate this." I give a soft kiss to her lips, and I can feel her smile spread.

"It's nothing. I wasn't sure how to approach gift giving at this stage and on such short notice."

I lean against the block and shake my head. "It's not nothing."

"And for the record," Jay chimes, leaning in to brush his lips against hers. "We would have been happy with just a kiss."

"Me, too. But I was hoping we could do this." She lifts the final box out, revealing a gingerbread house kit. Of course, it's no ordinary kit. "This is a traditional Swiss chalet—" she explains with excitement and points to the assortment of candies, frosting mix, and marshmallows, "—complete with all the architectural details one's heart can desire." Her eyes dart between us, and she bites her bottom lip. The small movement makes me want to do the very same thing to her. "My dad and I made one every year. I know it's dumb—"

I stop her right there. "No, it's not dumb. I love this." I take out my phone from my pocket. "Let me put some music on, and continue the family tradition."

The sounds of a winter wonderland fill the room, and I can't help but smile watching her open all the bags of candy, swaying her body to the music.

For the next few hours, we're so engrossed in our project, so consumed by laughter and jabs at each other's choices of building materials that we don't even bother sitting down for a formal meal. We eat the lasagna in between stuccoing frosting to the roof and constructing gumdrop trails.

As I attach tiny cinnamon candies to the roof's edge, I muse, "I'm so glad you had this with your dad. You must cherish these memories."

"What were your traditions? What were the holidays like for you as a child?" Cora asks, piping thin loops to a window ledge.

I can sense Jay stiffen at the question, for my sake. I want to tell her about my family, I do. I just—it's not an easy subject to talk about. There are exactly three people that know about my childhood traumas: my sister, Jay, and my therapist. This moment we're in is so blissfully perfect, I don't want to ruin the moment. Thankfully, Jay intercepts the question.

"My family goes big. I've got so many aunts and uncles and cousins it's hard to keep track. We all gather at my grandparent's house, eat too much and talk over each other. Grams will get tipsy accidentally, *her words*, and start singing *Joy to the World*, forgetting most of the lyrics, so my cousins and I will provide her with the missing words, but they're always wrong." He chuckles at his own memories. "Like she'll go 'Let earth receive her—' and then I'll tell her 'Schnauzer.'" He starts to belly laugh, and Cora and I giggle along with him. "She doesn't realize it at first, but she'll sing it and then let out the sweetest drunken cackle."

I witnessed this very thing last year when he took me to the big Bishop family Christmas. It was a stark reminder of the difference between our childhoods and families. But I had the best time. They welcomed me, hugged me, and were genuinely interested in me.

Cora licks frosting off her finger but can't wipe the smile off her face. "I love that. They sound like a fun bunch. I'd love to meet them someday."

Her words instantly make me choke up. If she means what she's saying, she wants to stick around... she wants there to be an *us*.

Jay stands from his stool, sets his candy cane down, and hugs Cora from the back tightly. He scrunches his face and smiles. "They'd love you!"

Wanting to join this embrace, I step around the butcher block table and join them. "If they love me, they'll be enamored with you," I mutter into her hair. "But don't let him fool you; the Bishop family is full of characters—" I start, but a loud crash sounds off.

I hit the ground, shoving the civilians against the closest interior wall and covering their bodies with mine.

"Stay down!" I bellow and grab the radio on my shoulder, only it's not there. All thought is erased from my mind except what my next move is. If I have no radio contact, I need to find a safe place for these people.

I assess the room and see no damage, but I have to get them out of here before anything collapses. I jump up and haul them with me, shoving them towards the door, and I open it to survey my surroundings before the cold air hits me.

What the hell? Why is there snow?

Then I hear a familiar deep voice like a light shining through clearing fog. "Marco! Marco! It's not real, baby." I turn around and stare at the man next to me. He's touching my shoulders, worry evident on his face. "It's me. It's Jay. Breathe deep."

Staring into his deep brown eyes, I do as he says and take a deep breath. I didn't realize I was holding it until now. It feels like all the blood rushes back into my brain, and my vision refocuses into reality.

"That's it. Look into my eyes and keep breathing with me." We take a few more breaths in sync with each other. "You're home. You're on vacation with me and Cora. We're in a cottage, and we're safe." A few more deep inhales. "Now tell me where you are."

Still looking into his eyes, I repeat, "We're safe. We're on vacation." Reality finally sets in, and I turn to look at Cora, who's at Jay's side. Standing in our socks on the porch, I can start to feel the cold wet snow soaking through.

"Come back inside, baby," he drawls, and I follow them. He leans me against the wall and peels off our socks in silence, then takes Cora's and puts them in the washer next to us in the foyer.

He steps back into my line of sight and says in a calm, slow voice, "I think you had a PTSD episode." I nod my head in agreement. "George was on top of the cabinets and knocked off a large ceramic bowl. It shattered on the tile floor, triggering you."

He leads me around the shattered bowl and sits me on the couch. "You guys stay here, and I'll clean up the mess," Cora says softly.

Jay folds his legs in and faces me, holding our hands together. "Let's keep breathing together until your heart rate returns to a normal pace."

After several minutes, my body starts to feel like itself again, and my thoughts fully return to the here and now. "Are you okay? Did I hurt either of you?"

"I think we're okay. I might have a little bruise from the impact of being flung on the ground, but other than that, I'm fine."

Cora sits next to me and puts her hand on my shoulder. "Same. I'm okay. More importantly, are *you* okay?"

I release Jay's hands and haul her to sit on my lap, her legs draped across Jay's. I bring their heads to lay on my chest, soaking in their scents and safety.

I sigh, "I'm okay now. I'm sorry if I scared you."

"How often does this happen?" she asks.

"It varies. Last time was about a month ago. I'd say I've probably had ten episodes since returning home."

"Plus the nightmares," Jay adds.

I stroke the hair on his head. "Yeah. But it's been getting better. I've been seeing a therapist since I got out. I started seeing one while I was still a soldier, but I didn't trust him. I felt like he was there looking out for the best interest of the Army and not me. As soon as I got home, I found a new one."

I kiss his forehead. "Jay has been my rock through everything."

"Would you like another rock?" Cora smiles sweetly, and my heart skips a beat.

"I would. Maybe rock collecting can be my new hobby."

Jay lifts off me and pinches my side. "It better not be! You get *two* rocks, and that's it."

Smiling and wincing at the playful pain, I chuckle, "Yes, okay. No more rocks."

Cora draws an idle circle on my collarbone. "What do you need right now?"

I look at Jay, and he gives me a knowing look. He knows all too well what I need at this moment. I swallow hard and breathe in. "What I need is both of you. When I get like this, I need to make sure you're safe and cared for. It's kind of... primal."

I pause, hoping she'll understand what I'm asking. She sits up and looks me in the eyes. "You need to fuck us?"

"No, baby. I need to make love to you."

Chapter 23

Bare

Cora

"Are you comfortable with that?" Marco asks me, his voice like a breeze against my face.

Am I? The whole point of this trip is to pretend this is real, right? Though *pretending* doesn't seem right. I'm certainly not pretending. They're not. I want to be swallowed up by them. I want to give everything I can to them, especially Marco. If this is what he needs right now, then I want to give it to him.

Running my fingers through the thick dark curls on the top, I scratch his head, and he closes his eyes. "Yes," I reply and lean in to kiss him. It's slow and lingering, and I feel Jay's hand snake up my leg.

He stands up and pulls me off Marco's lap. Silently, they each take one of my hands, and we make our way to the bedroom. Much like the rest of the cottage, the room is mountain Americana at its best. The walls are rich wood panels like the living room. The massive bed is a simple wrought iron frame topped with a deep red, cream, and tan quilt that ties in the fabric of the curtains and ornate rug.

I love it when homeowners get it right. They leaned into the design of the house and didn't try to make it something it's not. It feels authentic.

Jay and Marco feel authentic. They're letting me in and showing me the real them, scars and all. Maybe it's time I do the same.

When we reach the bed, my eyes dart back and forth between them. They're staring at me with the same intensity I'm feeling. Marco guides me to sit on the edge, and they both start to undress me, tossing my clothes on the floor.

Weird. I know Marco is picky about that, but right now, he feels like an entirely different man with laser focus. Like the world around us doesn't exist.

They strip me completely naked, and Marco says in a hoarse voice, his face serious, "I want you to sit back and watch for a bit. I need you to know that I am going to take and take and take from you, but I want you to make your own decisions, too. This is not a scene. This is us."

His words hit me hard; the weight of them feels like something I'm never going to lift off. "Okay," I reply a little breathlessly and situate myself in the center of the bed, propped against the pillows.

I watch Marco take Jay by his slim waist and pull him into his body, their mouths connecting like magnets. I can see their erections straining against each other, each of them grinding their hips into one another.

Jay makes quick work to undress Marco, his broad, muscular shoulders and chest converging into that perfect V of his Adonis belt. I bite my lip as Jay pulls off Marco's black boxer briefs and immediately palms his enormous cock. Maybe *palms* isn't the right word because Jay cups his balls, and Marco's thick length takes up most of Jay's forearm.

Marco moans at the touch, but just as quick, he takes Jay's clothes off and kneels in front of him. With one arm wrapped around Jay's ass, he holds his cock in the other hand and licks a long wet trail from sac to tip. Staring into Jay's eyes, Marco flutters his tongue over the small slit on his crown, and Jay rolls his head back as he holds onto Marco's hair.

I'm so turned on by watching this that I can't help but drag my fingertips to my folds and idly play.

Marco takes Jay's cock into his mouth and hollows out his cheeks, sucking deep.

"Fuck that's good, baby," Jay groans and turns his focus back on him.

With a sloppy *pop* sound, Marco removes his head and strokes and pulls with such force that I can't believe how aggressive they can be with each other. He's stroking him so much harder than I could ever manage.

"Wait, wait," Jay pants. "I don't wanna come yet. If you keep going, I will." Without a word or a moment's hesitation, Marco lifts Jay off the ground and throws him next to me. Jay grabs my arms to steady us both and looks down at my wet fingers circling my clit. He turns to his side, his hand finding mine, and with a deep, slow voice he rumbles, "Allow me," as he takes over.

Marco makes his way around the bed to my other side, and he's brought a bath towel with him that he lays on the bed under our bottoms.

Smart.

Snuggling behind me, he presses his massive warm body against mine. I can feel every muscle push against my soft body. Our skin touching feels like a drug—it's electric and heady and consuming.

He grinds himself into my ass and between my thighs. Between these two men, between their scents and skin and fingers, I'm a puddle of arousal.

Jay dips two digits inside me as Marco kisses my neck. Curling his fingers, Jay drags over my G-spot, and I can't help but clamp my legs together and thrust. Marco pushes his knee between my legs, and Jay does the same. Then Marco whispers in my ear, "Grind, baby."

I take one hand and pull Jay's neck to fuse our mouths together, and my other hand moves behind to hold Marco's hips as he thrusts himself against me.

My orgasm builds and builds, and when I'm almost there, rocking against their strong legs, my pussy filled with two expert fingers, Marco adds his hand to my clit and furiously rubs, sending me straight into the abyss. My legs clench tight around theirs, my pussy fluttering in appreciation, and the butterflies in my lower stomach feel like they're escaping.

I relax against them, my body going limp, and stars swirl around my vision.

Stars—and hearts.

"You did so well, baby," Marco murmurs against my shoulder, and he wraps his big tattooed arms around my chest. "But I'm going to need more. Jay, can you grab the condoms? I think they're in your bag."

"Wait," I blurt, mustering all the courage I have. "If you guys are okay with it, I'd like to go without. I'm clean, and I'm on birth control."

Jay's eyes grow wide, and Marco's body tenses behind me.

"We're both clean," Jay confirms, his expression a mix of excitement and worry. "Are you sure?"

"I'm positive. I trust you both." And it's the truth. Maybe I'm too quick to trust, too quick to see the good in people, but there is something about these men that my heart sings for and my mind feels at ease with.

I feel and hear a low growl rumble behind me, sending shivers down my spine. "I can't wait any longer..." Marco shifts away and turns me to face him, my back to Jay. "You're going to take us both." He slips a hand around his cock and presses the fat tip against my clit, sliding it back and forth from my wet center, my arousal coating us both. "You're going to take us both right *here*," he grunts, thrusting inside my pussy with one jerk, and I grab hold of his massive shoulders. The invasion is both too much and exactly what I want.

I inhale sharply and gasp, staring directly into those feral blue eyes of his. "Both of you..." I start, thinking it over as he slowly moves inside me. The heat of his shaft, the feel of skin on skin, completely bare, is making me lose all inhibitions. Not that I have any around them.

Jay's hard body forms to mine, his hands moving to my full breasts and his erection pushing against me. "Both of you..." I repeat, squeezing Marco's traps. "Yes. I want both of you there."

"Good, because I need to look at both of you when I come, and I want you to flood our cocks together."

Oh my god, where does he come up with this dirty talk?

Marco stills his hips and lifts my leg up with the crook of his elbow, allowing Jay room to nestle his dick at my already full entrance. An entrance that, up until now, only had a maximum capacity of one.

"Are you ready, baby? I'm going to go slow. Let us know if you need to stop," Jay whispers into my hair, his breathing shallow and quick—like he can't believe what's about to happen.

Oh my god, now they're both calling me baby? I'm melting over here.

He moves one hand from my breast to his cock to line up.

I close my eyes and nod. "Okay."

Marco takes my chin between his fingers and presses his soft lips to mine; the friction of his short beard is driving me wild. Jay notches himself into me—and I *know* bodies can handle this; the vagina can dilate to an enormous size, but that tidbit of information seems impossible right this minute.

No way is he fitting.

Kissing me through it, Marco takes a deep breath. "Relax, baby. Breathe with me."

I stop kissing him, and our foreheads touch. I spread my palms on his bare chest and get lost in the design of his tattoos as we inhale and exhale in a slow, steady cadence.

I feel the head of Jay's cock make its way inside, and I will my body to welcome him.

"*Fuck,*" they both groan at the same time.

When Jay is finally all the way in, he gives me a few moments for my body to accept them before giving a push, and all three of us groan.

"Good girl," Jay croons.

"I'm ready," I pant, already worked up. I look into the sea of Marco's eyes. "Claim me. Claim us."

I think he likes hearing that because Marco lets out a quick growl before he attacks my neck, sucking hard and working his powerful hips into me.

When Jay starts thrusting, too, Marco stops him silently with his hand on his hip. "Let me, prince. I need to take care of you."

He obeys and lets Marco take full control, groaning as he lets our lover slide against his dick inside me. Jay cusses, and whimpers, and moves his hands back to my aching chest.

Marco's thrusts, like his gaze into our souls, are deep and meaningful. *He really does need this,* I think to myself. Marco looks desperate and powerful all at once—a combination I didn't realize could be such a turn-on.

I fling my leg over his hips and hold him tight, grinding myself against him. Wanting to feed his raw desire, I toss my head back next to Jay's, exposing my throat. "Marco... I'm yours. You have me."

He latches on the delicate skin beneath my jaw like a leech, sucking hard and biting me. "You're both *mine*," he says in a low, guttural voice. In a flash, he grabs hold of Jay's neck and pulls him as close as possible, taking his mouth in a brutal kiss above my head. "Say it," he demands, his hips still pumping without mercy.

Breaking away from the kiss for the briefest of seconds to reply, Jay breathes, "I'm yours. Forever."

I can't help myself when my mouth finds theirs and our lips and teeth and tongues war with each other. And I can't help myself when my orgasm crests so suddenly I don't even have time to warn them. Warm wetness erupts from my body as Marco keeps up his pace.

"Oh my god—fuck!" I scream.

"Holy shit, baby. That feels incredible," Jay praises from behind.

My orgasm isn't subsiding in the least. "Don't stop," I plead. "It's still going."

"Yes, baby—keep going. Jay, give it to her."

In a split second, Jay pumps into my channel, finding an agonizingly good rhythm with Marco.

How am I still coming? Not only is my pussy convulsing nonstop, but I can't stop the hot liquid squirting out of me like a fountain.

Using my chest like a life raft, Jay clings as he and Marco pound into me with abandon, my orgasm never ceasing.

"I'm gonna come, baby," Jay's hoarse voice cracks.

"Where do you want it, princess?" Marco grunts, his teeth digging into his lower lip as he scrunches his eyes.

"Inside me. Please." I beg, not really sure how I can manage the words.

"Do it," Marco grinds out through clenched teeth, sweat trailing down his face as his big arm lays over me and grabs Jay's waist. "Fill her up."

With a fierce shout, Jay's movements become erratic as he frees himself inside me. Marco follows him, holding my head to his chest and pulling Jay in as tight as possible. He grunts through his release, "I've got you. I've got you. I've got you." He chants as if it's a mantra to himself. But, no—it's not only for him.

As I finally come down from the incredible high I've been sustaining, his words seep into me. "I've got you."

Our chests heave, our breath hot.

"I've got you."

I close my eyes, and I feel Jay kiss my shoulder.

"I've got you."

Without moving my head from the heat of Marco's tattooed chest, I reach back to touch Jay—any part I can find. Feeling his hips, I give him a squeeze.

"You have me," I pant.

And I mean it.

Chapter 24

Opening Up

Jay

Once we splay out and catch our breath, Marco makes a dash to the bathroom and comes back with wet washcloths to wipe us clean. He tosses the towel that lay under us with the rags back into the bathroom.

When he comes back to the bed, he bends down and peppers kisses all over our bodies until we are both smiling with delight.

Which brings us here, a naked Cora, partially covered in a tangle of white sheets, leaning against my chest as we lay propped against the pillows. Marco lays the opposite way, leaning on his side, playing with Cora's ankle, delicately tracing lines up and down.

"How do you feel?" Cora asks, looking at Marco. "After everything, I mean. Did we help?"

He gives her a gentle kiss on her foot. "You were both perfect. I feel... stronger. Grounded."

Cora places a hand on my chest and smiles at him. "Good.

I liked doing that for you." He gives a lazy grin, and my heart swells.

This moment.

This woman.

This man.

Everything feels so right.

We bask in the silence, in each other's presence, soaking up every last pheromone and good vibe possible.

I take her hand in mine and stroke my thumb across it. "What does your future look like, Cora?" My own question catches me off-guard, but... I am curious. I very much want us to be a part of that future, and I want to hear from her about how we can make that happen.

But the positive energy that was dancing through this room is soon sucked out.

She goes a bit stiff and takes a long pause. "Um, wow. No one has asked me that in a long time. I think in a personal sense, I stopped thinking about the future after..." she sighs and closes her eyes for a long time. She's clearly working through something, and far be it from me to rush her.

I look at Marco and he's wearing the same concerned look as me.

"What's going on, sweetheart?" he soothes.

Her lip quivers, and she keeps her eyes closed when she says with an unsteady voice, "After I miscarried."

Did I hear her right? "You miscarried?"

She nods her head, and her mouth turns down, her chin wobbling as tears start to form. "When I was married. We got pregnant after trying for a while, and—" her voice breaks on a soft cry. "—we were so happy. Then one day in the first trimester, we went to the doctor's office for some testing, and we found out there was a strong chance the baby would have Down syndrome." She takes a deep breath, and I tighten my grip on her hand. "The doctor asked us if we... wanted to continue the pregnancy after knowing this. I had no doubt in my mind that this baby was everything I wanted. Of course, I wanted to keep my baby."

She wipes tears from her eyes, but they keep coming. I bring up the sheet to wipe her face and look at Marco, silently gesturing for him to cover himself up. That fucking cry boner of his was going to rise to full mast any second, and I won't have Cora's heartfelt memory dishonored like that. He leans up and stuffs a pillow on his crotch, giving me a look that says *I'm not an asshole, I'll get rid of it.*

With her eyes still shut, she continues, "When we got home, Theo told me he didn't want to keep the baby."

My stomach drops.

What a piece of shit!

Her tears fall hard as her face contorts, and my heart shatters for her.

"I told him there was no way I was giving them up. We fought over it for weeks. He said I was selfish, I said he was shallow, and ultimately, we couldn't get past it. I told him I wanted a divorce and that I would raise this child myself. It hurt so bad, and the love I had for him seemed tainted. I never expected that this one thing could rip apart a strong marriage, but it did. It was this wound that couldn't heal."

Cora takes another deep and shaky breath, and Marco shifts around so he's face to face with her and puts a hand on her shoulder. "Then, at the twenty-week ultrasound, I went by myself to find out how the baby's development was tracking and the sex. But... there was no heartbeat."

Tears now fill my own eyes, I sit there listening to her pour out her heart about what must be the most traumatic experience of her life.

"I had to deliver her two days later."

Still holding her to my chest, I weep along with her. Marco sandwiches her, his own tears gleaming. "I'm so sorry, Cora," he offers, because what else can be said?

We give her time to cry through it.

Sitting there.

Embracing her.

Giving her space to feel.

When her breathing returns to a calmer pace, I ask, "What was her name?"

She opens her eyes and says with a sad smile, "Violet."

"Well, Violet was very lucky to have you as her mother."

"Absolutely," Marco whispers.

"Thank you," she murmurs through a watery smile. "After that, I really didn't have a plan for myself anymore. We got divorced about six months later." She huffs a small laugh, "And then I met *you* that night." She nudges me. "Angie and I were out celebrating my divorce, as bittersweet as it was."

"No wonder you ghosted me afterward. You weren't ready."

She shakes her head. "I wasn't—but you were exactly what I needed then. I needed to have carefree fun; and you made me laugh, and dance, and let go. It was one of the best nights of my life."

All the heartache she put me through following that night dissipates from my body, knowing I was able to give her that. Well, most of it.

"I still would have liked to stick around, even if it was just as a friend."

"Jay Bishop," she gives me an exasperated look, "after all this sexual chemistry, can you honestly say that we could have stayed *just friends?*"

I give her a roguish smile and a kiss, "I would have tried my hardest."

I reach to pull Marco's hand into ours and lay them back over my heart. With a calm and steady voice I ask, "Do you want more kids?" I can feel her stiffen again. "Be honest, baby."

She takes a long pause, really thinking it over. "I haven't let myself think about the possibility of having more."

"Maybe it's time you started thinking about it," Marco interjects "Because we like the idea."

"You guys want children?"

Trying to act nonchalant, I add, "We've talked about it. We're both interested."

"Did you have a plan before I came into the picture?"

"No. Just talks." That's the truth, technically. We didn't form any real plans on *how* we'd have children or when, but we've talked about wanting to be fathers and raising children together. Maybe we'd have a surrogate or adopt, but the thought of Cora being the one—being a mother to our future child—the idea has my heart racing.

She's quiet for a long time before Marco breaks the silence. "You don't need to give us an answer, sweetheart. Sit on that information for a while. If you ever want to give us an answer," he kisses her bare shoulder, "we'd love to hear it."

Chapter 25

The Date

Cora

I wake up to the low, thunderous sound of George purring. She usually falls asleep on me at some point in the night, but when I don't feel her, I open my eyes to see her lying atop Marco's chest, her arms stretched to his shoulders and face nuzzled into him.

What the hell? George hates men. She hated my father, Theo, and any man that ever came to my home. She barely tolerates women, yet here she is, acting like Marco is her own personal heating pad.

I'm so distracted by this glitch in the Matrix that I don't even register that Jay's no longer clinging to my body like he did all night. It isn't until he pads through the doorway with three empty mugs, a carafe of coffee, and wearing nothing but a grin that I notice.

Damn, he's beautiful. Even with his hair askew, he looks absolutely perfect. His golden skin glows in the late morning light, making him look like some kind of sun god.

He sets the coffee down, careful not to make a sound and disturb our sleeping beauties. He looks at Marco and George, then glances at me and mouths *Oh my god*.

I mouth back to him, *I know,* and then gesture for him to take a picture. He finds his phone and snaps a few shots with me next to them, mouth agape.

"Are you done taking non-consensual pictures of me?" Marco rumbles, his eyes shut.

Oops.

"She made me," Jay tattles.

"Only because this is the cutest thing I've ever seen," I tease quietly, trying not to disturb George. "The only time she's this lovey with me is when I'm having some kind of breakdown. She's like a little fuzzy therapist." Then it hits me, and even more imaginary hearts pop out of my eyes. "Oh my gosh, she's comforting you after what happened last night."

He chuckles softly, causing George to bump up and down. Without opening her eyes, she stretches out and rolls on her back, exposing her undercarriage to the room.

Wow. She's really making herself at home with him.

Jay hands me a cup of coffee as I pull myself up against the headboard, then pours one for himself and sits down on the edge of the bed.

Marco opens one eye. "I don't get one?"

"*You* have a job, and it's being a cat bed right now," he replies.

Marco grumbles, "Then I guess no one is going to make banana bread french toast for us this morning."

I stop sipping my coffee and bug out my eyes. "No, wait! Fuck off, George." I touch her belly, and she instantly jumps up and scurries away.

"Great," Marco sighs and turns into me, planting his face

into my hip and wrapping his arm around my legs. "How am I supposed to bond with my cat daughter if her mother chases her away?"

My stomach does a little somersault at his sweet words. He thinks of himself as a cat dad already? And he really does want to stick around? I don't know why this keeps surprising me. Jay and Marco have done nothing but show their genuine interest and vulnerabilities with me. Why is it so hard for me to wrap my head around that?

"I'm sorry. My mind is foggy. I can't think clearly on an empty stomach," I pout.

He lifts himself up onto an elbow and leans down to kiss my soft belly as he runs his big warm hand across it. I'm not sure if he's doing this just because he wants to touch me, feed me, or if he's trying to imagine me pregnant. I truly do not have the mental capacity to go through that talk again so soon, so I'm pleased when he says, "Well, we can't have that."

He then sits up and straddles me, taking my mug from me and setting it down on the nightstand. With a look of pure desire, he shimmies down my body and growls, "But I have to eat first." He buries his face between my legs, giving me one long swipe between my slit and inhales. "Are you hungry, prince?"

"Starving, Sir," Jay confirms, eagerly setting his mug down and joining Marco.

I sit back and enjoy the view, the feel, and the orgasm that two enthusiastic tongues provide at the same time.

After a beautiful brunch of the promised banana bread french toast, more coffee, mimosas, and fresh fruit, Marco and I bundle up and head out on a date. Jay brought up during our meal that he thinks we need to spend more one-on-one time together. I can't argue with that since Jay and I see each other almost every day at the office. We've definitely grown closer because of that, so even though it feels a bit strange to be without him, I'm more than happy to get to spend this time with Marco alone.

We decide to take a hike on a nearby trail close to the cottage. Clear signage is posted, and the snow is packed down on the trail, allowing us to find our way easily. If we take the trail long enough, we could end up at one of the local ski resorts.

"Did you ever hike growing up?" Marco asks, his long legs slowing down when he realizes I can't walk as fast as him.

"Yeah, sometimes. I had cousins that lived outside the city, and we'd all go hiking and play in the creek whenever we could." I chuckle to myself, remembering some of the activities we used to do. "My older boy cousins used to hold our wrists and ankles and swing us back and forth, then toss us across the creek."

Marco laughs deeply, "Why?"

Smiling, I shrug, "I have no idea. It was some kind of game. We'd also see who could catch the biggest fish and who could sit in the stream the longest in the spring when the water was ice cold."

"I'm happy you had that kind of childhood. I never really had the opportunity to get out of the city and explore like that—with no agenda." He looks around us at the snow-tipped branches. "I always dreamed of it. It's the kind of life kids should have."

It's not lost on me what he's implying. It's the kind of life he wants for his kids.

I grab his gloved hand in mine, and we walk for a while in silence before I ask, "What were your Christmases like with your family? What are your parents doing for the holidays?"

I feel his hand tighten on mine, and I look up at him to see his jaw clench. "Dad's in prison." His words are as cold as the air.

That catches me off guard.

"He's been in for a couple years already. Assault and battery of a police officer, his ex-girlfriend, and possession of methamphetamine. He's a real winner."

"Oh my god. What the—how do you feel about that?"

"He deserves it and so much more. I wanted to talk about this last night when we were making the gingerbread house, but," he raises his eyebrows and tilts his head. I nod, remembering all too well how that scene ended. "My past isn't something I want to keep from you." He takes another deep breath, "The traditions we had weren't exactly merry and bright. When my mom was still around, the holidays usually consisted of heavy drinking, verbal and physical fights, and my sister and I hiding out or going to friends' houses to get away from my parents. If they actually managed to remember to get me a gift, it was usually hand-me-down clothes from my dad that were too big.

"There was one year they got us a goldfish we named Figaro. Rebecca and I were so excited, and we thanked them endlessly. But before we even went back to school, he stormed into the house one day, yelling and cussing at me because I hadn't shoveled the walk when he was at work. He told me if I couldn't take care of my responsibilities, then I didn't deserve to have a pet. So, he took Figaro's fish bowl, dumped it down the kitchen sink, and turned the disposal on."

I halt my steps and jump back a little at that frightening image. "Oh my god. How old were you?" I gasp.

"Nine, I think. Rebecca would have been twelve."

"I'm sorry," I offer, my heart filling with sorrow. I take both of his hands in mine as we stand there facing each other. "Your whole childhood was like that?"

"More or less. When my mom left, I was thirteen. When she walked out, I assumed she would come back in a couple days like she always did. She didn't say goodbye. She didn't try to contact us." I watch his throat swallow and tighten, and his eyes shudder.

"About four years later, she was found dead in a hotel room. The cops came to our home and gave us the few belongings she had. She had written a letter to me and Rebecca, telling us how much she loved us and how sorry she was. Then Dad burned everything."

He clears his throat and focuses on the stitching of my gloves. "Somehow, after reading her letter, I was even angrier—and I let that anger control me. The only good thing in my life was my sister, and I did everything to protect her from our dad. It was like he saw our mom in her more and more with every passing day and hated her for it. I took every beating I could for her. She moved out as soon as she could, and when I turned seventeen, I graduated early, moved out, and fucked around for a couple years. I worked odd jobs and got myself into bad situations with bad people."

"What kind of situations?"

He takes a long pause, and finally looks up from my hands to my eyes. "Like stealing cars."

I'm stunned. My tender, nurturing, Marco? The massage therapist who cooks and cuddles? How did he go from this hellish background to become the incredible man he is today?

As if reading my mind, he answers, "I recognized I needed to change something, or I was going to end up like my parents, so, I joined the Army. It gave me structure, but it still fucked me up.

He sighs again. "I never want to see him again, and I especially don't want you or Jay to meet him. He's the scum of the Earth.

He'd also have an absolute conniption if he found out I'm not only dating a man, but I'm also in a polyamorous relationship. And you know what? Him knowing is not something I owe him."

"I understand."

He pulls me into an all-consuming bear hug. I'm a voluptuous woman, and I'm wearing thick layers of outwear, but when he wraps his arms around me, I feel positively petite. He's so tall and broad, and even through the crisp, earthy smells of this wintery forest, I still smell his lavender and sandalwood scent.

"Just talking about him makes my blood boil," he grumbles. "Come." He steps off the trail into the fresh powder, our boots sinking a few inches on each step. "Would you lay here with me?"

I agree and he guides me down, the sound of snow crunching softly around my body and head. He lays next to me, our arms outstretched but still holding hands.

We simply lay there in silence, watching the canopy above us. The occasional branch swaying in the wind and releasing its ledge of snow and floating to the ground. In the distance, I can hear kids laughing.

When I look over at Marco, his eyes are closed, his dark lashes fanned out, and he's breathing deep, purposeful lungfuls of air. This is what I love about him. He exudes this calmness and tranquility that I find incredibly attractive. I'm like a moth to a flame.

"Can I ask you something?" he says, and I look at him and nod. "The night we met, when I gave you that massage... what was the real reason you left crying?"

Oh.

Well, he already knows the origin story, I guess.

I clear my throat. "You mentioned attending your niece Viera's fourth birthday party. Hearing her name and her age triggered me."

It dawns on him then. "Violet would have been about that age now, too?"

I nod. "It's not your fault. You couldn't have known. Even if you did, you should be able to talk about your niece without me spiraling."

He rolls on his side and sidles up next to me. His nose and cheeks are red as he looks at me. "I'm sorry, baby." I give him a weak smile. "Would you like to talk about this more or not?"

"Not right now," I mumble.

"Then let's reset. Close your eyes," he tells me, and I shut them. In a slow, low voice, he rumbles, "Inhale slowly. Listen to the sounds of the forest. Exhale and empty everything. Inhale love and peace. Exhale your stress and control."

He guides me for a few more rounds, and then we stay there in silence once more. When I open my eyes, he asks, "How do you feel?"

I reach my gloved hand to cup his face. "Good. I love the way you make me feel, Marco; and it's a beautiful thing to watch you be so present."

He puts his hand on the side of my neck and lowers himself to kiss me, our cold noses touching, our warm mouths searching.

"Ow!" he exclaims, his body jerking back.

"Get a room!" a small but loud voice calls out as we turn to see three young kids charging for us with arms full of snowballs.

More snowballs pepper us as we quickly get to our feet, trying to duck each one. "Let's get 'em!" Marco bellows as he picks up the still-intact snowballs and throws them back at the kids. They start to retreat when each one hits its mark, but he doesn't give up. Laughing, we run after them, careful not to slip, and over

THE DATE

the ridge of the hill, we see a fortress of snowballs waiting.

Bingo.

It may be their stockpile, but Marco doesn't seem to care. "Show no fear, Cora! Take it all and regret nothing!" he screams as we charge into their zone, grabbing ball after ball and chucking them at the kids.

"Hey, this is ours!" one of the boys shouts.

"No one owns the snow!" Marco yells as he barrels one right at the kid's chest.

When we use up most of their arsenal, Marco instructs me, "Grab the remaining few and run down the trail. They're going to want to restock, and we need to be prepared later."

I can't wipe the stupid grin off my face as we take the last armfuls and run down the winding path. When we get far enough away, we turn back and see that no one is following us.

Laughing, Marco finds us a spot to drop our weapons against a fallen tree and chuckles, "Those kids have it coming when we come back through."

"Do you feel proud of yourself?" I chortle. "A trained soldier attacking innocent children like that?"

"Hey, they had it coming! Child or adult, you don't back down from a snowball fight."

We keep walking along, recounting the play-by-play and laughing until we come upon the ski resort.

"Would you like to warm up in the lodge and get something hot to drink?" he asks.

"Oooh, baby, talk dirty to me," I tease and give him a wink.

He chuckles and leads us to the main lodge where we find a couple chairs and warm up with hot chocolates. When I look around, I can see skiers everywhere, but then my eyes catch on one run of tubers. "Oh my gosh! They have tubing here."

He glances at where I'm overtly pointing and smiles. "Would

you like to?"

"Yes!" I gasp, clutching his thermal Henley shirt.

"Then let's go, baby."

We make our way to the rental counter and purchase our time and tubes. They give us a quick safety spiel, and we make our way to the run. It's a classic tow-rope system with a young man at the bottom and at the top that helps hook us up and unhook.

When we stand at the very top, we look down at the large easy slope, and I start running, calling back to him, "Last one down is the sub!" My heart races when he chases me, but I'm already falling onto my tube and leading the race.

"You sneaky woman!" he yells, trying to usher himself closer to me, but it's no use. We can only go as fast as the tube and the snow let us. I'm almost to the bottom, and I can taste victory when I run into a couple of other tubers who have stopped short, allowing Marco to whiz past me with a maniacal laugh and arms raised high.

I apologize to the laughing tubers next to me and make my way down the rest of the hill to a tall, grinning man.

"That doesn't count!" I protest. "There was an obstruction. Flag on the play! Uhh... another sports term!"

"Don't make a bet you can't keep." He taps my nose with every word.

"Best two out of three?"

"You're on, lady."

The best two out of three turned into the best four out of seven which turned into the best eight out of fifteen. I rarely won a race, but I was having too much fun to care. We ended up linking arms when we rode down together, run after run.

We didn't realize we'd been at it for hours on end until the big slope lights came on. Neither of us wanted to leave, but when the darkness settled in, so did my hunger.

Reading my mind, Marco asks, "Why don't we head inside, get a bite to eat to hold us over, and call Jay to pick us up?"

I groan, "Yes, please. I don't think I have the energy to hike back anyway."

When Jay drives up to the lodge, Marco opens the passenger door for me and hands me my giant soft pretzel as he hops in the back with his.

Jay's face lights up when he sees the warm and salty snack, and he bites at the air between us. Giggling, I let him take a big bite.

When he pulls away from the curb, he says through a mouthful, "You guys went skiing?"

"Better. I got to watch Cora knock families off their tubes."

"They kept stopping right before the natural end of the slope! It's not my fault. You're the one throwing snowballs at children!"

We recount the day's activities to Jay on the short drive home. When we pull up, Marco opens my door, but I'm still chattering away. It isn't until I reach the porch and Jay opens the door, and I step inside, that I shut up.

The whole living room, kitchen, staircase, window casings, and doorways are covered in colorful Christmas lights. They gleam against the wintery darkness, making my heart swell.

Stunned, I finally manage to look at Jay. "You did this?"

He stands behind me and wraps his arms around my shoulders. "We planned this for you the night before we left. We brought the lights with us. Didn't exactly have time to get you a proper gift."

I huff a disbelieving laugh. "A proper gift? *This* is incredible, you guys. It feels magical and sweet and warm. It's perfect." I turn to face both of them, several ideas popping into my head. "Can we take pictures with the lights?"

Marco's lips curve up slightly. "I *would* like more than just a picture of me and George cuddled together on this trip, so yes."

"Then, can we eat dinner and fuck like rabbits under them?" I add.

Jay crowds me between Marco and, with a low chuckle, says, "In the living room or in the hot tub? I strung lights up over that, too."

I gasp and start shedding my coat and boots. "Hot tub first! I need to get warm." Then I'm bustling away to the bedroom to peel off my clothes.

I hear Jay and Marco laugh at my giddiness. But when only Marco joins me in the bedroom, he drawls, "Jay's gonna finish up dinner, and *we* are going to finish our date, woman."

Marco

As I settle into the hot tub and give Cora my hand to help her step in, I can't help but marvel at her. Spending this time alone with her has been wonderful. Watching her have fun and laugh is my new favorite thing, and I simply refuse to let go of that. Making her and Jay feel good is all I want.

When she settles in the water, she immediately straddles me. A look of pure seduction is all she's wearing. Thankfully there is a privacy fence around this back porch so the neighbors can't see.

She presses her breasts against me, and my cock can't help but stand straight up. She groans, and I can't tell if it's from the heat of the water or the heat between us.

She runs her hands over my pecs and shoulders, massaging me. "Baby, don't stop," I groan, closing my eyes.

I can feel her pussy rub against the fat head of my dick, and on instinct, I palm her thick ass, trying to guide her onto me, but the way she's squeezing my traps has my mind conflicted. Do I want to bury myself in her or let her keep massaging me?

She moves her hands to my hair and scratches my scalp. That's it. I'm done for. I fully recognize that men are dogs in more ways than one, but pet us like we're actual dogs and give us treats? We will fold instantly.

"Do you want me to take care of you, Sir?"

Good Lord, she's toying with control here. I won the races tonight. She's fucking *mine*. But then she kisses my neck and bites my earlobe, all while massaging my head, and I'm barely holding on.

"Mmm, yes, baby. Be a good girl and take care of me."

"Thank you, Sir," she whispers in my ear and then slowly nudges her pussy against my aching cock, sinking down.

"How are you this wet and slippery in the water?"

She bites her lower lip and focuses on seating herself completely. "I applied lube before we got out here for that very reason."

I toss my head back and tighten my grip on her ass. "*Fuck!* Horny *and* smart? I'm never letting you go."

She laughs, but it quickly dies off when I thrust into her. "Oh," she pants and buries her face into my neck.

I start with a strong pace, but I feel myself careening toward an orgasm way too soon. Like, embarrassingly too soon. I halt my movements and nuzzle against her face. "Hold on, princess. I'm too worked up. You're so fucking hot, and I can't help myself."

Then she contracts her channel around me, and I moan. "Ugh, baby. What are you doing to me? I can't last if you keep—*ahh*—doing that."

She starts riding me in earnest, and I pinch her backside, causing her to cry out. "Yes, Sir. Come inside me. Please let me take care of you."

My willpower dissolves, and I can't be bothered to think about how tragically short this will be, but damn it, I cannot stop. With only a few more thrusts, I clench my fingers deep into her ass and empty inside her.

When my mind comes back to reality, she's assaulting me with kisses and licking the sweat accumulating at my temples. "That was so hot," she pants between licks.

"How is coming in under two minutes hot?" I ask in disbelief.

"It makes me feel so sexy and desirable that you couldn't hold back."

"Well then, let me show you just how desirable you are, princess," I growl and stand up, taking her with me. I push her into the corner of the tub. "Swing your arms around the sides and hold on, baby."

She grabs on, and I sink to my knees in the center of the tub, hitching her thighs over my shoulders. "Cross your ankles and squeeze Daddy's head when he makes you feel good."

Her eyes go wide, and she drops her jaw at my words. I quickly wipe away the excess lube around her lower lips and dig in like it's my last meal.

I'm not gentle. I'm not slow. And I don't plan on stopping until she gives me at least three orgasms.

She squeezes my ears and moans, "Oh god, your beard feels so good. And your tongue. *Fuck, me.*"

With my right hand, I spread her open, exposing her clit, and flick my tongue over it mercilessly. I take my time and build her up, then back off and build her again until she's a squirming mess. When I feel her whole body start to get tight, I take a big bite and suck hard. I think she might pop my head off with her insanely strong legs, but it's all worth it when she arches her back, her hands white-knuckled on the edge of the tub. She lets out a cry that I'm positive every neighbor in a half-mile radius can hear. "Yesyesyesyes!"

But I don't let her sit down as I slip two fingers inside her, heading straight for her G-spot and coaxing it. Her body never fully stops contracting as I pull another screaming orgasm from her. Her chest heaves, and she is an absolute vision like this.

I'm rewarded with her stream, and I thrust my hand in faster, deeper, harder. I pull my face away briefly to praise her, "That's it, baby. Good fucking girl. Don't stop."

She doesn't. I watch her, for what seems like ten minutes, keep riding orgasm after orgasm, squirt after squirt, until she looks like she is in physical pain and begs me to stop.

I slowly remove myself from between her thighs and guide her to my lap. With her legs together and her side resting against my body, she slumps against me as I hold her in the water and stroke the loose ringlets from her bun away from her face.

When she gains her breath, she rasps, "Well, that's new. I didn't know my body could do that."

"Do what?"

"Sustain an orgasm that long. I can't tell if it was one long one that ebbed and flowed between ninety and one hundred percent the whole time, or if it was a dozen different ones all strung together."

I smile at that. "We will have to do extensive research and find out. You know, for science."

She giggles inside her post fuck haze, and it's a deep rumble instead of her high-pitched one. "Well, if it's for science..."

"That's it. I can't wait any longer!" Jay exclaims as he bursts out, swinging the door open and marching towards us, handing us our towels. "I heard everything in there, and I'm *fucking hard*. So, we need to eat right now and get to it."

Together, we laugh at Jay's serious tone. "She has a new talent to show you, prince."

Chapter 26

Christmas Morning

Cora

My phone dings nearby with an incoming text, waking me up. The midmorning light fills the space and there's no way I'm getting up from this sexy cuddle puddle we've formed on the floor of the living room.

Last night after we came inside and Jay basically forced us to eat dinner as fast as possible, we made a little nest in front of the fireplace with every blanket and pillow found in the cottage. We fucked and made love well into the wee hours, crying from pain and pleasure all under the colorful twinkling lights.

I don't want to move my body yet, but I know I'm going to be sore. Jay was downright feral last night. He admitted in the throes of it that he was jealous of my date and hot tub sexcapades with Marco—but it was all in good fun. He said next time Marco and I fuck, we are required to video call him.

Pervert.

Jay squirms a little behind me, poking his morning wood into the crevice of my backside. With his arm already lying over my waist, he pulls me in tighter and murmurs in a cracked voice, "Mmm, Merry Christmas, baby."

I smile. "You think Santa saw us fucking like animals and turned around?"

"Oh, we definitely got coal this year."

Marco chimes in from the other side of Jay with his rough and sleepy voice, "Nah, Santa is a dirty voyeur. He was watching."

All three of us chuckle.

Extracting myself from Jay's embrace, much to his chagrin, I sit up and grab Marco's discarded Henley and put it on. It's tight around my hips, but it's enough to cover up for now. "I'll start the coffee, and then I want to give you guys your gifts." I look around for a second. "I wonder where George is."

"She's curled up behind my knees," Marco says with a smile, still spooning Jay.

I make my way to the kitchen, start the coffee and scoop some food for George. She comes barreling in, and Marco follows.

"I'll get breakfast started," he grumbles, rubbing his sleepy eyes.

"And I'll lay here like the pillow prince that I am," Jay calls out from his position on the floor, making us giggle.

When breakfast is ready, we all sit in the living room with our plates and mugs. I take a bite of the omelet Marco made and groan, "God, Marco, you spoil me. I friggin' love you."

As soon as the words come out of my full mouth, I stop chewing, and I know my eyes are blown wide. My heart stops beating. A blaring alarm is going off in my brain. Heat rushes to my face as I see both men look up from their own meals to stare at me. Marco's shocked expression matches mine, and Jay is beaming.

CHRISTMAS MORNING

I swallow and stammer. "Uhhh... Th-that just came out. I-I don't. No! I mean, I do, but... *Shit. Fuck.* Not like that. I mean, kinda like that. Wait. Ohmygod *ohmygod*. Pretend you didn't hear anything."

I cover my mouth with both hands to stop myself and close my eyes, but there's radio silence. I can't look at them, but I uncover my mouth and blurt, "I only meant that you're a really good cook, and I appreciate you."

I cannot believe I said I loved Marco. It just slipped out. There's no way I can say it this soon; we're not there yet. *Fuck,* they probably think I'm insane.

When I finally open my eyes, Jay is sitting against the couch, his plate discarded on the floor and his arms crossed over his chest. He gives a smug smile and huffs a laugh. "Sure. You *don't* love him. Let's go with that." Sarcasm drips from each word.

My eyes move to Marco, who has a giant smile he's trying to hide by rubbing his hand up and down his dark bearded jaw. He glances at me, bites his bottom lip, and asks, "Would you like to take a lap and restart?"

I nod and stand up instantly, walking away from them as fast as possible. I hastily put on my snow boots and long coat and walk outside in the freezing cold air. The temperature difference is shocking, and it jolts me out of my own head. For good measure, I walk to the end of the driveway and head back.

That should do it.

I walk back inside, shuck off my boots and coat and join them back on the floor. Jay hands me my coffee with a smile, and I take a fortifying sip.

I'm just going to pretend I never said that.

"Would you guys like your Christmas gifts?"

To my relief, they nod and don't bring up the situation that shall not be mentioned. I lean over and grab the two envelopes from the Christmas tree and hand them over.

They break the seals, and each pulls out thick cardstock paper that I've painted a watercolor portrait of each man. Marco opens a painting of Jay, and Jay opens a painting of Marco.

"You painted this?" Jay asks, his expression is soft and sweet.

"Yeah."

Jay leans over to Marco to look at his own portrait. "They look just like us. You captured us so well. Thank you, baby."

"Sweetheart, these are beautiful. I want to frame this." Marco smiles and then looks up at me from his hands. "Thank you." He leans over and kisses me, making my insides flip. "But where are you?"

Nervously, I stumble on my words. "Oh, I... didn't really know how to... If I should... I didn't know..."

Thankfully, Jay cuts me off. "Well, I want one of you."

"Me, too," Marco adds. "It's the three of us, right?"

This is it. It's time to make the call. These men make me feel safe, and make me have fun. They appreciate what I give and support me—and yes, their dicks are huge, and they know how to please. No one is supposed to have it all, and here I am with two? I need to stop second-guessing this and claim them. Fuck what people might say about us. I need to hold on to what makes me happy.

I lean towards them and touch one hand to each of their legs, lightly squeezing their strong thighs. "It's the three of us. I'm all in."

They both grin, melting me on the spot and meeting me in the middle to share a tender kiss, and I think maybe that little verbal slip up earlier wasn't so far off the mark.

Jay pulls away from the kiss a little to whisper, "I want a naked painting of you."

I can't suppress the giggle that bubbles up, and I hope I never stop.

We spend the rest of the trip doing much of the same. Lazy cuddles by the fire and in bed, eating and drinking to our hearts' content, talking about our families, our past relationships, and yes, copious amounts of sexy time. I'm pretty sure every hole in my body needs a vacation from this vacation.

We went tubing again, this time bringing Jay, and it was a blast. We spent all day there, laughing and racing each other. Marco and Jay were being taunted by these two little girls, so they each flung one of the girls down the hill from the top, making them squeal with laughter. The guys spent the next couple of hours doing the same thing to every kid who saw them at the top. It made my heart flutter watching them interact with those kids.

When we got back to the cottage that night, they were both sore from *throwing children down a hill*, so I gave each of them my poor attempt at a massage, but they groaned and moaned and really made a meal out of the whole experience.

On our last day, we decided we would throw a last-minute New Year's Eve party when we got home. It would be low-key, but kind of our way to let our relationship out in the wild. So, on our drive back to the city, we texted all our friends the invitation for the next evening.

I told the guys when we got back that I needed to go visit my mom and spend time with her and that I would come over the next day to help set up at their place. To my surprise, they both asked if they could join me. I was a little hesitant at first, but they said they really wanted to meet her.

After unpacking at my house, we drove to Mom's home

and spent the rest of the day with her. They were so kind and patient, and she was beside herself, blushing at every smirk and wink they threw at her. When Marco told her he was a massage therapist, she lit up and asked if he would give her a massage. He agreed, and now they have a date later next week.

When we got back to my place, I didn't want them to leave just yet. I wanted to express to them just how thankful I was for the trip, for the way they treated me, for everything.

I sat them down on the edge of my bed and sucked them off. I was mesmerized by the way they looked down at me. They may have been looking down, but their eyes told me I was on a pedestal. I may have been serving them, but they were worshiping me.

Chapter 27

New Year's Eve

Cora

After Jay and Marco left my house this morning and made a mental note to buy a bigger bed, I did all my laundry, checked some emails, cleaned up, and took a long shower, followed by an extensive skin and hair care regimen. I loved our vacation, but I am happy to be back home to recalibrate myself.

An hour before I'm supposed to leave, I get dressed, trying on a dozen different outfits. We said this was a casual, laid-back event, but I'm not feeling it. Opting for some gold glitter tights, a black mini skirt, and a tight black plunging neckline top with long sleeves, I feel like fire. My breasts are practically spilling out, and my curves are on full display.

I put on a little makeup, adding some gold shimmer to my eyes to match my tights.

I'm going to have to beat those boys off with a stick tonight.

I grab a small toiletries bag and fill it with sleepover essentials and stuff it in my purse. No point in grabbing pajamas, but I do pack a fresh pair of panties, leggings, and a sweatshirt for tomorrow. Then I remember the leggings and sweatpants the guys bought me, smile to myself, and put mine back. I want to wear what they got me. I think they would like that.

Feeling like a million bucks and ready to party, I head out to my car and drive to the guys' place to help set up.

When Marco opens the door, he has a tea towel slung over his muscular shoulder, an Army green t-shirt, and jeans. Upon seeing me, he smiles, takes my oversized purse, and pulls me in for a hug. "Hello, beautiful. I missed you."

Resting my head against his warm chest, I groan, "I missed you, too." *Jeez*, it's been like eight hours since I've seen him, but it's true.

He lets me go and shuts the door while I shrug off my long coat. "Let me take that for—" he cuts himself off and gapes at me, his eyes raking over my body.

Yes! Exactly the reaction I wanted to see.

"Baby! *Fuck me*, you look good."

I smile and run my hands up his biceps. "Thank you. I could eat you up right here; you look so yummy."

His stare stops at my chest, and he pulls me in tight to his body. "I'm gonna fuck those tits tonight."

I giggle, a rush of excitement flowing through me. "Where's Jay?"

"He's downstairs setting up a disco ball and a karaoke machine."

"I love it. I'll go help him."

"Alright. I'll be up here working on the charcuterie spread."

Tonight's menu was a mixture of what all three of us wanted: charcuterie, gumbo, and soft pretzels.

I head downstairs, where I find Jay wearing tight black jeans that show off his cute butt and a tan long-sleeved ribbed polo that he's pushed up to his elbows.

I check my mouth to make sure I'm not visibly drooling.

He doesn't see me just yet. He's testing out the microphone of the karaoke machine, singing in a low register ABBA's hit, "Gimme, gimme, gimme a man after midnight—"

I walk up close to him as he sings. "Can I have two?"

Startled, he spins around and takes me in. He drops the mic, pushes me against the wall and assaults my neck with kisses. He grabs the nape of my neck and sifts his fingers in my long curls.

"Mmm, you've got on that perfume I love—*and* your tits are out? Are you trying to kill me, woman?"

My chest rises and falls as I pant and laugh at him at the same time. Fondling one of my breasts, he snakes his other hand under my skirt at my center. I smirk, knowing exactly what's about to go through his mind.

He struggles with the tights, feels a lot of material and clasps at my crotch. Huffing out an exasperated sound, he pulls back and pins me with those dark brown eyes. "Tights *and* a bodysuit? It's like you don't want to come."

I laugh at his mock seriousness and trail my manicured nail down his chest. "Or am I just a tease?"

He narrows his eyes. "You did this on purpose."

"I dressed up for myself—and for you guys. If it just so happens that I'm a tease, then so be it."

His jaw ticks, and he growls at me, sending a pleasurable shiver down my body, causing my pussy to pulse. Dammit, maybe this outfit was a bad idea after all. Who am I kidding? I can't hold out.

Jay pulls me off the wall, turns me, and pushes me towards the karaoke machine, slapping my ass hard. "Then get to work, you tease. You better bend over from the waist to pick up that disco ball."

About three hours later, and after a tortuous amount of teasing each other, many of our guests arrive, and the place not only looks great, but the vibe is perfect. The music is a mix of 90s and early 2000s hits, and the entire kitchen island is covered in charcuterie. Shrimp gumbo sits on the stove for people to serve themselves, and in about ten minutes, Marco is going to pull out the first batch of soft pretzels from the oven, complete with cheese sauce and various mustards.

We rehung the strings of lights from the cottage in their living room and basement and then set out decks of playing cards.

I was honestly surprised that so many people showed up.

Sitting on Jay's lap on the couch, I chuckle and sip my cocktail, listening to Jay's friend Noah tell us about the time he and Jay held a photoshoot for his bulldog.

"She was turning five!" he whines. "She deserved it."

"We had the works for her," Jay remarks with a smile. "Tutus, pearls, flower crowns, painted nails."

I giggle, "Please send me those photos. I must see them."

Noah starts to scroll through his photo reel when the door opens, and I look up to see Angie and our friend Rafael walk in.

I jump up and squeal, not sure who I am more excited to see. "Raf! I didn't know you were in town!" I hug him tight, with wonderful memories of the three of us flooding me.

He laughs, "Only for a few days. Angie convinced me. She said the Mummers Parade just isn't the same without me."

"I'm very persuasive," Angie adds.

Memories pull me back to all the mornings we'd wake up on New Year's Day, hungover as hell but making our way to see the chaos that is the Mummers Parade. Rafael loved it so much he would attempt to make his own outrageous costume by wearing, attaching, and *gluing* anything he could find to his body. The more bizarre, the better.

"I'm so happy you're here! Come on in. I want you guys to meet my guys."

I lead them over to the living room, where Jay and Marco are now standing. "Angie and Rafael, these are my boyfriends, Jay and Marco."

Angie gives Jay a hug, "It's so nice to see you again. I'm so happy you're back in our lives." She breaks off and hugs Marco. "And you! My god, you're handsome, too."

Both men chuckle at Angie's complete lack of decorum. She's always been like this, treating people she barely knows like close friends.

Rafael shakes both of their hands. "It's nice to meet you guys. Angie and I have been friends since we were kids, and we met Cora in college."

Jay laughs a little sing-song tune and rubs his hands together in a devious way. "Oooh, I can't wait to hear about college Cora. Tell me everything."

I shut it down before it even starts. "You know what, let's go take your coats to the closet, get you guys some food and drink, and sing some karaoke, huh?"

"Sing a duet with me, and I'll tell you about the time she got tasered!" Angie yells at Jay as I push her out of the room.

An hour later, I'm finishing up a song with Angie, our signature song, *Nothing's Gonna Stop Us Now* by Starship, and I'm bouncing with joy. I hang up the microphone and skip over to Marco, who's clapping for our terrible singing. "Very impressive," he drawls, meeting me with a kiss and a squeeze of my butt.

I dramatically flip my hair back. "Thanks. We've had a lot of practice."

He chuckles as Jay comes over with a couple to join us, and Marco exclaims, "You guys made it! Cora, this is my sister Rebecca and my brother-in-law, Vinny. Guys, this is our girlfriend, Cora."

She looks just like Marco but with a slimmer stature and finer facial features. Her long dark hair is styled straight. Her eyes go wide with shock. "What? You have a girlfriend, too?"

Marco grabs hold of Jay's hand and brings him close, wrapping his arms around both of us. "Yes, we're a package deal, and you're going to be fine with that."

My body gives a little shiver at his command. So, it's going to be like that, huh? We're just going to demand people respect us? I'm fine with that.

"Well, color me surprised." She turns to her husband, a total beefcake of a man, and gasps. "Wait, can *we* get a third?"

He laughs at her. "You're officially drunk, my dear."

"Maybe, but think of the help we'd have raising the kids!" She takes out her phone from her back pocket and shows me the home screen. "This is our one-year-old, Leo, and this is Viera. She just turned four. We were..."

Rebecca's words fade away, and my vision narrows on the little girl. Her hair is dark and wild like she spent a whole day playing outside. She's smiling so big that her eyes are closed. An orange popsicle drips down her hand.

All the music and laughter from the party disappears, and I can only see that awful day's memories play in my head.

The nurse.

The doctor.

The monitor.

The itchy gown.

The tears.

The pain that never truly goes away.

The pain is so powerful that it numbs me. I don't realize I've changed locations until I come to, looking around a familiar bedroom. A big warm body is pressed behind me, and big tattooed arms cling like a snake.

Marco.

His deep voice whispers into my hair, chanting. "It's okay, Cora. I'm here. It's okay."

I register that all my clothes are gone and I don't know why. I feel safe, though.

"Where are my clothes?" I whisper.

With a gentle voice, he murmurs, "I brought you up here to get away from everyone. You were panicking, tugging at your clothes, saying they were too restricting, so I took them off as fast as I could."

I don't remember that.

"What's the last thing you remember, baby?"

I take a deep breath, not wanting to say the words out loud about the picture. I mumble, "Your sister."

I feel him nod. "Breathe with me," he commands and proceeds to lead me through a series of guided breathing; inhaling for six seconds, holding my breath, and exhaling for six seconds. We do this repeatedly until I'm putty and my mind is clear.

The door opens slowly, and Jay slips in, holding a glass of water. When we make eye contact, he gives me a wary smile and makes his way to the bed, and sits on the edge. He gently strokes my hand that's clinging to Marco's forearm. "Hey."

"Where is everyone?" I ask.

"I sent them home. I made sure everyone had a sober driver."

"We got you out of there quickly before anyone could register what had happened," Marco reassures.

"Thank you."

"Do you want to talk about it?" Jay asks.

I haven't talked about this with anyone other than the guys and Angie. It's not something I've been comfortable talking about, but with them... they make me feel comfortable and safe enough to try.

I take another deep breath, thankful for the clarity Marco has helped me find already. "Rebecca showed me a picture of Viera, and I... thought about Violet. Losing Violet."

Jay nods his head, his face solemn, and squeezes my hand. Neither of them speaks, allowing me space.

"I kind of panicked and blacked out."

Silence.

"How often does this happen?" Marco asks, still spooning my naked body, holding me close.

"It doesn't always get this bad. I don't know. Sometimes I can go a month without losing it. Sometimes, only a week."

More silence.

I feel like I'm absorbing their calm energy when Marco finally speaks up. "In no way am I trying to diagnose you or tell you how to process, but... based on my experience, what you're going through sounds a lot like post-traumatic stress disorder. What you went through, what you endured was traumatic. It was awful, Cora, and I'm sorry it happened to you."

More tears prick at my eyes, and Jay wipes them away with his thumb. "What do you need right now, baby?"

I don't want to talk about this anymore. I'm wiped out. Drained. I need a lighthearted distraction.

"Can we just lay here and watch HGTV?"

"Of course." Jay leans down and kisses my lips so sweetly I could cry from that alone.

A half-hour later, I'm snuggled between my men, watching the Property Brothers show off their remodel and their winning smiles. I have a clean and hydrated face thanks to Jay bringing me my makeup remover and skincare stuff. It's amazing how much better I can feel with a clean face. I can feel myself resetting.

Drifting off to sleep with the glow of the TV, I feel two faint kisses and the words "Happy New Year, Cora."

I try to say it back, but I'm too far gone. I think I murmur nonsense as I leave reality and sleep consumes me.

I hear a soft voice, but the words don't register.

"I know, prince. But it wasn't the right time to tell her."

Chapter 28

Recoil

Jay

I walk into the office on January 2nd with a positive outlook. At least I'm trying to stay positive. I've just spent an amazing week with my partners; Cora is officially ours and we're officially hers. But when she left yesterday to go home, I felt such a loss. It feels unsettling living with only Marco now. Knowing Cora is by herself in that big townhouse doesn't sit well with me.

She spent most of New Year's Day with us, talking about the party, and watching movies, but not bringing up what happened to her—and that's okay—we don't want to pry. We want her to talk when she wants to, but when she left to visit her mom, I could tell she was holding back.

"Good morning, Jay! Happy New Year!" Katie chirps from her desk as I pass by. She waves her hand while holding a donut, and I can see remnants of previous donuts peppering her pregnant belly, making me smile.

"Good morning, Katie. Did you have a nice break?"

"I did! I napped the whole time and ate everything I could."

"Perfect. That's the way to do it." I keep walking to my office. "I'll see you in the morning meeting."

I check to see if Cora is in, but she's not, so I head to my office to unpack.

Before turning to my computer, I check my text messages, specifically one I've been feeling anxious about. The one I have with my mom. I texted her on Christmas, wishing her a merry one, but no response. I texted her again on New Year's Day, but again no response. Guess she's really holding out for that apology from me, but I really don't think I'm in the wrong here.

When I finally open my inbox, there are hundreds of unread emails, and I go stiff. I relax when I see it's mostly reminders that every employee needs to update their annual goals and retake training. By the time I sift through everything, I get a new email that pops up from the hotel security team. My pulse races as I open it up and read the message.

Dear Mr. Bishop,

Attached is the security footage you requested for the night of your company's holiday party. This video recording was taken outside the empty room you were located in. Please let me know if there is anything else I can provide you.

Sincerely,

The Hotel Franklin Security Team

Immediately I open the video and press play. The date and time stamp on the video is a match. My pulse picks up, and I can feel the blood pumping in my ears. I watch as two men walking come into view. The camera angle is obviously from the ceiling, but it's clear enough. That's Jonathan and Chris. There is no audio to the footage, but I don't need it when I see them walk out of view, and seconds later, I see myself emerge from the room with Marco.

Bingo.

The clip ends, and I forward it to Horatio and Cora. As soon as I hit send, the goddess herself walks into my office holding two white to-go coffee cups. As gorgeous as ever, her long camel-colored wool coat hangs open, showing her billowing black dress slacks and a navy blue silk dress shirt. She's the picture of sophistication. Her heels click softly against the floor as she rounds my desk with a soft smile and a knowing look.

With the door still open, she leans down and presses a gentle kiss to my waiting lips. Momentarily paralyzed, I breathe in her spicy vanilla scent.

She pulls away slowly. "Good morning, Mr. Bishop."

"Good morning, boss."

"Are you ready for our meeting with your team today?" Yesterday we discussed how we would address our relationship with the company. Both of us liked the idea of keeping it a secret, purely for the kinkiness aspect, but we knew we needed to disclose it to Human Resources. Being that I am the head of said department, we have to tell my direct reports. We're going to do our best to keep it a secret from everyone else, though. I'm sure news will trickle down eventually, but for now, we'll keep to ourselves. So, her keeping the door open during our little kiss... my god, we're downright exhibitionists.

"I am. They are going to be in for a treat with this news. Shall we prepare the fine china tea cups for them?"

"Absolutely," she teases with a smirk and an eye roll.

I look back at my computer for a quick moment, and I remember the video footage. "Wait a moment, Cora. Shut the door. The hotel sent the tape."

She gives a little gasp and quickly shuts it. She leans against the desk, and I watch her watch the clip.

Anger and disbelief mark her face as she sits in silence, watching the clip replay. Finally, she speaks. "Do you know who said what?"

"Now that I've seen this, I'm certain Chris was the one who said, 'The case is heating up' and Jonathan was the one who said, 'That bitch is going down.'"

Cora lets out a deep sigh. "Do you think they're working against me?"

"I don't know. They've both been vocal about not being your biggest fan."

"Yeah. You sent this to Legal?"

"Yes."

She pushes off my desk and sighs again. "Okay. When we go into our morning meeting, as much as I want to cuss out Jonathan in front of everyone, we can't disclose this information until Horatio tells us what to do."

"Of course."

She makes her way to leave my office, and I grab her by the waist before she gets too far and stand up to give her a scorching kiss. "Thank you for the coffee," I growl with a devilish smile. "I *owe* you."

Over the next week, Cora and I worked with Horatio and the other legal team members on the case. We investigate heavily into Chris Francis' work on the project and discover he signed off on the soil reports, knowing the ground wasn't structurally feasible. We found reports from other soil engineering companies showing their refusal to build similar structures over the last two decades. This leads us to believe Chris either didn't do his research or he had malicious intent.

Then that leaves the city inspector. Horatio looked into the city's records of every property inspection sign-off, looking for similar signatures to the one Bob Sabin supposedly signed. No matches came up, and since Chris was the only other signature on the report, that leads us to believe someone forged the signature.

Horatio also started collecting the evidence for a new defamation lawsuit. Once we find out who is responsible for the first case, we'll be pursuing this one.

During this entire week, Cora has been so engrossed in her work and the case that she looks re-energized. At first, it seemed counter-intuitive, then I realized she has me and Marco now. We've been making her take more breaks, eat complete meals, and turn off her brain from work in the evenings.

Our after-work routine the last week has consisted of her and I going to visit her mom while Marco finishes up his evening clients and meets at either her place or ours.

Last night Marco came with us to the assisted living home to make good on his promise to give Connie the massage she requested. Of course, she didn't know she asked for one, but when Marco showed up with the strap of his massage table strung over his shoulder, his big biceps on display, and his crisp white t-shirt, Connie practically melted.

Now Marco is the talk of assisted living. Even the staff were fanning themselves, asking for his number and scheduling appointments. I think he's working out a plan with the home to come by once a week and give massages to the residents.

But the thing helping her most is relinquishing her control every night. It's to the point where Marco can snap his fingers, and she will scurry to her knees and obey. It's not every night we have a scene, but when he simply takes control, she melts. To watch it, to be a part of it, is mesmerizing. Marco has made it his mission to give her and I matching bite marks, welts, and beard burns in the exact same places. I know it gives him a caveman-like possession to see, but it makes me feel an even stronger connection to her.

We are his.

I got to work early the next Monday so I could go for a run at the office gym. Cora had spent the day at our place Saturday but left in the evening to hang out with Angie. As much as we didn't want to let her go, we knew we were hogging her, and she needed to spend time with her friend.

As I ran, I kept having this nagging feeling. We hadn't heard from Cora at all Sunday. She texted us Saturday night when she went to bed, but there was radio silence all day yesterday. Maybe I'm too clingy, but I like hearing from her every day. It was probably nothing. I was going to see her in a matter of minutes anyway.

I climb the stairs to the main office from the lower level, and head right to her office. She isn't in yet.

Hmm. Okay.

When I gather up my stuff and head to the morning meeting, I know I'll see her there. I enter the room, and most of my colleagues are there already with a couple minutes to spare before the meeting starts.

I notice Katie is missing, too.

I ask the room, "Does anyone know where Cora and Katie are?"

Dayo speaks up. "I don't know about Cora," they say directly to me and then turns to the rest of the room, "but Katie had her baby yesterday, everyone!"

Soft cheers erupt from the whole room, but I go still.

"Here, let me pull up the pictures she emailed last night," Dayo says, connecting to the projection monitor in the room. Sure enough, there are several pictures of a tiny pink faced baby with giant blue eyes.

Dayo reads the caption aloud. "Amelia Josephine has made her arrival three weeks early, but she and mommy are in perfect health. Please feel free to pass along this announcement to the rest of the company."

I block out the rest of Dayo's words when I see the recipients of the email. Dayo, a few other members of Katie's team, and Cora.

I read the timestamp. 'Sent Sunday at 8:05 am.'

Oh, no.

I rush out of the room, not caring to excuse myself. I can't think about anything else other than Cora and how she's handling this. Running to my office, I dial her number, but she doesn't pick up. I grab my coat and bag and call Marco as I rush out of the office. He picks up on the first ring.

"Good morning—" he says before I cut him off.

"Get to Cora's!" I shout. "She's not at work, and her employee just had a baby yesterday. I think she had an episode, and she's hiding away."

I hear him grunt like he's getting up, and he cusses. "I'll be there in ten minutes."

"I'll meet you there."

"Call Angie, Jay. She might be able to help."

I remember getting Angie's number at the New Year's Eve party. "Good idea. I'll see you there."

We hang up without saying goodbye, and I push my way out of the office doors and run to my car, finding Angie's contact and calling.

She answers on the third ring. "Hi, Jay. What's going on?"

"Cora's not at work. Her employee had a baby yesterday, and I think she's freaking out."

"Oh, shit. Wait, what's today's date?"

I look at my phone as I turn on my vehicle. "January 8th."

"Oh, no, Jay. Yesterday was Violet's birthday."

To be continued...

Acknowledgements

Please don't hate me for that cliffhanger! I'm so sorry, but I had to. The next book in this duet, Structural Support, will be coming out sometime between December 2023 and January 2024, but you can pre-order it now. In that, you're not only going to read more about our sexy trio, but you'll also read about Jay and Marco's origin story.

I want to thank you, my dear reader, for taking a chance on me. I hope I was able to create something you loved as much as I do. Please consider rating and reviewing this book on Goodreads and Amazon—that's the biggest way you can support me.

A big thank you to my best friend, Rachel, who served as a cheerleader and alpha reader. Thank you for forcing me to send you each chapter as they were completed. I also love calling you my alpha now *wink*

To my husband, thank you for all your support and encouragement. It's easy to write about cinnamon roll men because you give me the best material. You're forever my teammate.

To my friend, Angie, thank you for letting me use your name

ACKNOWLEDGEMENTS

and that actual night out in Manayunk as the kindling that sparked this story. That really happened, dear reader. Well, most of it. Neither of us actually kissed or slept with a stranger (I'm happily monogamously married!) Maybe someday I'll show y'all the picture of a puppy bulldog chomping on my nose as proof.

To my wonderfully talented illustrator, Vera Osipchik, you simply blew me away with your cover art. Thank you for bringing my characters to life.

To my ARC team, thank you for your support! I absolutely love you all.

To my editor, Alli Ferguson with Falcon Faerie Fiction, thank you for all your hard work polishing my story to its brilliant shine.

Trigger Warnings

[BDSM] [Degradation] [Dirty talk] [PTSD] [Threesomes] [Gay sex] [Double penetration] [Mentions of pregnancy] [Miscarriage] [Raw doggin'] [Squirting] [Sex toys] [Anal sex]

About the Author

Sloan Spencer lives in metro Detroit with her husband, two kiddos, and dogs. She loves nature, scandalous stories, and thick thighs. You can follow her on her social media accounts or visit her website:

Instagram: @sloan_spencer_author
TikTok: @sloanspencerauthor
Facebook: Sloan Spencer's Reader Group
Author website: sloanspencerbooks.com
Be sure to follow her on Goodreads and Amazon!